MOONLIGHT AND MISCHIEF

BRACKEN CREEK WOLVES

Campfires and Canines

Moonlight and Mischief

Secrets and S'mores

Wolves and Watercolors

Snowdrifts and Soul Mates *novella*

Blood and Brambles *short story*

MOONLIGHT AND MISCHIEF

Aly Hollis

TAWNY
BOOKS

Friends,

In Campfires and Canines, Hazel came to Bracken Creek Pack to visit her uncle, having no clue the little mountain community her father grew up in was actually a wolf shifter pack.

This story picks up about six months later. Jasper joined Bracken Creek Pack at the end of Book 1 and is trying to establish his place within the pack.

In the end pages, you can find reference pages of character's pack positions and family trees. I hope this helps!

On a more serious note, some content in this book may bother readers who are sensitive to certain triggers. The narrative contains characters drinking alcohol, explicit sexual scenes, use of guns and crossbows, hostages, serious injuries and (non-main character) death, and profanity. Please protect your mental health!

aly

For best friends who would come pick you up in the middle of the night.

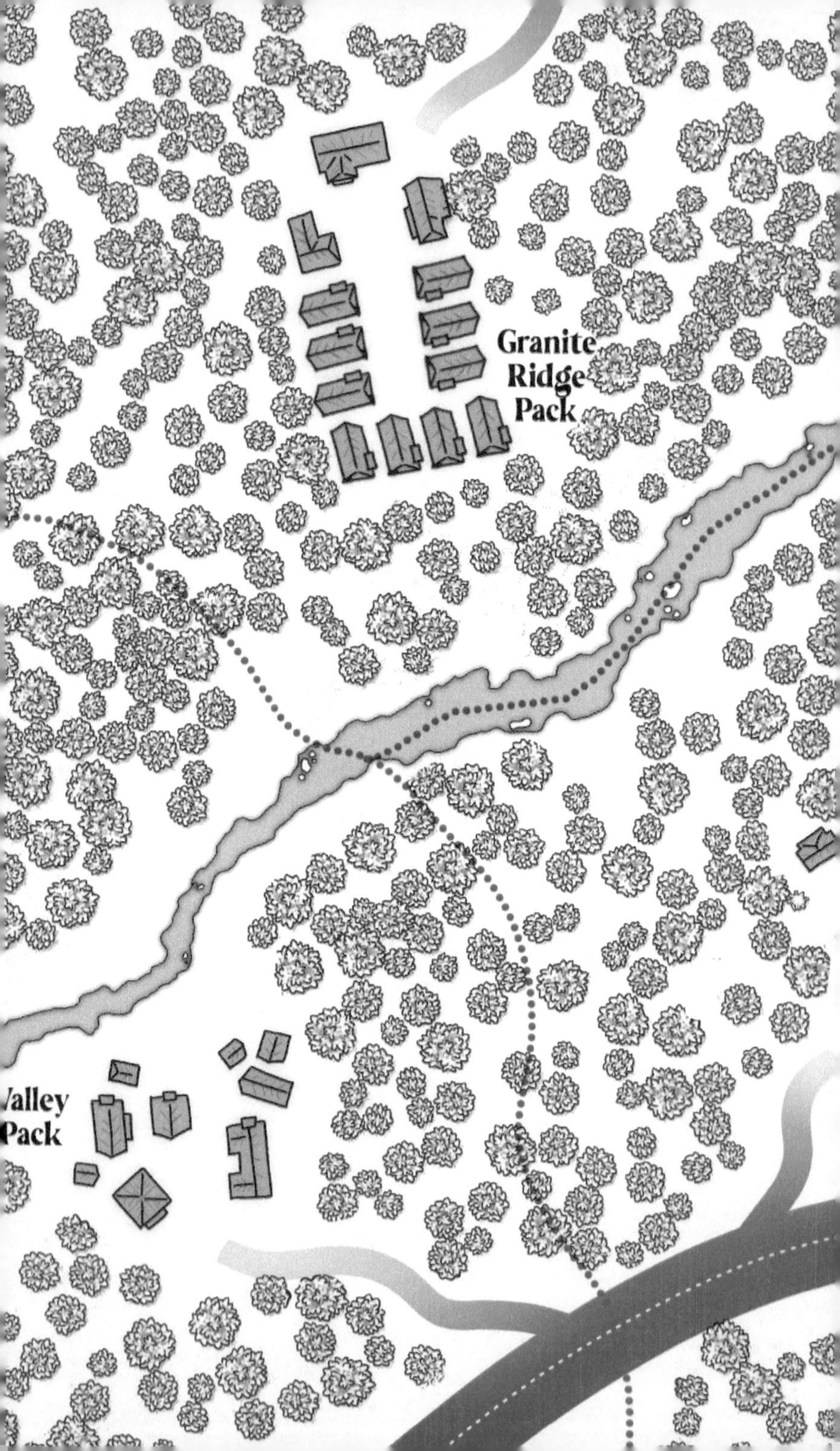

Granite
Ridge
Pack
Valley
Pack

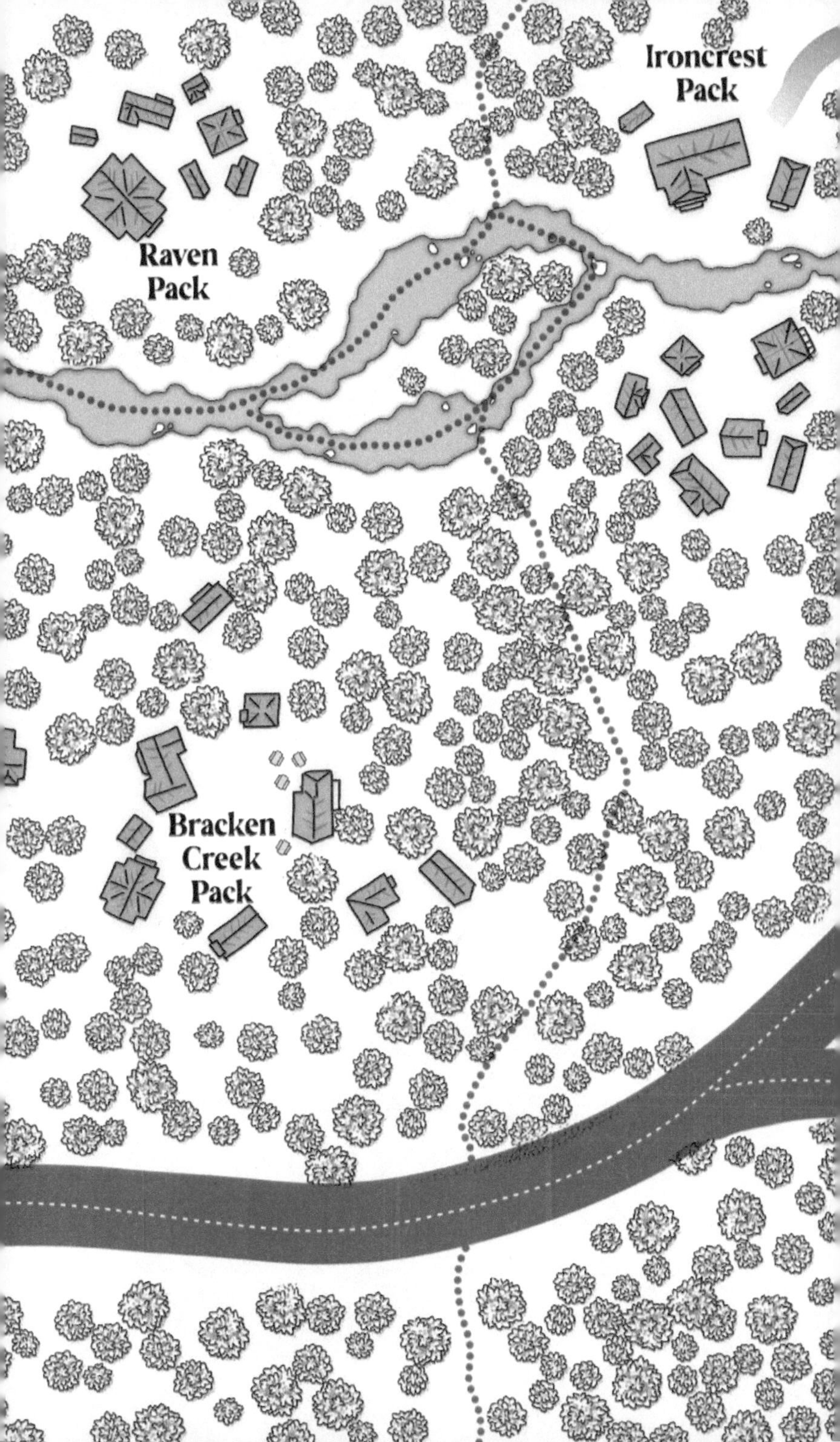

Ironcrest Pack
Raven Pack
Bracken Creek Pack

CHAPTER ONE

WOLF PUPS & WRESTLING

Marigold

Suppressing a smile, I tip Daisy's chin up to get a better look. "Did you have to stick a crayon up your nose? Really?" The end of a broken green crayon peeks out of her nostril. "Goddess help us when you start shifting," I mutter under my breath while stretching to reach the nearest tissue box.

"Hold one side closed." She pokes at her nose on the wrong side, wincing. "No, baby, this one. And then blow

your nose hard. If it doesn't come out, we'll have to get your mama."

Leaving the tiny menace to her task, I survey the rest of my class. My job isn't difficult with such a small class, but these students are a bit wilder than typical human children.

"Wrap it up, friends! It's almost two," I command, gathering spare art supplies from the closest table.

Buttery light streams in the massive windows. The walls of my one-room schoolhouse are wallpapered with their paintings and drawings between multiplication charts and historical timelines, handmade by yours truly. Students sprawl across benches, paint brushes and markers in their hands.

"I'm serious, I'm not cleaning up after you pups. Five minutes!"

At the sound of my scolding, a dishwater blonde head leans around the door frame. "Doing okay, Goldie? Need me to teach any of these kids a lesson?"

"Hey, Onyx," I plant a hand on my hip, a wry smile curving my lips. "I think we're good, but thanks."

"Got any more of those cookies you made for your class?" he asks.

"They're for my students," I say, rolling my eyes. Wandering to the back table, I wrap a napkin around one of the remaining chocolate chip cookies and bring it to Onyx.

"You're the best!" He says, a grin lighting up his face.

Leaning past him, I wave at his twin.

"You want a cookie too, Cedar?"

"I'm good." The afternoon sunlight streaks his hair amber, contrasting with the deep tan from his hours outdoors. He's handsome in a golden-age movie star way.

Onyx is more of a rebel, always dressed in grungy band shirts and ready with a joke or prank, but he's a sweetheart under the shenanigans.

"You guys busy?" I ask, hearing a chorus of giggles behind me. Nosy little stinkers.

Cedar nods, "Getting some training in."

"Have a good time! See you later."

Ducking back inside, I find that Daisy managed to shoot the crayon out of her nose and now holds it up triumphantly. At least her mom won't be mad at me, even if I now have to confiscate a booger crayon.

"Alright, my little artists, let's get this place cleaned up!"

After the school day ends, I wander across the sun-drenched meadow toward my family's cabin. Even though I moved in with my grandmother a couple of years ago, I like to check back every so often. A household of three men can get messy quickly and my father is hopeless with housekeeping.

It's empty like I knew it would be. Dad is out patrolling, Cobalt is playing soccer in the clearing, and Indigo is finishing up his afternoon internship with my grandmother. She's the pack's healer, and Indie will take over for her someday.

The cabin smells like old leather and my father's aftershave, with an undercurrent of sweaty socks. The warm wood kitchen is fairly tidy, but I toss the breakfast plates into the creaky dishwasher and start it. Padding across the ancient brown carpet toward the bedrooms, I pause to transfer the laundry from the washer to the dryer before it gets musty. My siblings' shared bathroom needs a quick wipe down, and then I'm popping out the front door.

Sure, the boys could handle everything themselves, but my brothers are busy and my dad works so hard. My job ends early in the afternoon, so it makes sense for me to tackle a few chores and lighten the load on my dad's shoulders.

On the way to my grandmother's cottage, I dodge my students kicking a soccer ball back and forth. Despite my fatigue, I cheer them on. They love to play in the clearing between the diner, the school, and the supply shop.

Cedar's garden spans the north side, centered around an archway covered in snow pea vines. The delicate tendrils climb the frame but it's still too early for the soft pink flowers to bloom.

Cedar loves to talk about his garden, and I'm always happy to listen. With his smile in my mind, I veer toward the training building tucked into the edge of the trees. The garage doors are rolled up in the back, and two men grapple in a spray-painted circle.

A tall, tattooed figure leans against the steel siding beside Cedar. Slate serves as the pack's Beta or second-in-command. He's quiet like Cedar, but in more of a brooding artist way, instead of being lost in thought.

At the moment, their attention is fixed on the duo currently throwing punches and evading kicks. Onyx's swirling black tattoos curl over his biceps and across his chest. Opposite him, Slate's brother Jasper dodges Onyx's offense.

Jasper joined the pack last fall. He's all sharp lines and high contrast - startlingly bright teal irises and pale gold hair, against warm tanned skin. He defected from our rival pack and has been trying to earn his place here ever since.

Onyx ducks as Jasper swings high, but Jasper is clever and he jabs with his other fist, hitting Onyx in the shoulder. Onyx lurches back and attempts to turn his motion into a rotating kick, but Jasper darts in and sweeps his feet, tossing him onto the dirt.

With a dramatic groan, Onyx pushes up to sit. "I'm getting tired of that. Someone else needs to go next."

"Sorry, man," Jasper says with a laugh, offering his hand. Pulling Onyx to his feet, he turns my way, his bright eyes widening. "Marigold, do you want to join in?"

My nose wrinkles. "Not today, thanks."

"Too bad. I'd love to see what you can do," Jasper murmurs. A blush blooms over my cheeks. I avoid sparring with the boys, preferring to fight Hazel or even Cassia, one of the pack's Zetas, or warriors.

I settle against the wall beside Cedar. Slate stretches his arms and arches his back to loosen up before he faces his younger half-brother. Slate is leaner and taller, though Jasper has a few more pounds of muscle on him.

Jasper clenches and unclenches his fists. Swallowing, I avert my gaze from his glistening back and the way the muscles narrow to his waist.

"Did you have a good day with your students?" Cedar asks quietly.

My mouth curves into a smile. "Yeah, aside from a crayon incident with Daisy, it was a quiet day. Oh, and Starling brought a lizard in after lunch."

"Was it one of those geckos?" His head tips toward mine. He's a great listener.

"Yeah, I think?" I purse my lips, trying to remember. Once I saw the creature in her little hands, we hustled outside to release the poor reptile.

He nods thoughtfully. "Next time, let it go in the garden. I can always use more help with the grasshoppers."

"Sure thing."

My eyes are drawn back to the sparring brothers. Last fall, they fought in a formal challenge in this very ring over Hazel, Slate's mate. Jasper's birth pack attempted to steal her, but the end result was Jasper being disowned and joining our pack. He's proven himself loyal with how hard he works and how grateful he is for a life away from the militant pack his parents lead.

Like lightning, Slate steps closer and swings. Jasper's forearm knocks it away, but he's ready with a roundhouse kick. Slate's strike lands on Jasper's side and he grimaces. Stumbling back, Jasper sucks in a breath, as if he's in pain. I bite the inside of my cheek.

Regaining his footing, Jasper attacks, landing a succession of boxing-style hits before Slate hooks his leg around Jasper's ankle and shoves him backward. His back hits the dirt.

"You okay?" Slate asks, pulling Jasper up by the hand.

"Fine. I think I'm ready to call it a day. I gotta get cleaned up," Jasper says, wincing as he prods his ribs.

"Me too." Slate waves at us and walks into the training building to retrieve his belongings.

Still catching his breath, Jasper faces Cedar and me. Onyx laughs and shoves his shoulder, showing off the soil clinging to his sweaty skin.

Slate passes us, giving Jasper an apologetic shrug when he sees the dirt. "See you guys." I suspect his haste is an attempt to see Hazel before dinner.

Jasper steps closer to me, his typical cocky smirk in place. It softens his sharp features. "Did you enjoy seeing me get my ass kicked?"

"Always." I return the wink he gives me. Jasper wipes his bunched-up shirt over his forehead and neck. I take it from him and use it to gently brush his back off.

"Thanks," he says.

Cedar straightens. "See you at dinner," he says. Onyx follows after his twin, waving his goodbye.

Jasper strolls beside me, the evening light highlighting his blonde eyelashes. "We were talking about a campfire after dinner. Sound good to you?"

"Yeah, of course."

Looking pleased, Jasper waves before turning back to his cabin.

I finally resign myself to checking on my grandmother before dinner. The door jingles as I step into the stone structure Sable has lived in for decades. Her cottage sits just north of Cedar's garden, making harvesting herbs and medicinal plants convenient.

Grandmother hovers over the dining table, bundles of herbs spread around her hands as she sorts and stacks leaves of lemon balm. Her rolling pin thuds on the table, startling me. With gusto, she flattens the spikey leaves before tying twine around them and setting each in the pile. Lemon balm is good for insomnia, something that often bothers shifters with all of our wolf energy.

"Good afternoon!" I chime, slipping my sandals off and plopping onto the floral couch serving as my bed. The card table I use as my nightstand has been overrun by tiny bottles of pink liquid - rowanberry concentrate. It's not toxic like wolfsbane, but the bitter juice incapacitates our magic for a few hours and is helpful during a crisis. Superstition says rowan wood blocks enchantment, and I've always wondered if the berry's effect on our physiology may have played a role in that mythology. As fascinating as the compound is, I would prefer it if my space wasn't covered in individual doses of it.

"Hello, dear," my grandmother murmurs absently.

I draw a calming breath. "Grandmother, can I move these bottles somewhere for you?"

"Why would you do that?" She doesn't even look up.

"I'm trying to keep my area tidy."

"That's not necessary." Her eyes are stormy when she glances back at me. "Indigo will move them tomorrow when he finishes the task. You know better."

"I'm sorry, I wasn't thinking."

Her silver braid undulates like a snake as she shakes her head. "I'd think you'd understand by now - healing others comes first. Before personal space." She exaggerates those last two words, repeating phrases I've said in previous arguments.

I flinch, but she's only prioritizing her work over our comfort. It's understandable. Shame weighs me down, causing my shoulders to round.

"I'm sorry." My chest aches with resentment, but I won't upset her, not when everyone relies on her constantly. More than a few times, I've been woken by an injured packmate stumbling in at three in the morning.

Her frustration is clear in the way her fingers crawl across her plants. Sable is an incredible healer, but her compassion and gentleness seem reserved for her patients only. Her sharp words cut me.

I don't need personal space. I have a warm bed and a roof. The mantra repeats in my head as I change my shirt and wash up to my elbows. We don't get sick often, but I have no interest in being covered with children's fingerprints and whatever dirt or germs they carry on them.

My grandma forgot me in my two minutes at the sink, her face serene as she stacks the herb bundles into woven baskets. I should offer to help her or something useful, but it's easier to slip out the back door and enjoy the peaceful lull of the forest for an hour or so before dinner.

Jasper

My cabin is all knotty pine and classic plaids. It might be small and several decades out of date, but compared to the cold concrete houses of my birth pack, it's a haven. It's one of the older structures in the pack's community, serving as a guest cabin when needed.

I'm welcome to stay here as long as I need, but eventually, I'll get my own place. I've considered finding a roommate or maybe buying a trailer like some single wolves in our pack have done, but nothing seems like the right fit.

The front door squeaks as I push it open. I've learned no one locks their doors here. There's a sense of mutual trust and safety that feels like I've won the lottery.

I shed the remainder of my clothing and step into a steaming shower. The hot water eases the soreness in my muscles and the pain from my fresh bruises. For a few minutes, I tip my head back and let the water sluice down my body, feeling utterly content.

Scrubbed clean, I pull on black sweats and a fresh t-shirt before heading out. But as my hand lands on the doorknob, a knock echoes from the other side. Swinging the door open, I'm greeted by my mentor.

Hawthorne is the pack's Gamma, a mediator and ambassador, as well as our Alpha Heath's cousin. With his tall frame and dark hair, he's imposing, which serves him well in negotiations. When I first joined the pack, he questioned me about my father, and that became an ongoing discussion until I was helping him with gathering information on other packs as well. I'm endlessly grateful that Hawthorne took me under his wing.

Among our pack, he's patient and supportive. Watching him with his two daughters makes my chest ache. My father mostly ignored me during my childhood. So Hawthorne has become my role model for when I have my own family.

"Hey, what's up?" I dip my head in respect and hold the door open.

He waves his hand, indicating he doesn't need to come in. "I wanted to stop by and tell you the news. It looks like the Alpha Counsel is going to happen."

I want to pump my fist in the air and holler "Yes!" but I restrain myself. The Alpha Counsel is our most recent project. It used to be an annual meeting between all the local Alphas, but it hasn't happened in many years. Hawthorne feels that it's the most effective way to begin repairing the relationships between our neighboring packs and I agree.

"That's awesome," I say, unable to stop my giddy smile.

"They still haven't agreed to a location, but your dad finally confirmed, so that makes four of the five Alphas."

"Still no Nyx?" I ask, frowning. The sole leader of the Raven pack avoids gatherings when she can help it. I've never met her, but it still seems strange she would refuse to meet with all the other Alphas.

"We can't win them all." He quirks his mouth. "And Ironcrest wants to meet with us tomorrow. So that should be interesting."

"Really? What do they want?"

"I believe it'll be some sort of apology. Anyway, I'd like you to join in," Hawthorne rests his hand on my shoulder.

"Okay, I'd be honored."

"You did good, Jasper. You deserve the credit for making this happen. I know how many messages you had to send to finally convince them to participate."

"Thank you," I say, pride surging in me. It feels like I'm finally earning a place here - as long as the Alpha Counsel goes well.

"Let's head to dinner, I need to get the girls from Marigold," he says, pulling me from my mental celebration. Still smiling like an idiot, I follow him toward the diner.

Most of the pack is milling about waiting for Heath to arrive. Marigold stands chatting with Slate and Hazel, a toddler balanced on her hip. Her strawberry blonde hair tumbles from a claw clip and cascades down her back in gleaming waves. I love her hair.

"Dahlia," Hawthorne croons, lifting her from Marigold's arms. The toddler's brown hair is barely long enough to be pulled into two curly pigtails atop her head.

She excitedly squeals, "Daddy, dadda!"

"Ready to see what Mama made for dinner?" he says, his voice pitched higher. His mate, Crickett, serves as the pack's lead chef, and she makes most of the dinners we share together.

"She's so cute," I say to Marigold, watching Dahlia bob her little head. She hums in response, rubbing the spot on her arm Dahlia has been sitting against.

"I'm flipping-dipping starving," Hazel mutters.

Alpha Heath strides across the meadow. His pack members lower their heads in a sign of respect that ripples through the crowd, though conversations continue. He's an Alpha who is loved and respected, not feared. It's been enlightening to learn the difference.

True to shifter etiquette, Heath gets his food first. Slate and Hazel follow him through the line. Hawthorne goes next, taking food one-handed while holding Dahlia and coaching Daisy on how much food to put on her own plate.

After those senior leaders, it's open to anyone.

"Come on." I usher Marigold in and grab a plate.

Onyx bounds behind us, jostling Marigold. "Tamales!"

"Watch out," I warn, my hand going to the small of Marigold's back. She smiles prettily at me. But then Cedar walks in after his brother, and Marigold immediately diverts her attention from me to him. Sighing, I stack two tamales on my plate with a sizable scoop of rice and beans.

We eat at our usual table on the outskirts of the clearing where the trees cluster in as if to swallow us up entirely. Conversation is light, while Hazel reviews her training for the day and Marigold entertains us with her students' antics. I soak up every second, reveling in the connection and affection between everyone.

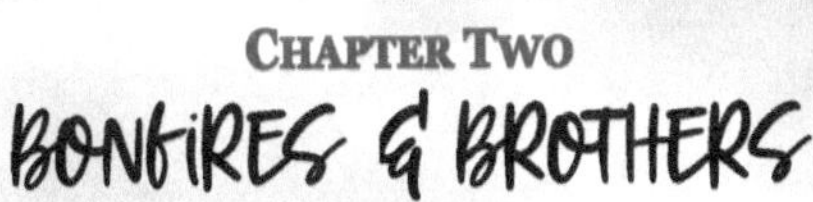

The campfire crackles as we settle on the split log benches and old Adirondack chairs weathered gray. The scent of woodsmoke mingles with the crisp pine air.

Cedar gathers an armful of kindling while Jasper snags the blankets we use during the winter months from the covered porch. Spring is solidly here, but the winter chill still creeps in once the sun sets.

"Feeling cold?" Jasper stands, a blanket draped over his shoulders with one side held out in an offer to share.

When he first arrived, looking like a kicked puppy, I sat with him and shared a blanket, and since then it's been our tradition.

I let out a long sigh. It's been a day. I broke up two squabbles today and comforted crying children three times. When talking about school, I only share the cute moments, but the truth is most days, it's draining. As if sensing my tension, Jasper rubs his hand up and down my arm. I can't help melting into him.

Slate pulls Hazel into his lap in their favorite chair, tucking another blanket around them. She nestles her nose into his neck, placing a kiss across the ring of tiny scars that show they're a mated pair who have claimed each other.

"Do we have any s'mores tonight?" Slate asks. Hazel has a major sweet tooth, and he's always looking for ways to spoil her.

"I think the store is out of marshmallows," Cedar says apologetically. Onyx lets out a dramatic gasp.

"Are you serious?" Hazel pops up. "Do we have any at home, babe?"

Slate shakes his head.

"I think our mom made some brownies. Do you want some?" Onyx asks. Their mother is our resident baker and makes the most incredible desserts.

Hazel nods enthusiastically.

Happy, I tip my head against Jasper's shoulder. Onyx hands me a napkin with a thick chocolate confection, the top glossy and crisp.

"This is so mother-fudging delicious," Hazel moans through a mouthful of brownie, causing me to snort. She holds it out and Slate takes a bite. My heart squeezes at the gesture. It's what mates do, feeding each other. I hope someday I'll have that.

The first bite of brownie is gooey and chewy and intensely chocolatey. "Yeah, this is a foodgasm for sure," I murmur.

Jasper coughs on his own mouthful.

"Careful, don't choke," I warn. "You've had enough embarrassment today already."

Clearing his throat, he argues, "Hey, I landed Onyx on his ass. Just because Slate beat me, it doesn't mean anything. I was tired already."

Smirking at him, I lick a smudge of chocolate off my finger.

"Dude, I took it easy on you," Onyx says. "Hey, who do you think would win in a fight right now between me and Cedar? He hasn't agreed to fight me in ages!"

"You guys are pretty evenly matched. It's usually a toss-up," Slate says.

I have to agree with him. Neither twin seems to have the upper hand since they are the same build, trained by the same father, and neither one is particularly motivated to take their combat training seriously.

"I think I'd need to see you guys go at it again," I say, brows arching.

"It's a waste of time. Any real opponents will have a different fighting style," he says with a shrug.

Onyx scowls. "You sound like Dad."

"At least sparring keeps us in shape," Jasper adds, and I can't help but notice the corded muscle in his forearm as he crumples his napkin and tosses it into the fire.

"I have a better question," I interrupt. Time to lighten this conversation. Campfires are supposed to be fun! "My students were arguing about this yesterday. If you had to shift into any other animal, what would it be?"

"That's easy, I'd be a bear," Onyx declares, puffing up his chest.

Hazel gives him a knowing look. "No, I think you'd be a raccoon," she jokes, her lips twitching.

"How about a tiger?" Onyx asks, pouting.

Fighting down giggles, I add, "Maybe a possum!" Jasper lets out a laugh and I turn to him, raising an eyebrow in question. "What about you?"

Jasper bites his full bottom lip, his eyes drifting upwards to the stars peeking between the branches. "Maybe something that can fly, like a hawk."

"Oh, I love that idea," I murmur. My fingers press into the rough edge of the bench beneath us.

"I'd be a goat." Cedar states. Everyone stares for a moment.

Slate's brows draw together as he cocks his head. "A goat?"

"Yeah, they're helpful and they seem to always be having a good time."

Hazel wipes away a tear from laughing so hard. "Yeah, that checks out." She twists, cupping Slate's jaw. "What about you?"

"No idea. What would you pick for me?"

"Oh, let me think." She sucks her cheeks in. "How about a golden retriever?"

Onyx guffaws, nearly tumbling off the bench as he throws his head back.

"You don't think I'm more of a german shepherd?" Slate asks, his dark hair falling across his forehead as he leans back to narrow his eyes at his mate.

"How would you know? You guys don't have dogs," Hazel argues, her eyes sparkling.

"But we still know about them!" Onyx blurts, his words blending into laughter.

Jasper leans forward, arms resting on his knees. "What about something like a stag? Like those big elk. Very majestic. No one messes with them."

"Yeah, let's go with that," Slate agrees, gesturing toward his brother.

Watching Jasper's smirk, I have an idea. Bumping him with my shoulder, I say, "Actually, I think you'd be a fox."

"Why?" he asks, his voice dropping. I can feel his breath on my temple.

"You're clever and a smooth talker," I tease, fidgeting with the edge of the blanket. It's getting too warm under here.

"I'm not sure if I should be offended or flattered," he says, his smile far too charming. The brightness in his eyes reflects the dancing firelight, flames within seafoam.

"Better a fox than a golden retriever," Slate grumbles, though his voice is gentle.

Hazel traces the dark trees tattooed across his forearm. "I love you just the way you are." He leans in, catching her lips in a kiss.

Onyx lets out a cough that sounds remarkably like "Get a room."

"They have a room, several of them," Cedar answers automatically, his eyes on the flickering fire.

"What about you, Marigold?" Hazel asks, breaking away from her mate. Her amber eyes glow honey in the firelight.

Tugging my fingers through my hair, I debate. "A dolphin?"

"I love that idea," Jasper says quietly. My cheeks flush, his praise setting off a flurry of butterflies in my stomach.

He raises his voice for the group. "I've got one, what superheroes do you think could be wolves?"

"Wolverine," Cedar says.

"Obviously," I agree.

The fire snaps, a few sparks floating into the air and up into the purple sky.

Slate adjusts in his seat, his hands curling around Hazel's hips possessively. "What about Black Panther? He's all about family, community, and helping people, right?"

"That makes sense to me," Onyx says, producing a second brownie for himself and taking a huge bite.

The conversation lapses while we all try to come up with another answer. Hazel finally shrugs. "I have no clue, I'm not a comic girl."

"It's okay. You can't be perfect in every way," Slate teases, earning a pout from his mate. He murmurs apologies in her ear as she curls into him.

Onyx has that gleam in his eyes that means he's starting trouble. "Hazel, did we tell you about the time Slate peed his pants over seeing some raccoons?"

"No!" She shoots up. "I haven't heard about this."

Jasper chuckles. "This sounds good."

I press my lips between my teeth, trying to prevent my laughter from interrupting the story.

"It was nothing," Slate growls, "I was five, and we were having a sleepover, and Onyx dared me to run around the cabin in the middle of the night."

"In his boxers," Cedar adds, a reluctant smile brightening his features.

"He was such a chicken!" Onyx says, his grin showing all of his straight, white teeth.

"There were over a dozen raccoons on the porch and when I tried coming back in, they all hissed at me. Of course, I was scared," Slate explains.

I can't hold my giggles in any longer, laughing so hard that tears come to my eyes.

Cedar nods, "We accidentally left snacks outside. That's why there were so many."

"You peed yourself?" Hazel asks between fits of laughter.

Slate shakes his head. "I don't remember that part."

"I do!" Onyx says brightly.

Hazel softens, hooking her hands behind his head. "That sounds fun. I wish I had grown up with you guys."

My laughter dies away, seeing Jasper's expression dull. There's a stiffness in his posture that wasn't there a moment ago. Jasper and Hazel are the only ones who didn't grow up here. I know he doesn't like to think about the years he spent under his parent's rule.

Clearing her throat, Hazel changes the subject. "Hawthorne told me that almost everyone finally agreed to an Alpha Counsel! So it sounds like that'll finally happen."

"That's amazing," I yelp, grabbing his hand and squeezing it. He's spent hours over the last few months negotiating with our neighboring packs to arrange such a meeting, and it hasn't been easy.

The barest flush colors Jasper's cheeks. "It's a good step forward."

The moment is perfect until Onyx adds, "And your shit-head dad can't ignore you there."

"Onyx!" I grimace. At least he hadn't mentioned Sienna, the mother Jasper and Slate share. She's the one I'm frightened of between the two Alphas.

Jasper laughs bitterly, "I'm sure he'll do his best. But it doesn't matter. I won't be participating in the meeting, just assisting, if I'm there at all."

It has to be hard to face your parents after they publicly announced you were dead to them.

I give his hand another reassuring squeeze. At some point, his fingers have threaded with mine, and it feels too nice to break away.

Cedar stretches. "It's getting late and I have an early morning with Cheddarbelle and Cheesette." Hazel barks a laugh at the goat's names.

"Don't make fun of my baby girls," Onyx snaps, though his voice is playful. I burst into my own fit of giggles until we're both wiping away tears. Jasper smiles indulgently at me, his thumb stroking across my knuckles.

Cedar stands, smothering the flames and tidying up with practiced efficiency.

"You guys have been extra cozy tonight," Onyx observes lightly, raising an eyebrow at me. I drop Jasper's hand instantly.

What's his problem? We always sit together. And I'd share a blanket with Onyx if he offered.

A blush creeps up my neck. "It's cold, do you want me to freeze? I didn't exactly see you offering to sit with me."

"Don't be mad, I'm just saying," Onyx responds, lifting his hands in an offer of peace.

Hazel levels her gaze on me, her lips pursing. "Maybe you guys have been a little extra touchy tonight," she says hesitantly.

Jasper is silent beside me, and I can feel how uncomfortable he is as he wipes his palms along his sweatpants.

"So what?" I say, "he's *basically* my brother."

"He's not your brother," Cedar points out, straightening.

A growl escapes me. "I said basically." Swallowing, I plaster on my kindest smile. "Jasper is Slate's brother, and we grew up together. So he's like family, and if we were anything more, it would be kinda ick."

Jasper finally reacts, shrugging the blanket from his shoulders and letting it pool beside me. "You don't have to say it like I'm a toad," he mutters.

Oh, shit.

"I'm sorry! I didn't mean it like that." His frown deepens as I continue to babble. "Besides, if you were a toad, you'd be one of those adorable little tomato frogs."

"Toads and frogs aren't the same," Cedar says quietly, walking away.

Jasper raises an eyebrow, eyes sharp with skepticism. "A tomato frog?"

"They're my favorite reptile," I say, goading a smile out of him. "Amphibian?"

I study his face for a moment, begging him to ignore my stupidity. The last thing I want to do is hurt his feelings. Even after these last few months, he is still sensitive about fitting in. I know Jasper belongs here with us. He's a piece we didn't know we were missing until he arrived. But he doesn't see it that way.

"We okay?" I ask quietly.

"No harm, no foul," he says as his lips curve into a smirk. Jasper winks at me and my breath rushes out, relieved he isn't truly mad.

He stretches and steps away from our bench. "Night, everyone."

"Good night." I fold our blanket and hand it to Onyx.

Jasper gives me one last look, reassuring me that he isn't upset before I make my exit.

Hazel wraps her arm around mine as we both stroll home, our paths intersecting until we meet my grandmother's cottage.

Hazel and Slate's home stands a short distance northeast. It's a sprawling two-story cabin that sat unoccupied after Slate's father passed away. Over the last season, the couple has renovated it, keeping the original charm while modernizing fixtures and appliances. It's only been a few weeks since they moved in.

We walk in silence until my worry overcomes my good sense. "I feel like crap," I tell her in a hushed voice. "I can't believe I said that."

Hazel cocks her head, waiting for more context.

"About him being ick." Hearing the word again makes me cringe.

She raises her shoulders up and drops them with a sigh. "I shouldn't have said what I said. I wasn't thinking and I put you in an awkward position."

"It's fine," I say automatically.

Hazel's cheeks hollow as she weighs her words. "Honestly, I think it was on my mind because I've been concerned," she says.

My brows furrow as I look at her. "Why?"

"Like I said, you guys have been touchy-feely."

Scowling, I open my mouth to argue.

"I know shifters are more physically affectionate," she says, cutting me off. "And I get that he can't be physically close to me, so you're the only cuddly one available."

"That's all it is," I say, nails biting into my palms at the swirl of anger and embarrassment heating my cheeks.

"He really values your friendship. And it would suck if you accidentally led him on."

"That's not going to happen."

She's right though. I've enjoyed comforting and encouraging Jasper over the last few months, but maybe we've gotten a little too close. Holding hands was perhaps over the line.

"I'm probably worrying for nothing. And I don't think you'd ever do something like that intentionally. But he didn't grow up with close friends like you did, and frankly, you're always busy staring at Cedar, so I'm not sure you'd even notice if Jasper was staring at *you* that way."

I bite my tongue. I should listen to her. Hazel is shockingly insightful and usually correct in her assessments. The situation calls for more thought on my part.

Slate catches up to us as we reach the corner of Cedar's garden.

"Good night," she says as her mate takes her hand and pulls her against him.

"Thanks for watching out for us, Hazel," I say, even though she's thoroughly distracted by whatever Slate is whispering in her ear. The lovebirds walk into the darkness, stealing kisses as they go.

Jasper is a good friend. Someone I can rely on. But that's all it is. He's never given me any indication otherwise, and I've been hung up on someone else for most of my life. It's just a close friendship. Nothing to worry about. But maybe we should curb our physical affection, so people don't get the wrong idea.

Creeping into the cottage, I open and close the front door at a glacial pace to avoid making any noise. Slipping my shoes off, I tip-toe into the hall.

My grandmother's bedroom door is closed. I quietly visit the bathroom and change into an oversized t-shirt I stole from Cedar years ago. Recoiling at the rusty squeak, I ease the sofa bed out and crawl under the covers.

Fatigue presses down on every one of my muscles. But before my eyes can drift closed, I hear a door latch click and swing open. My grandmother emerges from her workroom, a tub full of glass jars clinking in her arms.

Sitting up, I rub my eyes. "Good evening, Grandmother."

"Oh, you're back. Good, you can help me," she announces, setting the tub on the table.

Laying back, I sigh. "Sorry, I'm really tired."

"Don't be selfish, we need to prep these," she says dismissively.

I bite back a groan and pull the covers off. There's no arguing with her when she's like this, though I'm too tired to deal with it.

Fifteen minutes later, I'm cautiously pouring rowanberry juice concentrate into the tiny jars. Even with a funnel, it's tricky. My hands slip several times.

"Watch it," Sable hisses. She sounds nothing like a grandmother. She's the pack's crabby healer and I've had enough.

"I'm too tired to be any help. Let me get some sleep and I'll work on it before school."

She whirls on me, careful to not slosh the pink liquid she's holding in a quart jar. "You're always staying up late with those friends, and now you can't be bothered to help your pack?"

Tears prick my eyes. This feels like the last straw. I should keep my mouth shut, but if I saw a friend or one of my students being spoken to like this, I would tell them to stand up for themselves. Time to take my own advice.

Jasper

It would be kinda ick. Apparently, I'm ick.

The heat of her, through two layers of fabric, went from a comforting warmth to a searing burn when compounded with my embarrassment.

Stripping off my shirt, I grab a glass of water and lean against my kitchen counter. Not that I need Marigold to think that I'm desirable, but surely I'm better than a tomato frog.

My glass makes a plink as I set it aside and pull out my phone. What the fuck is a tomato frog? Bulging gold eyes stare back at me. Its vivid orange-red skin has a black stripe down its pudgy sides. Damn, it is pretty cute.

I'm wound too tight to sleep yet, so I settle across my bed with an old detective novel I found on the shelves of the cabin when I moved in. The pages are yellowed and someone has written notes in the margins, which somehow make the book more enjoyable.

As the protagonist stumbles across a second victim's body, someone raps against the front door.

Apprehension prickles through me like frost, leaving a primal alertness in its wake. It's after midnight. Pulse racing, I pull open the door.

"Hey."

Marigold's doe eyes stare back at me. "I'm sorry to bother you."

A huge t-shirt drapes over her lean build, bunching around the waistband of her joggers. She's scrubbed her face free of any makeup, leaving her looking raw and somehow ethereal. Darkness smudges under her eyes, triggering a protectiveness that has me stepping closer to her.

"Are you okay?" My stomach clenches.

Her smile wavers for a split second. "Yeah, I'm good."

Placing a hand on the small of her back, I lead her inside, closing the door to block out the gloom and cold. Marigold looks around my cabin, her lips parted slightly.

Seeing her like this, my heart rate is not slowing. She's always making sure everyone else is comfortable and happy, but I can see sadness beneath her sunny smile.

"So what's up?" I ask, hooking a thumb into my pocket.

Her fingers curl around the strap of a backpack thrown over her shoulder. "I sort of got in an argument with my grandma."

"That sucks," I say cautiously.

"It's fine," she says, "It's just... There isn't room for me in her cottage. And she's so focused on her work, she doesn't give me any space. I'm tired enough after a day of teaching, I can't be her assistant when I get home. It's too much."

"That does sound like a lot." My hands travel to her upper arms, steadying her as her words spill out of her like a damn breaking.

"And today she called me selfish! It's not like I was sitting around doing nothing all day, but she expects me to jump to whatever task she thinks of at all hours of the night. There's been times lately when I can't even open up my sofa bed because she's packed the room with her projects. I don't think I can wait until I save up for my own place."

By the end of her rant, she's deflated, gaze on the ground, lashes wet.

"Marigold, I'm sorry. That's really unfair."

She sniffles. "Thanks."

"How can I help?"

Those blue-green eyes meet mine and her tongue swipes across her lips. "Well..."

"Anything." And I mean it.

"Can I stay with you tonight? Until I figure something else out?"

My stomach flips. "Really?"

I expect she'd have potential housemates fighting to have her. She's wonderful. The idea of sharing a space with her is unexpectedly exhilarating.

"Never mind, it's rude of me to just show up." Her face closes off.

"No!" I blurt, "I was only wondering why I'm the lucky person you asked."

"Oh," she answers, hesitating, "Well, my brothers like having their own rooms, so I don't want to take mine back. Not to mention I don't want to face my dad over this. And I first thought of staying with Hazel. But.."

"But she and Slate are all over each other," I finish for her. "I wouldn't want to stay with them either. Who knows what you'd see or hear?"

She giggles, pressing a hand over her mouth. "That's about right. So that left you."

Nodding, I cross my arms. "Sounds like I'm your last choice."

Her brows furrow. "I think my last choice would be the twins. I can't deal with that much Onyx."

She says nothing about Cedar, but I'm not an idiot.

"I can go, don't worry about it, Jasper." She shrugs, turning toward the door.

No way am I letting her go.

Taking a wide step, I place my palm against the door so she can't open it. "Why would you do that?" I ask, putting on an air of confidence I don't feel.

"Cause you don't want me here," she answers.

"Absolutely not true. I would love to have you. I have an extra bedroom and you're my best friend," I say, "one of my best friends, I mean. You should stay here as long as you need to."

She flings her arms around me in a hug, her face pressed into my chest. For a moment, I'm floating, a wonderful friend who smells like lemon and rosemary snug in my arms. The instinct to protect and provide surges in my chest.

Breathing through the rush, I finally say, "It's late, let's get your room set up. You'll probably want some extra blankets. That room gets cold."

She steps back, a teardrop sliding down her freckled cheek.

"Hey, none of that. This is a fun friend's sleepover, right?" I say.

"Sorry," she says, batting away her tears and smiling brightly.

"You don't have to apologize,"

The door to the spare room opens with a creak. A twin bed sits against a window framed in rounded wood trim. Marigold pads across the thick rug and slouches onto the coverlet, slinging her backpack onto the small desk beside her with a thud.

"Is this okay?" I grip the top of the door frame, leaning in without stepping across the threshold.

"It's great, thank you." Marigold pulls her feet up and wraps her arms around her knees. She looks so vulnerable, it takes all my self-control to not scoop her up. But that feels like crossing a boundary. Instead, I locate a thermal blanket and drape it over the foot of the bed.

"Okay, well, the bathroom is the middle door and my room is at the end. Come get me if you need anything."

Her breathing has slowed, her expression softening. She deserves a comfortable space and a roommate who appreciates and respects her. That's something I can provide.

Tapping the door frame, I wander to my bedroom and lay back on my bed. Eyes closed, I listen to the sounds of her closing the bathroom door, running the faucet, and then a few minutes later, closing her bedroom door.

This woman called me *ick*. But her luminous eyes don't say ick to me, they're full of the warmth and affection I'm starving for. But if I'm not careful, I could mess this up. I'll never forgive myself if I hurt or upset her.

She's one of the best people I know, the first one I look for at gatherings, and one I linger to talk with. And now she's in my home. At this rate, I'll never get to sleep.

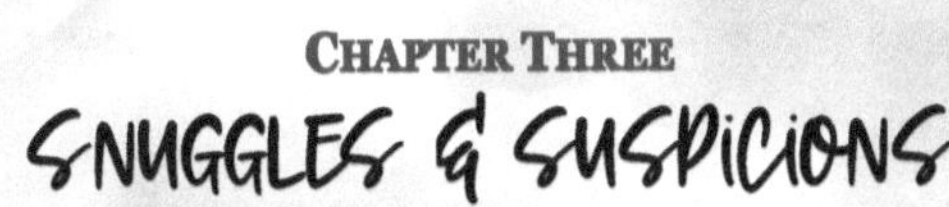

Sleeping in a real bed for the first time in almost two years is a revelation. I want to moan from how good my muscles feel as I stretch and pull the covers higher under my chin, sinking back into the warmth. Maybe I'll steal this mattress when I find my own place.

My phone beeps, warning me it's time to get moving or I'll be late.

Rolling out of bed, I stumble toward the bathroom, grateful I put away a few toiletries last night.

The bathroom door is closed. I stare for a moment, comprehension slowly creeping into my brain.

The door swings open and my new roommate faces me. A dark towel wraps his waist, and his platinum hair looks ashy as water drips down his neck. His bare chest gleams.

This isn't anything like watching him spar or strip before shifting from across the training room. He's so close I can smell his soap and see water droplets like pearls across his shoulders.

My inhale turns jagged and I step back carefully. Not an appropriate time to swoon.

"Good morning," he says, a cocky grin showing off his dimples.

My mouth opens and no sound comes out. His confidence wavers, his expression flickering. "Went for a run this morning."

"Sounds fun." I finally say, failing to keep my eyes from roving. Across his ribs blooms a green and yellow bruise.

For a bruise to still be visible overnight is surprising, meaning it's either very fresh or he was hit hard. "Jasper, what happened?" I motion to my side.

He blinks and looks down, huffing when he realizes what I mean. "It's nothing. Slate got me pretty good yesterday."

"Why didn't you go see my grandma? That looks nasty, she could have helped."

His clear aqua eyes meet mine. "It's fine. It'll be gone by lunch."

"Please take care of yourself," I say, holding his gaze. With a wink, he reaches over and lightly tugs on the fluffy braid I put my hair in at night.

"How'd you sleep?"

Pulling out the hair tie, my fingers unravel the braid into loose waves. "Honestly, really good. I didn't realize how poorly I was sleeping at my grandmother's."

"Good," he says. For once he doesn't seem quite so sure of himself. With an odd smile, he steps around me.

As Jasper disappears into his room, I shudder, trying to shake off all the tension from our encounter. I didn't realize having a male roommate would involve quite so much bare skin and bulging muscles.

Today feels like a day to look cute. A few swipes of makeup, and my favorite sweater with strawberries stitched down the sleeves paired with black leggings, and I'm ready to go.

Jasper's already left when I come out of my room. I'll have to learn more about his work schedule, now that we are roommates.

The cabin is further from the school building than my grandmother's cottage. I keep to the trees instead of cutting into the meadow. It'd be too easy for someone to spot me walking up from the south instead of my usual route.

Today will be busy. The children have a book report to finish and after lunch, we are taking a nature walk to look for insects. Science is a close second to my favorite subject after art.

I can't help but scan for my friends as I pause at the doorway. A few pack members walk in various directions, but no Jasper. Not that I'm looking for him specifically. I'm sure he's busy today too.

Jasper

The Alpha of Ironcrest arrives in a gray SUV. As he steps out and adjusts his jacket, the sunlight glints on his short silver hair. Zephyr has sharp features and dark eyes. Everything about him reminds me of a blade - polished, sharp, and as likely to help as harm depending on the situation.

His pack's Gamma trails behind him, dark hair falling over his eyes. He's noticeably shorter and wider but has laugh lines that suggest he's friendly.

Zephyr's Beta is conspicuously absent. But likely she was left at home as de facto leader.

Hawthorne greets them, walking across the gravel lot to shake the Alpha's hand. Apprehension skitters across my skin. Ironcrest's request to meet before the Counsel could be for any number of reasons, but I don't trust Zephyr.

Spying from the hallway window, I watch the trio walk around the side of the office, where a door leads straight into our largest meeting room.

Heath strides toward me, followed by Slate and Hazel. "Go ahead and wait in the room, Jasper. We'll be in after they're settled." Entering last is a power play.

My breathing is slow and even as I pull a calm mask over my anxiety. This is the first time I've seen anyone from another pack since defecting from Granite Ridge and joining Bracken Creek. An heir leaving their pack is unheard of, and I'm not sure what reactions to expect. Hopefully none. This meeting isn't about me.

A live-edge conference table stretches the length of the room, surrounded by heavy, cushioned chairs for a dozen people. Zephyr lounges in a seat toward the center, facing the door. His cold eyes flick over me and stop on my face. I hold his gaze for a moment before looking away. Long enough that he knows I am not afraid of him nor am I ashamed of myself. Any longer, and it would be a challenge.

Muscles coiled tight, I take my place against the wall, off to one side. Hawthorne sits across from Zephyr but down two seats.

"Alpha Zephyr, you remember Jasper. He is a Zeta in our pack now," Hawthorne says. Zeta, a guard. A respectable ranking, though it's not an accurate description of my position. But Zephyr doesn't need to know I was the one pulling the strings to arrange the Alpha Counsel.

"A Zeta? How ambitious of you," Zephyr says with a cruel smile. A flush crawls up my neck and my hands ache to clench into fists, but I don't give him another sign of my discomfort. His opinion doesn't matter. He doesn't need to respect me, as long as he respects our Alpha and Betas.

Finally, the door opens and Heath fills the entire frame, Hazel and Slate hidden behind him. He's taller than I am, and wider too, so he dwarfs everyone seated. The three wolves rise, and Zephyr reaches out to shake his hand.

"Good to see you again, Zephyr," Heath says.

"Likewise." Zephyr sits at the same moment as Heath. Hazel and Slate sit on either side of him, and Hawthorne is at Hazel's left hand. I take the seat beside my brother.

"Hello, Dell," Heath says.

"Alpha Heath," the Ironcrest Gamma tips his head respectfully.

"I hope your pack has been well," Zephyr says.

Heath folds his hands, resting his forearms on the table. "It's been a good winter for us. And yours?"

Zephyr picks lint off his sleeve. "Successful. We have two newly mated pairs and welcomed a set of twins."

I've only visited Ironcrest once, but I know it's one of the larger packs. Close to Bracken Creek's size, but smaller than Granite Ridge. But I don't remember many teenagers or young adults. Perhaps they have been recruiting. The idea prickles like pins and needles through my body.

"Congratulations," Heath says warmly.

Zephyr's smile is smug. "Thank you."

Heath pauses a beat, his eyes never leaving the other Alpha. The dominance struggle between them is suffocating, and the hair on my arms rises. But Heath's authority feels like loyalty and encouragement, and Zephyr's feels like arrogance.

"I'll admit, I'm curious to know what you'd like to discuss," Heath says expectantly.

Leaning back with his fingers steepled, Zephyr takes his time deciding what to say. His relaxed pose reeks of arrogance. "I felt we should clear up any misunderstandings about the unfortunate difficulties your heir faced last fall."

"Ah, misunderstandings." Heath echoes, his face betraying nothing.

We all knew Ironcrest aided Granite Ridge in taking Hazel hostage. So far, their denial has kept a shaky peace. If he admits to it now, it will have to come with apologies and reparations, otherwise Heath will be forced to take action.

Hazel's knuckles are white where she grips her chair arms, though her shoulders are relaxed and her face politely serene. Beside me, Slate is slowly leaning forward, lining his feet up under him to prepare for a fight. I take a slow audible breath, hoping he will join me on instinct. He ignores me.

"I'm eager to hear any new information. Last time we spoke, you were unaware of any involvement," Heath prompts.

Zephyr swallows, dipping his chin in a show of remorse that no one would believe. "Unfortunately, I did uncover something."

Dell drops his gaze to the table. Heath and Slate make quite the overbearing pair. Though Zephyr and Dell are not in our pack, and therefore felt none of our shared emotions, even a human could sense the rising tension.

"Granite Ridge took Hazel and held her for several days before she was returned to you, correct?" He knows damn well what happened, and that Hazel escaped with assistance from me. We poisoned the entire pack and I defended her while she raced for the border and Slate.

Heath plays along. "Yes, I believe Sienna wanted a foothold in claiming our pack by forcing Hazel to become mates with her heir."

I appreciate Heath leaving my name out of it. But Zephyr's gaze travels to me anyway. His neutral expression slips for a second, showing pure disdain. Hawthorne leans forward, a defensive barrier between our visitors and me.

"That always seemed like a foolish plan to me." Zephyr sighs. "She wasn't even a pack member, not really. What claim would she have even had? Your pack never would have accepted a rival's heir mated to an outsider who only shared a familial connection."

My hands clench under the table. Zephyr's jab at Hazel annoys me, more than his offense toward me. Down the pack bond, irritation ripples, and I can't tell if it's primarily Slate, or perhaps the entire room.

"What information did you have for us?" Heath asks, redirecting the conversation.

Unfortunately, Zephyr isn't finished. "It's a good thing your Beta took a liking to her. Keeps anything from getting," he says, pausing, "messy."

"My heir would be quite capable on her own. But paired with a powerful mate, my pack's future leadership is secure."

It's true. Slate is even stronger than I am. Not because he is about two years older and a few inches taller, but because of his natural drive.

"Yes, of course. You are blessed," Zephyr continues.

He is antagonizing us, purposefully drawing this out. Heath must have realized it sooner because his pose has relaxed to match Hawthorne's. Only Slate still looks murderous, and that would be the case regardless.

"Ferris approached me for help but never specified any plans. He must have known I wouldn't support him in something so-" He searches for the word. "Deplorable."

"Afterwards, I discovered some lower ranking wolves went behind my back." His repentant expression seems sincere, but Heath's mouth stays a flat line. He doesn't give any indication that we were already aware of their involvement.

"It's unfortunate those wolves forgot their place. I've banished those involved."

By banished, I have to assume they went straight to Granite Ridge.

"And I've made it clear to Ferris that if his alliance means standing against our other allies, then Ironcrest is not interested."

Silence stretches, Heath cocking his head as he regards Zephyr, reading little clues as to his truthfulness. Apprehension churns in my gut.

"I appreciate your apology and that you took their punishment so seriously," Heath finally answers. "I hope you're addressing any issues of loyalty. It must be difficult to manage such a large pack."

It's as close to an insult as Heath can get without outright disrespecting him. He's baiting him back, testing his intentions.

"We've been assessing to be sure our remaining members are obedient," Zephyr answers. Dell nods.

"Are loyalty and obedience the same thing?" Hazel says. Her voice is strong and steady. The corner of my mouth curves at her boldness.

"I guess not. But both are required, are they not?" Zephyr's smile is snake-like. Slate bristles at how Zephyr's eyes slide over Hazel.

"Perhaps," Heath says, pacifying.

"If there is anything we can do to assist your pack and rebuild our friendship, please let me know," Zephyr says.

"Your offense was against my heir so I will leave that up to her," Heath says, nodding toward Hazel.

Her eyes narrow at Zephyr and his smile fades. "You were our ally once, but that relationship had deteriorated even before Granite Ridge's actions, correct?"

"Unfortunately, yes. It's past time for us to correct the situation." Despite his respectful words, his lip curls for a split second before he regains his composure.

Hazel considers for a moment, causing Zephyr to grind his teeth.

"Alliances are built on communication. In addition to your participation in our upcoming Alpha Counsel, I think it would be wise for our Gammas to speak on a regular basis. I'm sure they can find ways we can collaborate." Her voice is soft but firm.

"A commendable idea."

Dell leans forward in his seat. "I look forward to hearing from you," he says to Hawthorne. "It will be good to stay in closer contact."

Hawthorne nods curtly.

"How has your contact been with Ferris in the last few months?" Slate asks.

"Minimal," Zephyr answers, "I have tried to keep the channel open, but his belief that Granite Ridge is superior to all other packs makes it difficult to find any common ground. I'm afraid we aren't the ally he was hoping for."

Interesting word choice. It's true that Ferris and Sienna believe they are above the other packs. But they wouldn't withdraw from negotiations.

"Hopefully we all can find a way to reconcile peacefully," Heath says.

"We will see," Zephyr says.

Neither leader seems to believe that reconciliation is likely between Granite Ridge and the surrounding packs. Knowing their misdeeds, I am not surprised.

"You've given us a lot to think about. Was there anything else we needed to discuss before the upcoming Alpha Counsel?"

"Nothing that needs to be addressed today."

Heath straightens, his hands falling to his knees. "Well, would you like to enjoy the lunch our chef prepared?"

My brows crease. Offering a meal to Zephyr is a way to offer alliance and friendship again. I know that's the goal, but warning bells are still ringing in my head.

Zephyr shakes his head, pushing his chair back and standing. His fingers adjust the sleeves of his coat while his eyes travel over each of us. "I'm afraid we must be heading back. Our work is never complete, is it?"

"Such is the role of a leader," Heath says, his tone a little colder than before.

Hawthorne steps forward to open the door for our visitors. "Another time."

"Of course."

Heath remains standing so I hover nearby, waiting. After our guests have driven away, Hawthorne returns, his expression unreadable. The two men exchange looks.

"Well, how do we feel that went?" Heath asks.

"Interesting," Slate says, "He seems sincere, but I'm not eager to trust him."

"I'm not sure I expected him to own up to the role they played," Heath says, his hand running over his short beard. "Perhaps Zephyr still has a sense of morality."

"If he was telling the truth," Hazel says.

"It's hard for me to believe that he had pack members acting outside of his command," I say.

Hawthorne crosses his arms. "Their pack has never been as close-knit as ours, but you have a point."

"Do you think he ordered their actions?" Heath asks, his dark eyes boring into mine.

"Honestly, yes, I do," I answer.

Hawthorne frowns. "No Alpha would lend out their wolves for hire."

Despite my nerves, I raise my chin. "I know our Alpha would never do that, but Zephyr has shown to be unpredictable. And it's not like Ferris to seek out individuals from another pack when he has plenty of his own."

"Did you know anything about the Ironcrest wolves?" Hazel asks, her amber eyes wide.

"No, I wasn't told any details. I wouldn't have known at all if I hadn't smelled them on you."

"Okay," Hazel says, bobbing her head. Her hands go to Slate's arm and he tugs her closer.

"It might be a good idea to increase surveillance," Slate suggests.

"We can look into it," Heath says.

"I also feel that we should consider more offensive training," I say.

Hazel nods. "I think so too. We've been training in how to defend our pack, but we might need to attack at some point."

Slate frowns, "Fisher would disagree with you."

"Fisher will train what I ask him to," Heath says. "I think we all need some time to process, and we can revisit the idea of offensive training tomorrow."

"Yes, Alpha," we echo.

Marigold

As the school day ends, a certain gleefulness bubbles up inside of me. Rather than my grandmother's sofa, I'm going home to a cozy cabin and a good friend who is extremely nice to look at.

The smell of fresh cut pine, cinnamon, and wool wraps around me once my feet step onto the knotty pine wood floor. Under the homey scent of the cabin, I can detect Jasper - he's faintly spicy like cardamom, coffee, and something sweeter like vanilla.

But Jasper isn't in the living room or kitchen, and his bedroom door hangs open. Hesitantly, I peer in. A queen bed stands with the headboard against a wide window with a line of little plants on the sill. A shirt is tossed over a chair and his quilt is thrown back to show crimson sheets. Apparently, his meticulous personality doesn't extend to keeping his room perfectly tidy. It makes me smile even as my fingers itch to fold his laundry and make the bed.

I trudge to my own room, slip off my shoes, and flop onto my newly beloved bed. The house is so quiet, but it isn't a lonely sort of stillness, it's peaceful. As I relax, my exhaustion becomes harder to ignore. Maybe one solid night's sleep isn't enough to make up for the last two years. I can't help but slip into a late afternoon nap.

If I dream of anything, I can't remember when I wake. The cabin is tranquil, like when I drifted off, but the light from my window has faded. Hopefully, I haven't missed dinner.

Stretching, I take a few deep breaths and try to wake myself up. The scent of food filters in, telling me that either I've missed dinner or I'm very late.

Grabbing a hoodie, I rush out of my room toward dinner, but skid to a stop in the open living room when I spy an overflowing plate of barbequed meat and a loaded baked potato on the kitchen peninsula.

Jasper brought dinner back for me. My throat clogs and my eyes prick. No one has ever gotten me dinner when I was too busy to attend. I'm always the one making sure everyone else is fed. Not the other way around.

Grabbing my plate, I head toward the back door. It's propped open with a rock that's painted with a paw print, a relic of a previous tenant.

Jasper sits on the edge of the porch, one knee drawn up to steady his hand while he drags a small blade across a chunk of wood, shaving off thin curls.

"Is this for me?" I ask to be safe. Amusement flickers across his face in response to my silly question. "Thanks. I really appreciate it."

"I can't let my roommate go hungry," he says. His smirk twists my stomach.

"Did you tell anyone about our... situation?" My voice drops off.

He shakes his head, causing his pale hair to flop over his forehead. "I didn't think you'd want people knowing. I can see how it would look weird." With a sigh, he rakes his fingers through his hair and sweeps it away from his face.

"I've got a lot to thank you for," I mutter between mouthfuls of potato.

"How about you start by taking it easier on yourself?" He bumps his shoulder against mine. The familiarity is comforting, but I have no idea what to say to him.

We sit quietly, his knife scraping and cutting away slivers of wood, and my fork steadily clearing my plate. I finish the last bite and take my dish to the sink. On the way back, I snag a pair of beer bottles from the fridge.

A lone overhead light illuminates the porch, casting long shadows down the steps. Jasper's night vision is superior as a wolf shifter, and he's able to continue his whittling when a human would have had to stop.

I hand him a beer. "So what are you making there?"

Jasper holds up the rough shape, rotating it for me to admire. "You can't tell?"

"It's a bobcat." I guess the first thing that pops into my head.

He scowls. "Really?"

"Oh, an owl?"

"Not even close."

"A hedgehog?"

"Stop, they're getting worse," he says, laughter breaking through his serious demeanor. "It's gonna be a fox."

"Oh, it looks exactly like a fox. Really great job." My hand clamps over my mouth, stopping my giggles.

"You said I was like a fox, so I figured you might like a little fox," he says absently, digging the tip of his blade under the bulbous top, now carving out what might be the muzzle, though it's hard to be sure.

"This is cool, actually," I say, trying to encourage him, though it looks like a blob to me.

His exhale is audible like an amused huff. "Well, Marigold, I've seen you do all sorts of crafty things with your students, but what activities do you like to do just for you?"

"I can't remember the last time I had spare time to do anything creative," I say, giving in to the urge to rest my head against his shoulder. He's warm and steady, warding off the night's chill.

"Well, what would you do if you had time?" he presses.

"Nap." The glass bottle slowly twirls as I twist my fingers.

Jasper holds the wooden figure up, turning it side to side and measuring with his thumb. Satisfied, he returns to deepening grooves that might be the sides of the legs. It's looking foxlike already.

"Other than naps. I know you're hiding more talents from me," he says, his smirk sending my heart tumbling.

"I like macramé."

His blade pauses and he regards me for a moment. "Like the knots with the rope? Making hanging plant holders and stuff like that?"

"Yeah," I answer, "it's called cord, but you've got the idea. I haven't gotten to do it since I was a teenager."

"That's actually pretty cool," he says, now cutting into the wood to carve out what looks distinctively like two pointed ears.

"Did you think I'd be boring? Like my secret hobby is watching paint dry or organizing socks?" I try to sound indignant.

"Don't diss sock organizing. You have no idea what I do in my private time," he says dryly, turning the little statue over in his hand to inspect his progress.

"I knew it," I mutter. Jasper rolls his eyes but then pauses. My arms prickle with tiny bumps from the cold. He's staring at my skin.

"It's late. We should go inside." Standing, he tucks his knife away and holds out his hand for me. Despite the dropping temperatures, his palm is warm.

He leads me inside, the patio door clunking shut behind us. I'm not ready to call it a night, and neither is he because he leads me to his sofa. I have to admit it's far more comfortable than my grandmother's.

A faint smile brightens his features as he wraps me in a rust-colored plaid blanket before building up the fire in the old cast iron wood-burning stove. Warmth fills the small cabin and I breathe in the scent of woodsmoke and sweet barbeque.

As Jasper settles beside me, I drape the blanket over his shoulders like we always do, but it feels different. We aren't around a bonfire with our rowdy group of friends. It's just us. His skin warms my chilled arm. Awkwardly, I smooth the edge of the fabric.

"Tell me more about your students." His voice is velvety and soothing.

"What about them?"

"I don't know much. Tell me everything."

My fist bunches up the blanket against my chest as I think. "Well, I've got the older ones, like Willow and my brother Cobalt. They've started some online classes, but aren't totally independent yet."

Jasper nods along like this is the most fascinating topic ever.

"And then I've got my younger students, who are pretty much all handfuls. I mean, Daisy keeps shoving different things up her nose every time I turn around. Starling fights me on everything - it's making her mom crazy too. Even Elwood, who I would have considered my easiest student, is starting to get emotional over the smallest things."

A slow smile spreads across his face as I talk. It's not the cocky smirk he wears most of the time. It's warm and genuine, with actual happiness shining through instead of an expression for show.

"How old are they?" he asks.

"Six, seven, and eight."

"Haven't shifted yet?"

"Nope, and I know that's why Elwood is being so difficult. It'll be any day now. As long as it's not during class." I pinch the bridge of my nose.

Jasper chuckles silently. "Have you ever had a kid shift in your class?"

He had no idea. "The older ones do it all the freaking time, especially if I'm being hard on them. It's impossible to argue with a wolf, after all. But I've never had a kid experience their first shift while in class, thank the goddess."

"Then maybe Elwood will be your first."

"Shut your mouth, you'll jinx me." There's no venom in my words, but I knock on the wooden coffee table for luck.

"Sorry," he says ruefully. Exasperated, I use my forearm to shove him away. He retaliates by wrapping his arm across my shoulders and holding me tight.

Mouth pursed, he looks thoughtful. "After spending so much time with your students, do you think you'll want a lot of kids someday?"

That's a loaded question and a complicated one. "I don't know. I see how hard it is for the parents sometimes. How exhausted they can be. And I'm barely getting by some of these days. I can't imagine being responsible for a pup all the time, making sure it gets fed and sleeps enough and doesn't disappear into the forest."

"No kidding," Jasper says, "I'm terrified of the idea of being a parent."

"Why?"

His teeth press into that bottom lip as he thinks. "I don't think I'd have any clue how to do it."

"No one has any clue, you figure it out together with your partner and get lots of help from everyone around you."

A certain solemness tugs at the corners of his mouth. The air is heavy and I can feel turmoil emanating from him. The silence feels like a rift between us that I can't cross.

His mouth creases. "My parents were not exactly involved when I was a kid. We got shuffled around, stuck with different training groups and watched by random guards.

"And when they needed us to project the right image, we were dressed up and told to act a certain way." He pauses, as if unsure if he should continue. I meet his gaze and wait. "And if we misstepped, the consequences were usually pretty painful."

"Are you kidding me?" I blurt, anger heating my skin.

Jasper exhales in a rush, leaning back against the sofa and looking at the ceiling. "Yeah, they weren't afraid of punishing us like any other pack member. Beating, withholding food, whatever."

He's quiet like he's trying to think of anything else and not relive some of those memories.

I knew his parents were awful. They've committed numerous crimes, and it's easy to deduce that they weren't warm and caring parents either. But the idea of them hurting Jasper as a child has me seething. My nails cut into my palms. But this anger doesn't help him, so I let it burn through me and quickly cool.

Rotating to face him, I wrap my arms around him and squeeze. He encircles my ribs and pulls me closer. Suddenly, I'm in his lap, my ass over his legs. His arms band around me with comforting pressure.

My breathing stutters, but Jasper doesn't seem to notice. Or he doesn't care. I focus on comforting him, running my fingers through his silky hair.

"You didn't deserve that," I murmur.

He buries his face in my hair and stills, each breath slower than the one before. He's calming down. The moment could be ten minutes or ten seconds. My brain shorts out and I've lost all sense of time and place.

Slowly, Jasper loosens his hold and I'm able to slide onto the sofa beside him, though his arm stays across my shoulders.

"You're nothing like your family," I say softly.

"Thanks." Clearing his throat, he untangles himself and stands. "It's getting late, and I'm gonna take an early morning run again."

"Good night," I say hurriedly, folding the blanket and setting it aside neatly.

"Thanks, Marigold," he says, his smile smaller and slightly sad.

I look into his eyes, noticing they're slightly red. "Any time."

The solitude of my room seems so vast after being wrapped up in Jasper's hug, cocooned in a thick blanket. The smell of detergent, dust, and dirt I've tracked in is astringent compared to his comforting scent.

Pulling the covers up to my chin, I force myself to relax. If I'm being honest, the proximity of him alone in his personal space has every nerve in my body on overdrive. I can hardly think straight.

He's just a friend. But hell, I'm not immune to utter masculine perfection. The golden stubble across his jaw and the way it feels against my cheek. The size of his hands over my hips as he embraces me. The more of his heart that I see, the more I adore him. I might be in trouble.

Chapter Four

Rosemary & Rejection

Jasper

My beautiful roommate dominates my thoughts all morning. She gets ready while I am running and then slips past me to grab breakfast at the diner before heading to her classroom.

Even after she leaves, I can smell her herbal scent all over my cabin. It's tempting to step into her room and bury my nose in her pillow, but that would be creepy - not to mention she might be able to tell, so I keep my feet firmly at the threshold.

Driven to distraction, my performance at training suffers. Fisher pairs me with Onyx, and normally I would have him on the ground in seconds. But he whirls around me and twists my arm, forcing me to my knees.

"See? I can absolutely whoop your ass!" he croons, turning to make sure there were witnesses.

"You're ridiculous," I say, brushing myself off.

Onyx grins. "Maybe, but I still won."

Fisher walks past and crosses his arms, scowling at me and his son. "Get your head in the game, kid."

"Yes, sir," I reply automatically.

"Want to go again?" Onyx bounces between the balls of his feet.

My wrist twinges as I rotate it. "Sure." I roll my shoulders before stepping back to the mat. "Hey, can we switch patrols? I'd like an earlier lunch today if that's okay."

"No problem."

Onyx doesn't win a second time, but I go easy on him when I pin him against the mat.

Across the gym, I spy Fisher grappling with Slate, the older man slowly losing ground.

Two and a half hours later, Onyx is taking my patrol with Cassia and Vale, and I'm headed toward the meadow.

Right on time, the wildlings pour out of the schoolhouse and tumble toward the diner to get their lunches. I wait for Marigold to follow them, but she doesn't.

Minutes tick by, and I begin to suspect that she is choosing to work through lunch, or is simply too distracted to remember to grab food.

Absolutely unacceptable.

Chewing my lip, I try to remember how Marigold prefers her hamburgers. Cheese, bacon, who doesn't love bacon, and maybe some veg? I take it easy on the sauce because I can't recall her eating mustard or ketchup in front of me. Surely she likes the secret sauce Crickett makes, but if not - I'll rush back to the lunch spread and make her a new one. She deserves to eat what she likes.

I push open the classroom door with my back while holding both lunch plates. Marigold putters around the tables, her long hair swaying as she moves, twisted into a thick braid. She's wearing a dress, a dark goldenrod color with tiny burgundy mushrooms scattered across the fabric. It hugs her trim waist and flares over those luscious hips.

With a cough, I force my gaze up to her head. I really shouldn't be looking at her hips. Or that ass. But the soft curls escaping her plaited reddish-gold hair are just as distracting.

She turns at the sound of my footsteps and smiles. It hits me like sunshine after a lifetime of shadow, warm and a little blinding.

"Did you forget to eat again?" I tease, holding up the food as an offering.

"You didn't have to do that," she protests, closing the distance between us. I have a sudden impulse to hug her, maybe lift her off the ground. Delicately, she takes the plate and hops onto the nearest table.

"Thank you." She stuffs three potato chips into her mouth at the same time.

Between bites of cheeseburger, I survey the classroom. I'm not sure I've actually been in here before.

"This is a really nice space. I love how much of the kids' art is on the walls. I'm sure they feel really special," I say, thinking out loud.

"Thanks," Marigold says, a rosy tint spreading across her nose and cheeks. Her ankles cross and uncross twice.

Wiping the salt off my fingers, I realize I should have brought drinks. Marigold must have the same thought because she takes a drink from her hydro flask and then holds it out to me. Sharing drinks, that's a new thing. I'm not about to turn her down though. With a slight hesitation, I close my lips around the built-in straw and take a long drink.

"Is this flavored water?"

Marigold shrugs with a guilty smile. "Yeah, I think today it's strawberry-watermelon, maybe? It helps me drink more water. Otherwise, I'm so busy chasing these kids around that I forget to drink anything and end up dehydrated."

"Smart." I take another sip, loving the way it reminds me of her. "So will you be home right after work or do you have plans?" Her lips curl into a smile at the word *home.*

Looking away, she shrugs. "I think I'll stop by my dad's cabin for a bit. Not sure I'll be back before dinner, but we can eat right away and then have some hang-out time afterward."

Her dad's cabin... her father is a Zeta and happens to have the late afternoon patrol, so he won't be home. Indigo will be with her grandmother apprenticing, and her youngest brother, Cobalt, always plays soccer with the other kids his age until dinner. Unless she's babysitting Cobalt, it sounds like she's visiting an empty cabin.

"Why?" I ask tentatively, against my better judgment.

Marigold hesitates, taking a bite of her hamburger. I watch her chew and swallow, not ready to let it go. "I like to check in on them."

That's evasive.

My eyes narrow. "Aren't your dad and brothers all out of the house between school and dinner?"

"Oh, yeah," she answers, her voice a bit higher. "Sometimes I like to help out a bit. You know?"

I didn't know, but I nod along and toss the last bite of my lunch into my mouth. Mentally, I catalog each of her words so I can mull them over later because it sounds like she's going over to help out with housekeeping and that would be strange.

Before I can question her further, Willow, Elwood, and Daisy storm into the classroom, arguing loudly. I catch the words wolf, gray, and biggest.

"Shush, you won't know what your wolf looks like until it happens, so chill," Marigold scolds, clearly familiar with the argument.

She shoos them to the table where she's laid out various math worksheets with the kids' names written in bold sharpie across the top so they don't grab the wrong one. It must be tricky preparing so many different grades at the same time.

"I'll see you tonight." She's busy, and I'd better get ready for patrol. At least she turns and waves at me before more kids run through the door and steal her attention.

My hand grips the door frame as I look back. She's beaming even as she instructs her rowdy students, like sunshine that can't stop shining. My afternoon duties suddenly seem dull in comparison, but I won't shirk my responsibilities.

Striding across the meadow, I'm joined by packmates also assigned to afternoon scouting. In the training building, we strip and shift into our four-legged versions.

Taking a deep breath, the scents of the entire pack stream through my consciousness. I can pick out Hazel's honey scent mixed with Slate's woodsy smell. Onyx, Marigold, Heath. And I can sense the general emotions of my packmates clearly, now that my human inhibitions are wiped away.

A gentle contentment simmers between all the members of the Bracken Creek Pack. I'll never get tired of these feelings, after twenty-plus years of jealousy, anger, pride, and greed from my birth pack. In lieu of avoiding my pack's bond, I sink into it, letting it fill me.

I lead our group northeast, toward Ironcrest. We circle the pack's boundaries, looking for any hint of invaders, rogue wolves or other packs. All is calm. Moving west, our group picks up speed.

Patrol isn't only about safety. It's about running together as much as enforcing our borders. The small groups are always varying, and today I run beside Slate and Aven, a reserved woman a few years older than us. She's talented enough to hold a higher role than her Theta title, but she isn't as dominant as other females like Cassia and Hazel. She's a steady presence as we venture deeper into our territory.

Pine needles churn under my paws, my nails gouging the soil. My ears swivel to pick up the sounds of little creatures and even larger prey. The sense of freedom that comes from running as a wolf is intoxicating. It's why I shift for my own short run every morning.

After a couple of hours, we head back toward our clearing, the day's work done. I slow near the school building, spotting a familiar strawberry blonde head of hair.

Marigold stands in the doorway, smiling and chatting with Cedar. She laughs, throwing her head back. My muscles coil and I have to suppress a growl as she reveals a length of creamy neck and chest to another male.

I've been so stupid. Every one of my thoughts has been taken up by this woman, and she's busy pining over someone else. I knew she had a crush on him, but it didn't seem real when she was touching me, curled up on my sofa, resting her head on my shoulder.

Feeling sick, I lope toward the training building to shift back. Even after dressing, I'm still fighting the jealousy I never expected to feel over my friend and roommate.

Marigold

The afternoon goes quickly. After lunch, my older students work around the pack, assisting adults with various jobs to gain experience. The remaining younger students are eager to finish math and earn some art time, and I'm happy to let them get out paints and paper.

Sitting beside Daisy, I doodle little cartoon wolves across a page while I praise the children around me. Their concentration is impressive as they build their own masterpieces.

After releasing my students for the day, I linger out in the meadow watching them play for a while. Honestly, I'm hoping to see Jasper come back from patrol.

Cedar steps out of the diner and heads toward his garden. "Hey, Marigold," he says in passing.

"What are you up to?" I ask. His feet slow.

"My mom wants some rosemary and chives for dinner," he answers. He grows all sorts of herbs and I love joining him in the pack garden.

"I'll help you!"

"I don't need help," Cedar says, "but I'd enjoy the company."

Beaming, I fall into step beside him. "Perfect."

We pass through the archway and my hand brushes against the trailing vines. He heads down the central path without glancing back.

"I love this time of year," I share, swinging my arms and enjoying the warmer weather.

"I do too. The transplants are all doing nicely. We're starting to see more bugs."

The walkway circles around the barrels that contain most of the herbs Cedar grows. Rosemary and mint overflow their containers, always trying to take over the rest of the garden.

He pulls a tiny pair of shears out of his pocket, making me smile at his quirky habits, and snips several sprigs. I take them from his hands, trying to be useful in some small way.

A lower, long garden bed with a protective screen arching over the top holds the delicate herbs. With practiced expertise, he harvests chives from among the thyme, oregano, and marjoram.

"Marigold, you smell like Jasper," he states, standing to face me.

My fingers run along the collar of my dress uncomfortably. It's such an unexpected accusation and his impartial tone gives nothing of his interpretation away.

"He and I hung out yesterday evening," I answer, biting the inside of my cheek. It's technically true. Hopefully, he's satisfied and lets it go.

His dark eyes study me. "Are you dating him?"

A flush crawls up my neck. This is the exact assumption we wanted to avoid.

"Absolutely not. No." I throw my hands up, almost launching the rosemary into the next garden bed. Whoops! Clutching the sprigs together, I cross my arms.

"So why do you smell like him?" he asks.

My mouth gapes open as my heart races. He isn't buying my excuse. Repeating it will make me look like a liar. The best option is the truth.

"I'm temporarily staying in his second bedroom," I explain.

"Interesting." His face stays passive.

"Nothing is going on! I needed a space of my own and he has the room, and it's been fun." My hands wave to emphasize my point, and I have to gather the herbs together to avoid losing them.

"Cool," he says. Apparently, that's enough of an explanation for him because he heads back toward the diner without another word.

After delivering the herbs, we head toward the training building to meet up with the patrol that has returned.

"Are you guys busy?" Hazel asks. Cedar shrugs.

"Not really, what's up?" I say.

Hazel glances behind her. Slate strolls across the meadow toward us, Onyx and Jasper beside him. "We were thinking about a short hike before dinner. It's too nice out to waste. Do you want to join us?"

"Sure," Cedar says.

"Yeah, sounds great." I have to agree with her, it's too lovely out to stay indoors. The trees smell fresh and green with new growth. Wildflowers have started to bloom.

"How was your day?" Slate asks Hazel. She swings their clasped hands as they walk. Adorable.

"Great," she answers, smiling up at him like he is her moon and stars. I find myself sighing and looking toward Jasper. His clear turquoise eyes gaze ahead, framed in blonde lashes lit up with filtered sunlight.

We wander north-east toward an area with an incredible view. Slate loves this spot. The musty smell of decaying leaves and the crisp scent of pine resin sink into my lungs as we get further from our community and into the thicker forest.

Jasper slows to walk beside me but stays silent. Our wrists brush and I lift my hands instinctively, clasping them together nervously.

"Did you have a good patrol?" I ask, making my voice cheery.

He nods, not looking at me. "Fine. How was the afternoon with your students?"

"Fine," I say slowly, drawing the word out.

"And you had a good time with Cedar?" he says, his tone cold.

My smile melts into a scowl and I study his expression for more information. He looks irritated, but I can't imagine why. "I guess. I helped him harvest some herbs for Clove. So we are getting her herb dinner rolls tonight if we're lucky."

He purses his lips, silent.

"Are you okay?" I ask.

"I'm good," he says, finally looking at me. I search for hints of anger or hurt in his bright eyes, but he's an enigma. I can tell he isn't happy, but whatever he's feeling is layered and he's keeping it contained.

Slate asks a question I don't catch, and Jasper speeds up to walk alongside his brother. Onyx takes his spot.

"Hey, Goldie," he says, "I'm sorry for giving you a hard time the other day."

"What are you talking about?" I ask. He's always pulling some prank or joke, there's no telling what he's referencing.

"About you and Jasper. At the bonfire," he says.

I shrug. "It's nothing. I owed him an apology after I put my foot in my mouth. But it's all good."

"Cool, yeah," Onyx says, his midnight blue eyes widening as he relaxes.

"Check out this view!" Hazel says, waving us forward. I stand beside her and Hazel drapes an arm around my shoulders. "I'll never get tired of this."

Being a new wolf, everything is still fresh for her. She reminds me why I love being in this pack. The sun is lowering on the horizon, but we still have an hour or two until it gets dark. The clouds skimming the distant peaks are tinted pink against the blue sky.

"Hazel, truth or dare?" Onyx asks. He settles on one of the boulders along the edge.

Hazel folds her arms, narrowing her eyes on him. "Truth."

"Does Slate use your skincare products?" Onyx asks.

Hazel bursts into laughter, looking apologetically at her mate. "I cannot confirm or deny that this handsome man likes to use the same moisturizer as me."

"It's got SPF in it," Slate says with a shrug.

"Knew it!" Onyx says, grinning.

"Okay, my turn," Hazel says, wrinkling her nose as she surveys potential victims. "Marigold, truth or dare?"

"Dare," I say, placing my hands on my hips.

"Alright, I'd like you to try yodeling. I've always wondered if we could get a good echo up here." Hazel grins wickedly.

Pressing my fingers to my eyelids, I shake my head. This is going to be so embarrassing, but a dare is a dare. Stepping closer to the edge, I suck in a deep breath and let out my best impression of a yodel. It's so off-key, I sound more like a goose than a Swiss cow herder.

When I finish, everyone is laughing. A blush colors my cheeks, but I'm pleased my friends are entertained.

"That was amazing," Hazel wheezes, squeezing my arm. It's worth it to see her laugh.

"Okay, Marigold, what's it going to be?" Onyx asks.

"Jasper," I say, smirking. "Truth or dare?"

"Truth." He stretches out his legs, a lazy confidence rolling off of him.

"What's an embarrassing childhood story of yours?" I ask.

Jasper taps his fingers against his mouth while he considers his answer. "When I was five, I shot an arrow through my foot."

"What?" Hazel asks, straightening.

Shrugging as if it's nothing, he explains, "I was messing around with a crossbow. I've got a nasty scar from it."

"Wow," I say, wincing as I picture one of my 5-year-old students with a crossbow. No one in our pack would let a child near the weapons we store in the training building.

"Satisfied?" he asks, something uncaring in his tone.

I wrap my arms around myself and nod.

"Cedar, truth or dare?" Jasper asks.

"Truth," Cedar says.

Jasper's jaw ticks, and his gaze lingers on my face in a way that sours my stomach. "Do you have romantic feelings for Marigold?"

"What?" I squeak, whirling on him. "What is the matter with you?"

Cedar quirks half in his mouth in an apologetic smile. "I adore her, she's like family. But nothing romantic."

I want to sink into the dirt. My skin is flaming. The whole group shifts their weight uncomfortably. Gaze on the ground, I can't bring myself to look at either Cedar or Jasper. His answer was casual enough, but everyone here knows what a loaded question that was. The back of my neck prickles.

"Cedar, it's your turn," Hazel prompts. I'm grateful we can move on, but my face is still burning.

Clearing his throat, Cedar says, "Slate, truth or dare?"

"Dare," Slate says with a bold grin.

"Jump into the creek," Cedar says.

"No problem." Slate's off, heading toward a less steep incline until he can reach the riverbed. I don't bother watching him strip and jump in. Onyx whoops and jogs after him. Hazel stands on the edge, shouting encouragement and Jasper joins her, though he keeps glancing back at me.

Cedar studies me, his dimple showing as he grimaces. "Did my answer bother you?"

"No!" I say way too brightly. "Of course not!"

"Alright," he says slowly, as if he doesn't believe me.

"It's fine," I say, holding his gaze to support my lie. The longer I stand here, the louder my blood rushes through my ears, until I'm in danger of swaying on my feet. "I'm not feeling great. I'm gonna head home. Can you let them know?" I ask with a wave toward Hazel.

"Bye, Marigold." Cedar dips his head, his eyes flicking away from me.

Sucking in a breath and slowly exhaling, I turn my feet south, trying to resist breaking into a sprint on my way to Jasper's cabin.

Jasper. Did he feel some measure of this embarrassment when I said essentially the same thing about him? It seemed like a good thing at the time.

But when Cedar said it, I felt so small, so disregarded. I guess being told you're like family is only good when the person wants to be close to you in that way.

Of course, Jasper didn't have a years-long infatuation with me, but if I caused him even a fraction of humiliation, I owe him an apology.

CHAPTER FIVE

CONFESSIONS & COOKIES

Jasper

My feet skim the steps and only hit the porch once before I'm through the doorway of my cabin. Sensing her in her bedroom, I slow my breath and knock softly on the open door.

Marigold sits cross-legged on her neatly made bed, her fingers tugging at the braid in her hair, unraveling it. Her nails snag on a tangle and she lets out a growl. I ignore what that sound does to my body.

"Hey, hey, don't take it out on your poor hair," I tease, crossing the room. Her face lights up in that dazzling smile she wears like armor, though it's looking dull at this moment like she can't quite fake it.

Tentatively, I sit behind her and start to untangle the knot. "You don't have to," she protests, covering the snarl with her hand.

"Just sit and let me do this," I say. Her hands drop to her ankles and her shoulders tense, but she obeys. Her hair is lustrous and I revel in running my fingers through it. Gently, I tug apart the braid until it loosens.

"Thanks," she says hoarsely, almost a whisper.

"Did my question bother you?" I ask, my chest tight.

"It's not that. I'm being ridiculous."

"I love it when you're ridiculous, but you don't seem ridiculous right now, so what's upsetting you?"

Twisting, she peeks over her shoulder at me. "I'm really sorry I said you were ick the other day, that was so messed up, I was put on the spot and felt flustered, and it was such a dumb thing to say."

"So I'm not like a brother?" I ask, a sly smile creeping in. She rolls those luminous eyes. The last few inches of the braid unravel and I reach for the hairbrush left on the desk.

"I can brush my own hair," she says, snagging it out from under my fingers.

I hold my hand out. "I want to. It's time someone took care of *you* for once." She blinks at me but lays the brush in my outstretched palm. "I see how hard you work for everyone else, all the time."

The first drag of the brush through her hair causes her to let out a soft hum of pleasure.

"Your hair is gorgeous," I murmur. She tightens her shoulders and then lets out a sigh. "You okay? Did I actually upset you?"

"I feel so stupid."

"You're not," I say.

"I've literally spent the last ten years crushing on Cedar and he feels nothing toward me. And everyone knows, and I'm so embarrassed. How could I be this idiotic?"

"I'm sorry, Marigold," I say. "It was horrible of me to ask that and put you guys on the spot in front of everyone."

"I think I'm glad you did. I'd rather know, and I'm not sure I would have listened otherwise. I'm not mad at you, just humiliated."

"Don't be. Everyone adores you, and you have nothing to be embarrassed about. I was a jackass. I was irritated."

"What was bugging you?"

Silence stretches between us. But after what she shared, she deserves an honest answer. "I was jealous."

My ears burn and I can't look at her, but I take a deep breath and keep speaking the truth. "There're times when we're talking and he walks in and suddenly he has all of your interest."

Her lips part in surprise. "I'm sorry. I didn't realize."

"I know I don't have any sort of claim to your attention. But you're not second to anyone else for me. And I guess I wanted to be your first choice too."

She's quiet, her expression thoughtful.

Section by section, I brush out her hair into gleaming waves. Her nails dig into the fabric of her dress across her thighs, wrinkling it.

"Better?" I ask. She gives me a mhmm noise of approval.

"Jasper?" she asks. I set the brush aside and run my fingers through her hair, smoothing it back into a sheet of rose gold down her back. She tips her face upwards and closes her eyes. "I think you are my number one. I'd rather be here with you than with anyone else."

I can't resist grabbing her around the waist and hauling her closer in a tight hug. Her hair falls across my face like a silk curtain that tosses back as she squeals and laughs. Every noise is like music and my heart races.

Her shoulders rise and a flush turns her skin from freckled gold to pinkish bronze. We both sink down until we're settled comfortably across her twin bed, her head against the dip of my waist below my ribs.

"I don't know why I didn't flat out ask him years ago or simply get over it and move on," she muses. Reaching out, she tugs my foot closer, running her fingertips over the scar from the crossbow, though she doesn't say a word about it.

"I get it," I reassure her. "It's nice to have someone to fantasize about, and he's a decent guy." I should stop talking, but I can't help myself. "But he isn't what you need. You deserve someone who is crazy about you. Someone who sees you as a partner and cares about your goals."

She turns her face against my shirt. "Don't say I need Onyx."

My laughter bursts out of me and she joins in. "Onyx doesn't deserve you. You're perfect." The moment tightens around us, her doe eyes widening.

She turns on her side and it breaks the tension. "You never told me about that meeting yesterday."

I describe Zephyr's dramatic apology, and the way he evaded responsibility and subtly snubbed Heath. Marigold curls her lip at the worst parts. When I finish, she rolls to her stomach and props her head on her hands, elbows on the mattress.

"I agree. His wolves wouldn't randomly go off and work for another pack. He ordered them to do it, and he's trying to make us believe otherwise."

"Yeah, but what bothers me is how thoroughly he blamed my dad. If they are such good allies, he wouldn't do that, unless he had a really good reason."

Pausing, she frowns. "You're right. That's really suspicious."

My hand flops down, brushing across her upper back. "Maybe it'll be obvious at the Alpha Counsel. I'm sure Hawthorne and Heath will see right through any shit they try to pull."

"Are you worried about seeing him?" she asks quietly, and I know she doesn't mean Zephyr.

"No, it'll be fine. He can't do anything to me." I say, wishing I fully believed it. I know my pack will keep me safe, but that doesn't mean my parents won't find a way to attack me with their words and accusations.

Before she can ask another question about my problems, I shoot back. "Why do you do chores at your dad's? It seems strange. I mean, your brothers are older, Indigo is almost an adult..."

Her lips thin, but she doesn't try to spin it or lie to me. "My dad is busy and it's hard for him to take care of the cabin. My mom always did pretty much all the housekeeping."

Her mom. I knew nothing about her mom. "I didn't know, you've never told me," I say quietly, hoping she'll continue. She obliges.

"She died from complications from having Cobalt. So it's been about ten years. I was twelve."

"You tried to fill her shoes taking care of the boys?" I guess.

Her voice shakes a little. "Lots of moms helped take care of Cobie. It wasn't like I was caring for a newborn or anything."

"How did your dad handle everything?"

Marigold wets her lips and I follow the motion as she presses them together between her teeth. "Not great. He kinda shut down. Indie and Cobalt needed all of his attention, so I took care of myself and tried to help as much as I could."

My hand runs down her arm again and back up. "That sounds hard."

She raises her chin and meets my gaze. "Honestly, the hardest part was missing my mom, especially as a teenager."

"I'm so sorry." Gently, I tuck her hair behind her ear.

"I feel awful, because there are people like Slate who lost a parent within the last few years, and for me, it's been a decade. I don't feel like I have a right to grieve after all this time. But I do. Something reminds me of her, like when Crickett makes her favorite snickerdoodle cookies, or rainy days, those were her favorite, and it feels like it's fresh. Like I just lost her."

Her confession hangs between us. I've never lost a parent, so I have no idea how that feels. After how terrible my parents were, I can't imagine missing them with any intensity.

"What would you tell a friend who was grieving?" I ask.

She exhales slowly, her face relaxing as she thinks. "Um, that it's okay to feel sad. That it's going to last a long time and never really go away," she answers, her words starting slowly and picking up speed, "and that your sadness will start to mix with happy memories eventually, and it'll be nice to remember them, even if it still hurts at the same time."

I study her face as her emotion seeps out. "So isn't that what you should tell yourself?"

A smile flashes across her face and she reaches out and smacks my abdomen. "I get it, you goober."

"Hey!" I yelp, grabbing her upper arms and pulling her hands out from under her chin. She shrieks, trying to swat me again, her smile becoming a genuine grin.

Marigold

"How are you doing?" Hazel asks, her amber eyes watchful as she sips her lemonade. It's hard to hide anything from her, and I don't want to, but there are a few things I'm not ready to share.

"Fine." My tone is light.

We're settled around a picnic table, kids running back and forth in a vigorous game of tag. Usually, our girls' lunch is the highlight of my week, but today I'm feeling a little wary.

"That was pretty awkward on the hike yesterday. I don't know why Jasper asked that. I wanted to smack him." She wastes no time getting to the source of my uneasiness. With a lopsided smile, Hazel sets her drink down and the ice clinks against the glass.

A blush creeps up my neck and I slowly exhale. "It's okay. We talked about it. He was being stupid, but I'm not mad." My fingers run over the worn grooves in the picnic table, smooth from years of daily use.

"I'll still smack him if you want," Hazel offers. Her nose scrunches up, making her look deceivingly unthreatening.

Chuckling, I go back to my cobb salad, loaded with smokey bacon, eggs, and sharp cheese. The only way a salad is acceptable. We are carnivores after all.

"So, are we not going to talk about your huge crush?" she asks pointedly. I choke on my bite and the lettuce sticks to my throat. It takes a few coughs to clear my airway.

"What do you mean?"

"Marigold," she says, "as long as I've known you, you've been hung up on Cedar. Hearing what he said yesterday must have sucked."

"Oh, yeah." I take a drink, needing time to think. "Honestly, I think I was kinda over it. I was more upset with Jasper being pushy than what Cedar said."

"Oh." Her eyebrows rise incredulously.

Shrugging, I set my fork down. "It was a teenage infatuation. I'm not sure when it faded. I didn't even really realize. But I guess I grew out of it."

"So it's nothing to do with the fact you keep going over to Jasper's cabin every night?"

I almost spit out my drink. How did she know? My impulse is to deny it, but Hazel is too perceptive for that to work. "I can explain."

"Oh, yeah?" she asks, a smug smile crossing her features. She loves having one-up on me, which is fair after all the times I teased her about Slate before they got together.

My fork scrapes my plate as I push a sliver of hard-boiled egg through the remaining lettuce.

"You know how I was frustrated staying with my grandma. It was getting worse." She nods sympathetically. "I finally reached my breaking point, so I asked if I could stay in the second bedroom in Jasper's cabin."

"Why didn't you come stay with us?" Hazel asks, not guilting me, but in a sweet way.

"You and Slate need your space. You're still newly mated."

"We would have loved to have you," she argues.

Rubbing my eyes, I finally admit, "You guys are all over each other all the time. I can't imagine how you are behind closed doors. I certainly don't want to be in your guest room for several weeks. I love you, but I have my limits."

Her cheeks flush and she bursts out laughing. "We're not that bad!"

My stare turns deadpan. "I'm pretty sure he was feeling you up the other night around the campfire."

"No!" she denies, though her blush tells me I'm not far from the truth. "You turned this around on me, but we were talking about you and Jasper." So much for the conversation moving on. "You're not over Cedar because Jasper is becoming a thing for you?"

"We're roommates. Totally platonic," I say, keeping my tone even.

Hazel scoffs. "I wonder if he sees it that way."

"He does." Scowling, I stab a huge piece of chicken and stuff it into my mouth to avoid answering whatever ridiculous question she comes up with next.

Her gaze connects with mine as she leans forward and drops her voice. "Marigold, remember, I know Jasper." She pauses, suddenly serious. "He's been denied the love he needs his entire life. And you are basically a fountain of encouragement and affection. If you're not interested in him like that, then you need to be careful."

Swallowing, I frown at her. "I've been keeping a normal distance. Not being touchy-feely, like we talked about."

"It's more than that. You guys are spending a lot of time alone together now. Even if you're not all over each other, having all that time to talk, I'm sure you guys are getting closer." She rakes her nails through her hair. "If you're not firm with your boundaries, I have no doubt he'll fall head over heels for you."

Shaking my head, I think about how comforting and sweet he's been. "He might be my best friend. But that's it." Hazel's mouth opens in mock horror. "Other than you! My other best friend. He's been so kind and supportive. And respectful."

"I know how great he is. But that doesn't change the situation. I'm not worried you guys are mistreating each other. I'm worried you're crossing lines you don't want to cross," she says.

"I think you're overthinking this. It's been months, and we're clearly only friends. A few extra hours together aren't going to change anything."

"So you're not going to rebound with him?" she asks.

"There's nothing to rebound over!" I say, annoyance creeping in. With a breath, I let it go. "Okay, well what should I do? Because I'm trying to be a good friend. But if you worry he's catching feelings, I'm not sure what to do. I'd rather not confront him about it. That would be mortifying, especially if you're wrong."

My stomach churns at the thought of confronting him. What would I say? *You're not allowed to fall in love with me?*

"I think you need to set clear boundaries with him then."

"Like what?"

She leans back, tapping her fingers on her arms as she thinks. "Avoiding being too physically close is a good start." If only she knew about the hours we spent curled up together in my bed last night talking about our feelings. "And not getting too deep with stuff. Baring your heart and all that." Too late for that one too.

Folding my hands, I cock my head and give her a relaxed smile. "No problem. Don't even worry about it."

That might be the biggest lie I've ever told my friend.

"Okay," she says, her eyes narrowing.

"So how are you guys? How's the new cabin? Did you finish organizing the kitchen drawers?" Thankfully, she lets me steer the conversation away.

"Yeah, but Slate already rearranged everything. Which I guess is okay. He's the one using it most of the time."

"You lucky girl," I say, laughing. Slate spent the holidays learning to bake her favorite chocolatey treats. "Hey, have you heard anything else from Heath about internship assignments for my students?"

The conversation wanders between lighter topics until we are out of time. Hazel heads off to lead a patrol and I dive into a research project with my class.

After school, I'm eager to head home. Jasper had today off work and I'm curious what he's been up to. A soft clink of ceramic drifts between the trees, audible over the crunch of pine needles under my feet.

The cabin smells like cinnamon and burnt sugar, cozy and slightly bitter. I'm stunned, pausing in the doorway. "Whatcha doing?"

"Good afternoon, Roomie," Jasper calls from the kitchen.

Stepping forward, I cock my head, trying to take in the scene. Jasper is standing in the kitchen, holding a spatula and a mixing bowl. "Are you... baking?"

His smirk is so smug, I want to wipe it off his face. "Maybe."

Walking around the counter, I can feel warmth emanating from the oven. Bags of flour and sugar line the counter. Leaning over his shoulder, I spy a bowl of cookie dough before he waves me off with a spatula.

"Before you get up in my business, I got you something." He plunges the spatula into the mixing bowl and sets it aside with a thunk.

Grabbing a shopping bag, he hands it to me, his mouth stretching into a wide grin. It's from the local hardware store. Inside sits a huge skein of woven cord, a couple of thick dowels, a pair of high-end scissors, a few s-hooks and metal rings, and a tape measure.

"Are you serious right now?"

"Did I get the supplies right? The internet wasn't exactly clear."

"Jasper, this is way too much," I say, clutching the bag to my chest instead of shoving it back at him like I should.

He shrugs like it's nothing. "I thought you could make something for our cabin."

Our cabin. That's a first.

"I'm serious, this is like sixty or seventy bucks worth of supplies," I argue, trying to remember exactly how expensive this stuff is. "Let me pay you back."

"You can, with a cool wall hanging." He raises an eyebrow, waiting for my argument. Sure, I'll bite.

"Hey, that's worth way more than sixty bucks," I tease, crossing my arms. "Don't push your luck."

"Even with the best friend discount?" His begging puppy-dog eyes melt my resolve.

"You are unbelievable."

"Believe it, baby," he murmurs, almost to himself, turning back to his baking.

Setting the bag aside, I follow him back to the mixing bowl. A darkly burned batch of cookies sits scattered across a wrinkled sheet of parchment paper by the sink. A fine dusting of flour lightens his black shirt into charcoal.

"Looks like your first attempt didn't go so well."

He scowls at me, though I know he isn't serious. "I've never baked cookies before. Give a guy a break."

"Hey, Jasper?" I ask and he turns to me. "Thank you for the craft supplies. It's really sweet." I hold open my arms, and he pulls me close. While he's savoring our hug, I dip my fingers into the bowl beside him - where a pyramid of flour sits mostly unincorporated over the creamed sugar and butter.

When Jasper releases me, I swipe my fingers across his face, leaving a streak of white powder across his tan skin.

"Did you?" he says, surprise dropping his jaw open.

"Yep!" I say, flouncing away with a gleeful cackle.

He grabs my wrist, pulling me back. "I don't think so. Come back here and help me, if you're so eager to get involved."

"No thank you!" I squeal, yanking my hand away and jumping back.

"Marigold! I really need your help," he whines, trying a different tactic.

Crossing my arms, I smirk at him. "Make me."

For a split second, our eyes lock, mine full of challenge and his full of shock melting into delight. But then he's lurching forward and I have to run.

Tearing out the front door, I dart around the side of the house and pull my shirt off in one smooth movement, leaping right out of my pants as my wolf form overtakes my skin.

That moment of transformation is exhilarating, my four legs stretching as I fall back toward the ground. The scents around me become high-definition, every rustling leaves loud to my wolf ears. The second my paws hit the earth, I'm off, dodging trees and leaping over the foliage.

Jasper pursues me, his huge white wolf faster. Glimpses of snowy fur flash in the edges of my vision as I listen to his steps. I wait for the moment he tackles me, but it doesn't come.

His shoulder pulls level with mine until we are running side by side. Our breathing syncs up, his stride shortening to match mine. Wanting to see what he's made of, I dart sideways and race north-east. Surprisingly agile, he keeps pace with me.

Bumping my side into his, I playfully snap at him. His teeth gleam as he bares them back at me. He can catch me, but can he keep me? I throw my weight into him, throwing him off course.

Finally, he takes the invitation to really play. Leaping forward, he throws his paws up, looping one over my back. I twist, pushing him back a step and trying to throw him to the ground. A growl rumbles out of him and I shiver at the rich sound.

On his second lunge, he allows me to take him to the ground. He rolls over onto his back, his paws framing my ruff. I snip at his muzzle, snapping my jaws closer to his nose.

For a moment we're suspended, me over him. His glowing teal eyes meet mine and I can see how much he loves being in his wolf form. Most shifters do. It's what we're made for. I've noticed his white fur streaking past my window in the mornings.

Gracefully, he rolls to his feet and bends into a classic play-bow. Why yes, I'll happily join you. As I lower my own front-half, he springs forward.

I chase him downhill toward the water, and then back up the slope across the north end of our territory. Faintly, we can hear the afternoon's patrol east of us.

Racing through the trees together is thrilling. As wolves, we can run for hours. But it occurs to me that he may have left the oven on, so after a wide loop, I lead us back home.

Jasper disappears around the corner, allowing me privacy to shift back and pull my clothes on. Rounding the edge of the cabin, I find a deliciously shirtless man standing on the patio waiting for me.

"Now will you help me bake?" he asks, looking far too pleased with himself as I avoid looking at his chest.

"Fine." Grabbing his hand, I drag him into the kitchen and start checking his recipe. It looks good so far. "I think you baked them too long."

"I baked them for twelve minutes like the recipe says." He's baffled and it's adorable.

I triple check the temperature. "Different ovens heat differently. This oven might run warmer or colder, but without an oven thermometer, I can't tell."

"Do I need one of those?" he asks.

"No, but it's a safe bet it does run ten degrees hotter, maybe fifteen. We can turn it down and see how they bake." The buttons chirp as he follows my instructions.

As he mixes the flour in, I tear off more parchment paper and lay the baking trays out. He sets the bowl of dough in front of me with a thud. "Look good?"

Nodding I scoop the first cookie and plop it onto the tray.

"Wait, you missed a step," he says, picking the dough up and dropping it into a smaller bowl and rolling it around. Cinnamon sugar.

"You're making snickerdoodles?" I say, spinning to face him.

He doesn't look up, finishing rolling the cookie dough in the sugar mixture and setting it back on the cookie sheet.

"Jasper?" I prompt.

Finally his cyan eyes flick upwards. "Yeah?"

"You're making snickerdoodle cookies after I told you about my mom." I speak slowly, wanting his confirmation. His smile turns guilty.

Shoulders tensing, he scoops another dough ball and tosses it into the sugar. "Maybe I'm craving them after you mentioned it."

"Asshole." He laughs as I swat his arm.

My assumptions about the oven temperature prove correct. The second tray of cookies come out golden and gorgeous. Some edges are a little too brown, telling me the dough wasn't mixed thoroughly. But I don't think he needs a critique, not when it's his first time baking cookies. Practice smooths out many mistakes.

His bright eyes watch my face as I chew my first bite. I nod, giving him a thumbs up. He visibly relaxes, taking a cookie for himself.

"Pretty good for a rookie, right?" he says, his cocky smirk back. As I turn back to scoop the rest of the dough out onto one last tray, I hear him say, "a cookie rookie," under his breath. Glancing back, I crinkle my nose with amusement so he knows I heard him. That earns an embarrassed laugh.

Jasper insists on doing the dishes and I settle on the sofa with another snickerdoodle cookie. He hums as he scrubs, the running water and clinks of bowls and measuring cups forming a dissonant accompaniment. I watch his profile, admiring the curve of his lips and cut of his jaw.

By the time the kitchen is clean, it's time to meet everyone for a community dinner. We don't bother arriving separately, though he stands a bit further away from me once we arrive in the clearing. I want to grab his arm, but I try to respect the silent boundary. Hazel is right, we should keep a little distance. Even if I don't really want to.

Jasper

Storm clouds roll over the treetops along the north-east edge of our territory. Onyx carries a box of electronics as Slate picks out spots to install security cameras. They're rated for all-weather outdoor use, so a few raindrops aren't going to interrupt our work.

The increased monitoring along our shared border will allow me to breathe easier. Heath allowed

Hawthorne and I to pick out the tech, and Onyx helped because he's good with electronics.

"Hazel told me Marigold is staying with you," Slate says, looking straight ahead. Onyx swings around, his mouth gaping. Thankfully, he manages to control himself long enough to hear my answer.

"She had some issue with her grandma and asked to crash with me." Shrugging, I say, "The cabin has two bedrooms. It would be dumb to tell her no." That might be downplaying it, but I don't like how stiff Slate's posture is.

"Wait, how long have you guys been living together?" Onyx asks.

Sighing, I rake my fingers through my hair and push it out of my eyes. "About a week."

"She could've stayed with us. We have a second bedroom too," Slate says. I frown, really not wanting to have this conversation, but luckily Onyx jumps in.

He snorts. "Really, dude? You guys are so handsy, we're all glad your cabin is one of the farthest away. No one wants to stay with you." My brother glares at Onyx with an expression that would stop me in my tracks, but Onyx just barks out a laugh.

"It's no big deal. I've got plenty of space and she's nice to have around," I say.

Slate halts, looking up at a gnarly oak tree. "How about this one?"

I breathe in, testing the scents. Our scent is starting to fade here, but the hint of Ironcrest is so faint, I almost can't smell it. "Looks good to me." Grabbing a low branch, I haul myself up, anchoring my back against the trunk and wedging my feet against the largest lower branches.

"So she's baking in your kitchen, singing in your shower, walking around in her bunny slippers." Onyx hands up a little camera along with the hooks and a screwdriver.

"I don't think you have a clue what women behave like," I say dryly.

He doesn't need to know I was the one baking in our kitchen. Marigold does have a lovely singing voice in the shower - also something I don't want to share.

Onyx gives me a strange look, his typical grin absent. Whatever he sees must irritate him, because he scowls at the tree trunk.

Flicking the camera on, I hold it against the trunk where there's a split that will camouflage the tech.

"Angle it down a bit," Slate says, monitoring the live feed with his phone. I adjust per his instructions. "Perfect. This one gives a really clear view."

It only takes a moment to affix the security camera in place. I hand the tools back down to Onyx and then lower myself onto the nearest branch before letting myself drop. Leaves flurry around my feet as I land.

"How many more?" I ask.

"Three," Onyx answers sullenly.

"What's wrong?" I ask.

"Nothing," he says, refusing to look back at me.

A fine mist of rain filters down between the branches and coats my arms and face.

"Let's hurry this up, I don't want to get soaked," Slate says.

We walk in silence, but Onyx's mood continues to decline. After he makes an angry scoffing nose low in his throat, I finally speak up.

"Just tell me what's pissed you off."

For a moment, he glowers at me. "We all saw how upset she was the other day. You were being an asshole. And she's always had a thing for Cedar and you forced them to face that, and Cedar wasn't ready. So now that's ruined."

He's right, but I can't bring myself to feel remorse. Cedar's feelings aren't my priority, Marigold's are. I don't care if I ruined anything for him. Onyx is delusional if he thinks anything would have happened between Cedar and Marigold given more time.

Sure, I could have handled things better, but it was worth it. She's freed from that one-sided relationship. I'll take any shit I get for what I said, knowing that Marigold is happy.

Voice level, I speak to Onyx in the most reasonable tone I can muster. "I'm sorry about that. I already apologized to Marigold. If they're meant to be together, I'm sure it'll still happen. But if your brother says he doesn't have feelings for her, maybe you should trust that."

Onyx's lip curls, some acidic remark brewing. But Slate decides to step in. "So nothing is happening between you two?" he verifies.

Huffing, I throw my hands up. "No. She's a friend who needed a place to stay. It's no different than if she stayed with you," I say with a pointed look at Onyx. If one more person asks if we are now dating, I'm going to shift into my wolf and eat them.

"Maybe she should," Onyx starts, but Slate has had enough.

"We need to get going. As much fun as this has been, I'm ready to be done for the day." Slate's tone leaves no room for arguing.

"Agreed," I say.

We secure the next camera, and I can see Onyx softening. He won't apologize, but he nods at me while handing over tools and is meeting my gaze again.

As soon as the last camera is in place, we head back. It's really raining now. My t-shirt clings to me, and Slate and Onyx's longer hair slicks to their necks. We stash the tools away before parting.

"So I'm the only one who doesn't have a beautiful girl to go home to," Onyx complains, back to his usual mildly irritating self. Slate rolls his eyes and laughs before taking off.

Marigold won't be off work for a while, but I don't see any movement through the classroom windows. Hopefully she's enjoying a quiet afternoon.

Knowing I shouldn't bother her at work, I go home.

Rain patters on the roof, filling the cabin with soft music. Perfect weather to curl up with a book and leftover cookies. The afternoon is quiet, at least until Marigold comes home.

Her scent reaches me right before her voice hollers, "I blame you!"

"What?" I call back, loving her sass.

"It finally happened." She leans around the doorway to my room and I set my book aside on the round table beside my armchair. Her hair is dark with water and her shirt and sweats cling to her.

"Elwood and Starling were fighting, and it was kinda bad, and then Elwood had his very first shift - while we were on a freaking nature walk! And he took off, and then it started raining so we couldn't even track him properly!"

"I'm so sorry," I say, jumping up and meeting her. "I wish I had known so I could have helped."

My hands go to her upper arms. She's chilled.

"It's fine. His brother was right there, we actually found him pretty quick." She shrugs with a cute half-smile. "Just not quick enough to keep me from getting totally stressed out and drenched."

She motions down her body as if I hadn't already been acutely aware of the way her clothes plaster to her figure. Her giggle is a bit manic and it leads to her entire body convulsing in an uncontrolled shiver.

"Geez, Marigold, you're freezing." The giggle redoubles followed by another shiver. "Stay here. You need to warm up."

Grabbing a blanket off my bed, I wrap her up and hand her one of the snickerdoodle cookies off the kitchen counter. While she nibbles on it, I crank the tub faucet all the way to the left. Once the water heats, I set the stopper of the vintage claw-foot tub.

Marigold follows me into the bathroom and stands by the sink.

"Since you had such a stressful day and you're cold, I thought a bath would be really good for you." The Epsom salts dissolve into the hot water easily and the air fills with the scent of lavender.

"A bath?" she echoes, like it isn't right in front of her.

"Yeah, it'll warm you up and the salt will help your muscles relax so you aren't sore tomorrow." Rubbing her arms, I slide past her in the narrow bathroom and pause at the doorway.

"You're spoiling me." Her smile makes it worth it.

"I'm not done. It's almost dinner, so I'm gonna grab us food. And after your bath, we can eat by the fire and I'll open a bottle of wine," I find myself saying.

"That seems excessive."

She might be right about that, but I can't help it.

"You don't need to do any of this," she protests.

Chuckling, I tug the blanket off of her and give her a little push toward the steaming tub. "I want to. You deserve it."

"I don't want to be a burden." Her vulnerability shows through.

My hands grasp her shoulders so I can look her square in the face. "You're always taking care of everyone else." She opens her mouth to argue. "Don't deny it, I've seen it. So now it's your turn."

She scowls at me. "That's not your job."

"Well, someone needs to do it."

She reaches up and tugs at my shirt. "Can I convince you to let *me* get food while *you* enjoy the bath?" She cocks her head. "You seem like a bath guy."

I know she doesn't mean to flirt, but my breathing slows as my heart rate increases. Deliberately, I step back. "Absolutely not."

"Oh come on." Even her whiny voice is adorable. Her lip pouts and I raise my hand to touch her on instinct. Catching myself, I twirl my finger, ordering her to turn around.

"Get in your bath now, or I'm going to put you in it myself."

"You wouldn't dare." She crosses her arms.

"Marigold, don't make me throw you over my shoulder." My thoughts fill with the image of her ass in the air, legs dangling, while I grip her thighs to keep her steady. Not helpful, but better than the image of climbing into the bath with her.

"Fine. But I'm washing dishes tonight." Rolling her eyes, she starts to lift the hem of her shirt.

Blood rushes in my ears as I shut the door and lean my back against it. Of course I knew she'd shower in my bathroom, but the idea of her soaking in that steaming bath is too enticing to dwell on.

This amazing woman bends herself into a pretzel caring for everyone else, encouraging them with her bright smiles and boundless energy. But after living with her, I see the exhaustion underneath. She deserves someone taking care of her. And until I'm forced to stop, that job is mine.

Dinner is a chicken stir-fry with snow peas and carrots over rice. I've had similar food in town, but my parent's pack would never have served anything so flavorful. I set the plates on my chunky wooden coffee table and locate one of the bottles of Sauvignon Blanc that the internet had said was sweet and mild.

Waiting for her, I attempt to read a few more pages, but all thoughts of reading fall out of my brain when she emerges wrapped in only a towel and tip-toes to her room. Freckles cover the expanse of skin across the top of her chest.

Make-up free, hair wet, but now flushed with heat from her bath, she's the most attractive woman I've ever seen. She comes out in the same oversized sleep shirt she arrived in the first night.

"Oh, I love stir-fry night," she says, grabbing the plate further from my seat and nestling down beside me.

"Yeah, it's great," I say, barely remembering to grab my own food.

She leans her cheek against my shoulder briefly. "Jasper, that really did make me feel a hundred times better. Thank you."

My eyes are on her shirt. There's something about the faded design that bothers me. It seems masculine, which is fine as long as it's hers. But what if it's not.

She dives into her food, stopping only to take a long sip of the wine.

"You like it?" I ask, smiling over my own glass.

It clinks as she sets it down on the table, and her hand drops to my thigh, squeezing. "It's delicious. I didn't know you're a wine connoisseur."

Shaking my head, I set my own glass down so I can wrap my arm around her waist. "I'm not, I have the internet on my phone."

"I've heard of that. Something the teenagers have," she jokes.

It's easy to laugh with Marigold. "Something like that."

"You are younger than me," she says, cooly, though a teasing smile begins to curl her lips.

"Not by much."

"Young hoodlum," she says, scrunching up her face into a scowl. She's adorable.

"At least I know how to use the internet."

Marigold snorts, covering her mouth with the back of her hand. "You're ridiculous."

We lapse into companionable silence, and I finish my meal before she does. Eating quickly was a survival technique growing up, and those habits are slow to unravel. But I'm happy to enjoy Marigold's warmth soaking into my side as she takes tiny bites and savors the last of her dinner.

When she stands, I stand too, but she pushes me back down. "I get the dishes, remember? You agreed." She refills my wine glass.

It's not a bad view. She sways to music in her head while she washes up the two plates and sets them on the counter. They belong to the diner, not the cabin.

Despite the fire, the chill of the rain seeps into the living room too. Once she's satisfied with the kitchen's cleanliness, Marigold ducks into her room.

A moment later, she lets out a little shriek.

I scramble around the coffee table and have her half in my arms before she lets out a laugh.

A slow drip falls from the ceiling right into the center of her bed. The leak has spread across her bedspread and surely soaked down into the sheets.

"Ah, shit."

"Yeah, not ideal," she agrees.

I strip the linens and place a huge bowl under the leak, but that's the best I can do for tonight.

"You should take my bed tonight. I'll sleep on the sofa," I say, grabbing a towel to clean up the spilled wine on the coffee table. Luckily the glass rolled and hadn't broken.

She scoffs. "It's a pretty big bed, I think we can share it."

The glass slips again, but I manage to catch it before it clatters down, giving away my surprise. "Are you sure that's a good idea?"

Shrugging, she leans against the kitchen counter. "We've cuddled up plenty of times. This time we'll be unconscious. That's less scandalous than laying in a bed awake."

It's weird reasoning, but I can't find any reason to disagree. Unfortunately, something is still bothering me.

"Is that your shirt?" I ask.

"Um, yeah? Well, I think it belonged to one of the twins originally, but I've had it for years."

It shouldn't bug me, but it does. She's in my house, and I don't like the idea of her wearing another guy's shirt.

Biting my lip, I stalk to my dresser and dig through the drawers for the softest faded shirt I can find. Marigold stands in the doorway, watching, bemused. Shoving it into her hand, I say, "Here, wear this one instead."

"Okay," she says, her eyes sparkling. Thankfully, she understands the possessiveness that drives shifters. She disappears for a moment, and I sink onto my bed, feeling like an idiot.

That sense of euphoria returns in full as she climbs into my bed and stretches out beside me on her stomach, crossing her arms and setting her chin on them.

My shirt drapes over her back and clings to her hips. It looks so much better on her than it ever did on me. I want to pull her to me, but I settle for admiring her.

The room is warm and the only light comes from the dim lamp on my bedside table. In sunlight, all of her colors are bright and dazzling, but in this low light, I notice the upturn of her nose and the curve of her cupid's bow, and she's somehow more lovely.

"You know, Hazel told me one time that your old pack has very few females," she says, surprising me. That was out of nowhere.

"Yeah, they like to recruit single guys. No distractions from work."

"That sounds awful. So are the guys absolutely feral over the girls they do have?"

I laugh, resting my head back against my pillow. "More like they compete that much harder for rank, since only the top positions get a mate."

"Wait, what?" She pops up, frowning at me.

"What?"

That bottom lip purses as she cocks her head at me. "Are you saying the Granite Ridge pack doesn't allow wolves to choose mates the normal way? It's assigned with rank?"

Shrugging, I roll onto my side to face her. "Yeah. Only the strongest should breed, or that's the idea."

"That's insane. And sounds miserable."

"They don't claim their mates. So if someone loses position or is killed, the other is still available. It's about duty, not love or even support." I try to explain the best way I can. Growing up, it was normal. It took becoming a teenager and seeing other packs and humans in town to realize it was odd.

"Definitely insane. Doesn't that seem terrible to you?"

I chew my lip. "Yeah, it is. But I was going to be the Alpha, so I always knew I would have my pick. Or more likely be paired with a political match."

Up this close, the interwoven tendrils of sapphire and malachite in her irises mesmerize me as her gaze holds me captive. She's studying me and I'm not sure I measure up.

"Are you disappointed you lost that opportunity?"

"No way, it's a relief. Now I can be with whoever I like and there's no pressure."

She hesitates for a beat, wetting her lips. "Did they ever try to pair you up with anyone?"

"Other than Hazel, not really. But they would have if I had stayed. There were lots of discussions about it, but most of them I wasn't involved in. Just informed later."

"Did you like Hazel at first?"

Oh, that's awkward.

I take a moment, thinking through my words. "I did, but she was the first person I had met who was sincere and kind. I barely knew her and I wanted to be around her. And then I discovered her entire pack was like that."

"Oh." She tilts her head slightly, her lips rounded.

"Honestly, she saved my life. I didn't know a pack could be like this."

"Jasper." Her voice is soft, empathetic. But I don't need her comfort, I need to express myself.

"And you are the kindest, brightest person in the pack. You made me feel so welcome and accepted."

"That's sweet, but anyone would have done the same."

"You're not anyone. You were the one I wanted to be around from the first day I arrived."

Tension thickens the air until I can't catch my breath.

She clears her throat, looking away. "What do you think you want in a mate? More of a housewife and mother like Crickett? Or a partner to go into battle with, like Cassia?"

"I don't care," I say, giving into the urge to run my fingers through her hair. When I brushed out her hair a couple of days ago, I learned how silky and soft those reddish gold waves were. Even slightly damp, it's divine to feel those glossy strands slip across my skin.

"Well what do you want in a partner then?" She's so serious, my chest tightens. I didn't expect her to care.

"Um, I guess someone who is loving. I want someone I can talk to and have fun with." A blush washes over my face, and we're so close, there's no way she misses it. "What about you?"

"I don't know." She presses her lips between her teeth, the way she does when she's nervous. "Someone who sees me."

The trust in her expression draws me in, making me feel wanted. I run my knuckles down her cheek, brushing her hair back. She leans into my touch, her eyes fluttering closed. My breath catches as she tilts her face toward me, and I can't resist, not when she's filled up my entire world in the last few days.

Impulsively, I lower my lips to hers, my nose brushing her cheek. She presses back, her mouth smooth and warm. The drag of her lips against mine is the single most earth shattering sensation I've ever experienced. My fingers tangle in her hair, trying to find an anchor as my world is destroyed and put back together in a single moment.

She draws back and stares at me, eyes half-lidded. "That was my first kiss," she says quietly.

What? The gravity of that truth crashes around me. I kissed my best friend and roommate. Fuck.

"I'm so sorry. That was so stupid of me. I wasn't thinking," I say in a rush.

She shrugs, her face pink. "It's okay. No big deal, really."

"We can pretend it never happened." What if she's angry that I robbed her of that experience with someone she really loves? Dread sinks in my gut.

"Sure, never happened." Her voice is higher, emotional. Is she going to cry? Fuckity double fuck.

Is she going to move out? Did I just ruin the best thing in my life? "Please stay, I promise I won't be an idiot again."

"Jasper, chill," she says, reaching out and running her fingers through my hair. Her nails scratch down my scalp, cutting through my panic. I'm able to take a slow breath.

"I'll sleep on the couch. You can have my bed. I'll give you space." I start to get up.

"Really?" Her voice is sarcastic. I freeze, half-upright.

"Stay. I like this." She tugs at my arm, and I'm shocked and thrilled to be pulled down beside her again. She could do absolutely anything to me right now and I'd happily go along.

My heart thumps in my chest so hard I'm sure she can feel it. But she rolls on her side and places my arm over her waist, not releasing me until I've scooted forward and pressed my chest to her back.

"Much warmer," she hums, wiggling her ass back into me. Surely that wasn't intentional. I have no way to hide the reaction my body has to her, but if she notices, she doesn't say anything.

I keep my head back, away from her silky hair or the warm skin of her neck, even though I'd love nothing more than to press my nose against her skin and breathe in the scent of rosemary and sage.

"This is really nice," I say quietly. She murmurs a soft noise of agreement, but nothing else.

Sleep seems impossible with her soft body against mine. But eventually her breathing evens out, and ages later, so does mine. Sleep is peaceful, and when I wake up with her still in my arms, I'm filled with this feeling of tightness I can't shake.

I kissed my roommate and best friend. And if I'm being honest, she's been my secret crush for a long time, even if I was too dumb to recognize it. Nothing else can explain my private obsession with her smell, her hair, the way she smiles. Everything about her.

Could she feel the same way? The way she clings to me gives me hope. But most likely, she hasn't realized anything yet. Maybe I can help with that. What's a little flirting between roommates?

CHAPTER SEVEN

SPARRING & SUBTERFUGE

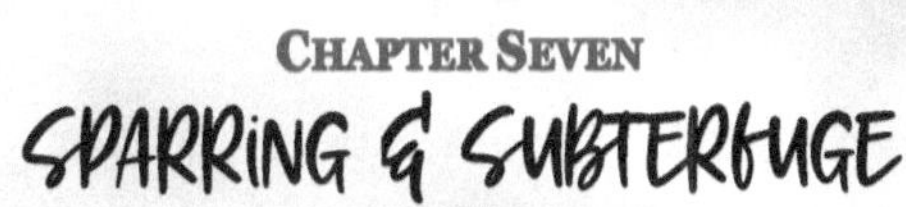

Marigold

"**G**ood morning, Sunshine," Jasper murmurs into my hair before he climbs out of his bed. My muscles are liquid and I couldn't follow him if I wanted to. The sheets smell like him. Burying my nose into my pillow, I breathe in the soft spiced scent. It's so comforting, I start to drift off again.

After his morning run, I hear the shower crank on. I'd better get myself up. But it's so cozy, I don't move until

he comes into his bedroom wrapped only in a towel, with an expanse of wet, golden skin that heats my blood.

Memories of his mouth against mine bombard me, urging me to leap at him, wrap myself around him like a deranged sloth. Suck on that full bottom lip.

Maybe I'm less okay than I said.

Scrambling out of bed, I head into my room to change, giving him privacy. And as I shimmy out of my clothes, I don't think of him taking that towel off. Not one bit.

Saturdays are for sparring. Every pack member takes either a position like Theta or Zeta, or a normal job, like mine. But regardless, everyone needs to train and be prepared to defend our territory at any time.

I meet Hazel in the training building. Her dark hair bobs in a perky ponytail. "Ready for some exercise?" she says, as if she doesn't work out every single day. Hazel's only been a wolf for a few months, and she trains harder than anyone else to make up the difference in experience. As the Alpha's heir, she has to be ready for challenges. Yet again, I'm glad to not have a leadership position within the pack.

Teaching might also make me sweat, but it's way more fun than the endless training exercises that leave bruises across Jasper's ribs.

"Yup!" I twist at the waist, swinging my arms and giving her a bright smile.

Hazel's eyes wrinkle as she smiles back. "You look peppy today. More than normal, I mean."

"Hey, ladies!" Onyx yells through the open garage door. A few older wolves are setting out for a run, but otherwise it looks pretty quiet.

I toss my jacket down on a bench. "Hey Onyx, ready to get your ass handed to you?"

"You couldn't handle me," he shoots back with a grin.

Warmth presses against my arm as a hand slides across my lower back to grip my waist, igniting sparks under my skin. "Don't waste your time with him." Jasper's voice leaves goosebumps along my arms.

"Think you can do better?" I flirt back, leaning into his chest.

One eyebrow arches. "You'll see." Sliding past me, he greets everyone. Cedar is missing, and Onyx makes an excuse for him, something about the chicken coup.

"Marigold, you up for a match?" Hazel asks.

"I'll take on Jasper, actually," I announce.

"Are you sure you want to fight me?" he asks, warning in his eyes despite the fact it's clearly what he wants.

Shrugging, I hold my arm across my chest in a stretch. "Hazel can train with Slate today. I want to see what you've got."

This leaves Onyx, and he decides to practice with weaponry, throwing slim daggers into a target nailed to a tree. Slate is more than happy to grapple with his mate, and within minutes they're trading punches and kicks in the graceful way partners do when they know each other's movements as thoroughly as their own.

"Ready?" Jasper asks, ushering me onto the blue mats. "Want to up the stakes?"

"How?" I bounce between the balls of my feet, psyching myself up.

"Loser has to give the winner a massage," he murmurs.

"Sure, I'd love a massage."

Jasper watches me, utterly relaxed.

Edging forward, I take my first strike, my fist flying at his shoulder. His arm knocks it aside, but instead of simply blocking, he surges forward, forcing me to step sideways and wrapping his arm across my upper chest and hauling me toward him. He could easily put me in a headlock. Biting my cheeks, I resist the urge to melt into him. The corded muscles of his forearm stand out, begging for me to run my fingers along them.

"I think you're my favorite sparring partner, Sunshine."

"What's with the nickname?" I ask, waiting for him to release me, instead of struggling against a hold I know I can't break. That is, without kicking his shins or scratching his face, or some other move that would injure him. And I like my roommate uninjured, to be honest.

"I think it suits you," he purrs, voice quiet enough it's private. The heat of his breath feathers against my ear. My body shivers and he releases me with a low laugh.

Frustrated at my reaction, I set my weight back and twist, aiming a hard kick to his ribs. Grinning, he grabs my ankle and uses my own momentum to throw me onto the mat. Walking past, he waits for me to scramble up.

That was humiliating. I thought I was a bit better than this. I've beat other opponents. But other opponents don't lean in and whisper distracting words.

"I'm going to get you back for that," I say, panting.

Taking my time, I look for an opening and feint a punch followed with a swift kick to his thigh, lower so he can't grab me. His smile returns, something akin to pride warming his face.

He likes when I successfully land a hit? Fantastic.

I step closer, ready to try the same trick again. But the scent of baking spices wraps about me, muddling my focus. He gets close, too close. I can't land a hit when his forearm shoves my chest, and his other hand grabs my shoulder, twisting me as I fall backwards. My torso hits the mat, arms pinned behind me in his grasp. His knees frame my hips as he kneels over me. "Had enough? I'm happy to throw you on your back a few more times if you're not done."

Growling in irritation at his teasing, I wrench my wrists free and roll to my feet, causing him to step back. His cocky grin usually amuses me, but right now I want to strangle him.

I throw another punch allowing him to block it, but then hook my other hand at the nape of his neck. Not a traditional move. He hesitates, trying to read my intentions. Putting my weight into it, I grab the arm he blocked with and tug, while pulling his entire body sideways. He goes down like a rock. My knee hits the ground beside him and I grin down triumphantly.

His blonde hair fans across his forehead and I like seeing his typical sleek composure ruffled. He smiles back, sweet and genuine. "Very good," he praises, his words lighting my whole body up.

Why is he so stunning? It's unfair to the rest of us.

After two more matches that include me landing on my back approximately five times each, Hazel suggests we shift and find the twins for a good run.

Jasper's hands find my hips as he leans in. "We can finish this later, if you like."

"Maybe, if you behave yourself," I flirt back, blushing at my own breathy tone.

That was interesting. Last night, he said it was stupid to kiss me and told me to pretend it never happened. But the way his hands grip my skin and pull me to him, I'm not sure what to think.

Onyx retrieves Cedar, and we all shift, stashing our clothing away in lockers. My reddish gold coat looks particularly bright against Jasper's snowy white as he rubs his shoulder along mine.

Slate leads us toward the doorway and into the trees. Energy floods me, excitement that is not only mine.

Jasper's white wolf dashes ahead, nipping at Slate's tail as the boys race. Hazel runs beside me. The forest chatters around us, swaying branches, scurrying chipmunks, and even the hurried chirruping of western tanagers.

The boys are out of sight when we hear the rustling and growling. Excitement seeps through our pack bond. We increase our speed until they come into view.

Onyx's dark wolf rolls on the ground with Slate, while Jasper bounces around them. As Slate pins Onyx, Jasper dives for him. They collide in a whirl of gray and white, snapping and shoving with paws.

Jasper subdues Slate for a moment, but the older brother squirms free and abruptly dives at him. With a bark, Jasper takes off running again. Onyx and Slate give chase.

Hazel watches them go, and I'm confident if she was in her human form, she'd be rolling her eyes. Stepping closer, I nudge her muzzle with my nose in a sign of affection. She tilts her head, ears swiveling. With a wag of her tail, she dashes after the boys, inviting me to give chase.

Our endurance as wolves is considerably better than as humans, and it's another hour before we are panting and finished with our play. I haven't won a single game of chase, but the attachment and loyalty between us is stronger than ever.

Jasper

Eight of us gather around the meeting table, the air heavy. Heath sits at the center, with his heirs beside him. Hawthorne rests across from him, with me at his right hand. Fisher, our Delta and trainer, sits on his other side.

To Hazel's right slouches Sable, Marigold's grandmother. The healer's long memory of the local packs has been helpful in preparations for the Alpha Counsel. And at the end perches Linden, our business manager. With mousy brown hair and a reserved demeanor, Linden often joins our meetings to take notes for logistics, budget, or supplies, but I don't know him well. Being a few years older, we've never socialized together.

"How large of a team do you think each pack will bring?" Slate asks. Hazel leans back in her chair, her fingers tapping against her chin.

Hawthorne exhales. "I would expect around ten. Their top three, and then half a dozen guards or so."

"We should set a maximum number," Hazel muses.

Sable purses her lips. "Setting a rule about how many wolves an Alpha can bring is a sure way to make them wary and trigger them breaking that rule." Hazel frowns at her.

"We already have some advantage as the hosts, though it's minimal. I don't think anyone will bring twenty wolves, it would make them look frightened," Heath says. "They'll want to appear confident and powerful in their own right."

Nodding, Hawthorne adds, "Ferris and Zephyr will likely display wealth in any way they can. And all of them are likely to bring not only their closest advisors, but also their most physically impressive."

"Displaying power without numbers," I conclude. Hawthorne's mouth quirks, his approval sending a satisfied warmth through my chest.

"So who do we want to bring?" Fisher asks.

"Everyone here, although I think I'd prefer you stayed behind with our pack as leader de facto in my absence." Fisher nods at Heath's edict.

"There is no reason for me to join you." Sable raises her chin. Heath nods in acknowledgment.

"So how many additional Zetas and Thetas should we bring?" Slate asks.

"Two," Heath says, "Lazuli and Cassia." The mated pair make an impressive team. Lazuli stands tall and intimidating with his athletic build. Cassia is smaller, but she is perhaps our strongest Zeta. She's quick, clever, and fairly ruthless, although only in a fight. It's quite the contrast to her calm temperament and role as a mother to Oliver, the youngest baby in our pack. He's six months younger than Dahlia and only recently started running.

"I'd like for us to have additional security measures," Hazel says.

"Yes?"

"Perhaps additional members standing by at a distance? Vale, Elm, and Aven?" Slate suggests, mentioning the last three of our warriors. Elm is Marigold's father and the oldest of our Zetas, and Vale is the youngest Theta at barely eighteen, though Vale's talents at scouting earned him the position as a teenager.

Several people nod at the suggestion. Taking a measured breath, I say, "Perhaps a hidden stash of additional weapons within easy reach?"

Fisher's lip curls. He knows I mean handguns, and he disdains them. Though we pack in shots of wolfsbane which disable our opponents instead of kill, he still sees it as dishonorable. That belief makes him a critic of me.

"Yes, please arrange that," Heath says. I fight to keep my face relaxed when I want to smirk. Hazel's gaze flicks to me and her mouth twitches in a subtle praise.

Heath sits up straighter. "What do we know about the objectives of each pack? We need to consider how their desires may conflict."

This is Hawthorne's area of expertise. He leans forward, speaking directly to his Alpha. "Zephyr seems intent on rebuilding an alliance with us, at the expense of his relationship with Ferris. So we are primed for a conflict between them in addition to Ferris's general dislike of us. But outside of them, I don't foresee any requests or complications from the Valley Pack. So it's whatever we bring to the table."

"What are we pushing for?" Hazel asks. Her wide brown eyes look up at her uncle.

"Peace and order," Heath says simply.

Slate frowns. "We need to publicly hold Granite Ridge accountable for their recent offenses toward us."

"Do we?" Sable asks. I scowl at her. Knowing the depths of her unkindness to Marigold has set the healer in a new light for me, and I see her compassion extends furthest for those she is healing, and least for her family.

"Everyone is already aware of their crimes," Hazel says, crossing her arms. As the chief victim, her word will weigh the most in this matter.

"Do you want a public apology or other repercussions?" Heath asks.

Hazel's face scrunches up as she thinks. "Only if it benefits the pack. My pride is not delicate." Her uncle nods approvingly.

Respect for Hazel rises up in me. Less than a year ago, she was living as a human in Los Angeles. But now she has blossomed into a generous and competent leader.

Smiling at her, I joke, "I mean, you already took their heir away from them, so there's that." She rolls her eyes at me. From the corner of my eye, I catch the slightest smirk on Hawthorne's face.

"We could focus on our requested agreements including a counterbalance for their slights," Linden suggests, surprising me.

"I like that idea," Hazel says. Slate's brows crease together. I suspect he'd prefer a public display of groveling and punishment.

Everyone pauses, the topic heavy. Finally Heath says, "We need to carefully consider what changes we may enact. And have variations prepared to adjust for the other pack's input.

"The goal is peace. So we must consider the actions that threaten our peace and what measures we can take to curb them."

"Granite Ridge's thirst for new recruits," Slate says automatically, and I have to agree.

Heath glances around, checking the faces of all of his subordinates. I give a small nod.

"They have outright stolen wolves from nearby packs," I say carefully, "but not from our neighboring packs, excluding their move against Hazel last year. So they have deniability. So whatever guidelines we push for agreement need to take that into account."

"What about using phrasing that better fits what they are claiming to do?" Hazel asks.

"They say the other wolves are *choosing* to join them," I say grimly.

"You could call it head hunting," Hazel says, earning confused frowns. "Or poaching. They're poaching wolves from other packs."

"How can that be monitored or enforced?" Fisher asks.

"They should be held accountable. If we push the point of their offenses toward us, we could ask for interventions such as inspections," Slate says.

Heath sighs. "Unfortunately, I think that's unlikely to work."

"It's more than fair," Slate says, his brow furrowing.

"That doesn't mean it's doable," Sable reprimands. Slate's mouth thins, his irritation a physical sensation through our pack bond. He's hot headed when it comes to his mate.

"There has to be solutions we haven't thought of yet," Hazel says, smoothing things over.

The debate trails off, eventually being set aside for a future discussion. As the last order of business, Hawthorne outlines the top leadership of each pack to remind everyone of names and positions.

My parents, Ferris and Sienna, of the Granite Ridge Pack, will likely bring whoever their current Beta is, though that role changes hands often so we have no assured name. And perhaps they will bring their heir, my younger sister Ember. I'm curious how her training has evolved in my absence, since she is now first in line and not a spare. Knowing her, she's probably ecstatic. I'm not doubtful she had been scheming to remove me at some future date, and I did it for her.

Zephyr leads Ironcrest, with a Beta named Beryl, and his Gamma, Dell. Beryl is effectively Zephyr's heir, for he has no mate or children that we are aware of.

Unfortunately, Nyx of the Raven Pack will not be joining us, therefore the only other pack participating will be the Valley Pack.

Cashel has led the Valley Pack nearly as long as Heath has led Bracken Creek. He's our closest ally. He's likely to come with his heir, Beta, and son, Malachite. Hawthorne reminds us that his Gamma is a cousin, Zinnia.

My head is swimming by the time we're done. But during the Counsel, my only role is to observe and interpret the actions of the leaders that I know. And to provide security. I won't even be at the table.

We've discussed and planned for this meeting for months, but now that it's concrete and fast approaching, anxiety gathers in my gut. Particularly with Zephyr's strange meeting a few days ago. I have no idea what to expect when I set eyes on my parents.

The tension in my shoulders uncoils as I approach my cabin and hear giggling from inside. Marigold is perched on the sofa with a stack of papers on her lap.

She looks up and her face brightens from relaxed amusement to affection.

"Whatcha up to?" I ask, settling beside her.

Holding up the pages, she says, "Just grading. Do you want to help?"

"How would I know what's correct?" I ask, spinning the pink felt marker from the table between my fingers.

"It's math from elementary school, I think you can manage," she says, giving me a lopsided grin.

"Sounds doable," I say, hand squeezing her leg pressed against mine. She extracts a paperclipped bundle from under the pages she's already marking up and sets it across my lap.

"Anything that's wrong, circle what's incorrect and they'll have to redo it in class. And if it's the word problems on the next page and they didn't show calculations, circle the empty space where calculations should have been."

It's easy enough. There's only six pages, and they're pretty close to perfect. Marigold leans over, throwing her head back in a laugh. "Check this out," she says, holding a page up.

"If you have eight apples," I read, "and eat five of them, how many do you have left?"

Marigold reads the scrawled answer, "An upset tummy." I snort, checking the name at the top - Daisy. "She is so sassy," Marigold says, giggles punctuating her words.

A few pages later, I hold out a paper toward her, it's from one of the younger students. "Triangle, square," I read, "hexagon, and..." pausing for dramatic effect, I point to the rhombus, "a squished square."

"Geez," she says, rolling her eyes.

I work through the rest of the pages fairly quickly, and help Marigold with a second bundle. Math finished, she pulls out a larger pile of multiple choice quizzes.

"These are super boring. I've been putting them off for ages. Do you want to watch a movie or something while I suck it up and finally grade these?"

"I don't have a T.V.," I say, frowning.

"My laptop has a bunch of movies loaded up. Pick whatever you like." An ancient, thick laptop sits closed on the coffee table, a charging cord snaking over to the wall.

Easing it open, I spot a folder labeled movies right on the desktop. Marigold's nose is in her tests, and she sticks her tongue out as she starts writing a note on one. I smirk, seeing her selection of cheesy early 90's slasher thrillers and chick-flicks.

"You've got some interesting taste in movies," I say.

She wrinkles her nose, pushing her knee into my hip. "Hey, these are classics."

"Any preference?"

"Pick something you haven't seen."

I'm familiar with most of them, but haven't actually watched most, save for a few horror movies. Trying to avoid overthinking it, I pick a particularly cheerful looking romantic comedy.

Marigold hums her approval, and I can't help reaching my arm around her shoulder so she nestles against my chest. I'd watch anything if it meant she was this close.

Eventually she completes her grading and she slides down until she's laying across my lap. My hands groove through her hair, marveling at how the reddish gold waves gleam in the low afternoon light.

"We need to get dinner," she realizes as the credits are rolling. I want to stay there with her, stroking her hair and enjoying her smiles, but she needs to eat.

We're late for dinner, and everyone else seems to be sitting with relatives. Many people are already finishing their meals and cleaning up.

Luckily, Crickett hasn't put the food away yet, and we're able to heap Chinese food onto plates.

Marigold picks a quiet table on the edge of the gathering. We sit across from each other, and I miss being close, but it's nice to watch her expressions as she tries the fried rice.

"So if you had a different job from teaching, what would you do?" I ask, curious.

She takes a big bite of sesame chicken and stares into the distance while she chews. Eventually, she says, "probably something where I get to help lots of people. Like being a hairdresser or handyman. What about you?"

"Environmental lawyer," I answer without thinking. I used to imagine life among humans, when I thought perhaps that would be my only escape. One I'm glad I was too cowardly to take. A wolf without a pack is cut off from a vital part of themselves.

"Why?"

"I'm not sure," I say. "I took a lot of classes on environmental sustainability in college. And it seems like something worth doing. If I wasn't involved in a pack, I guess."

"Interesting," she says, studying me. "Okay, new question. You win the lottery, what are you buying?"

I shrug. "I don't know."

"What about a fancy sports car?" she asks.

"I've got the car I want."

"What about something ridiculous like a lifetime supply of your favorite candy. Or a bathtub full of sprinkles."

"That sounds like *your* dream." And now I'm imagining her in a bathtub of sprinkles with whipped cream instead of bubble bath. Freaking fantastic.

"Maybe." Her giggle dances around me, infusing warmth into my skin. "But I think I'd prefer a swimming pool full of marshmallows.

"What would you buy?"

Marigold pauses, nibbling on the tines of her fork. "I would have said my own cabin. But I'm kind of enjoying staying in yours." She grins at me, and it draws out my own smile in response. "But a car would be nice. Something practical but also cute like a sunflower yellow jeep."

"I could see you in something like that," I say. It's tempting to make that vision happen, but a new car is not a gift you give to a friend. Maybe someday.

She asks more inane questions and we laugh over our answers. It's a luxury to eat together during a pack dinner. No one bothers us or even looks twice at us, or not that I notice. It feels normal, like we are a couple. For a few minutes, I can pretend.

CHAPTER EIGHT

METEORS & MAKEOVERS

Marigold

MTuesday goes by in a blur of teaching and cleaning, but on Wednesday, I'm committed to babysitting Hawthorne and Crickett's brood so they have a date night - or date afternoon, since their children are so young. It's something I do every other Wednesday. Hawthorne is cool with my temporary home, so I'm left with the task of entertaining a toddler and young child in Jasper's cabin.

Oh, and I may have forgotten to tell Jasper about it.

"Ready to add the salt?" I ask Daisy, holding my breath as she wobbles the measuring cup on the edge of the bowl.

Jasper steps through the front door and stops short, blinking at the young guests we have. "Hey guys, what's going on?"

Daisy spills the cup of salt half in the bowl and half over my hand and across the counter.

Smiling maybe a little too wide, I say, "I'm babysitting. Want to help make some playdough?" Sighing, I sweep the salt into my palm and dump it into the bowl.

He recovers quickly, shucking off his hoodie and crouching beside Dahlia's blanket to ruffle her dark curls before joining us in the kitchen. "It's like making cookies?"

"Easier, because you don't have to bake them." Daisy holds onto the edge of the spoon while I begin to stir in the salt.

"Cool, what's in it?" He pokes at the lumpy dough.

"Flour, salt, cream of tartar, water, and whatever we use to make it smell good or add color," I quote from memory. It's not my first time making playdough.

To my horror, Jasper pinches a blob of dough from the bowl and pops it into his mouth. His eyes go wide and with a quick jolt, he spits the dough into the sink.

"It's pretty salty," I say apologetically.

Turning back with a strained smile, he says, "I know that now."

Daisy snorts between laughs. Once she's recovered, she narrows her eyes at Jasper. "You can add the flavor if you want, normally it's my job. You can borrow it if you really want."

"Really? What flavor are we making this delicious dough?" he says, playing along. My hands tighten on the bowl, resisting the urge to hug him. He doesn't have to help entertain her.

"Pumpkin spice!" Daisy blurts.

Frowning, I look between her and Jasper. "But it's spring time. Pumpkin spice is for fall."

"So?" Daisy says, little hands going to her hips.

Jasper smirks and our eyes meet, exasperation mingled with amusement. "What makes up pumpkin spice? Because I definitely don't have any pumpkin." He opens the spice cabinet. I'm concerned how old most of those seasonings are because they probably came with the cabin, but it won't matter for playdough.

Clicking my nails on the bowl, I try to recall. "Cinnamon for sure."

"Done," Jasper says, plunking the little glass jar down.

"Nutmeg and allspice?" I guess. He has nutmeg but not allspice. "Oh, and ginger, of course."

"And again, we have success. Three out of the four isn't too bad."

Daisy nods enthusiastically. She reaches for the ginger. Jasper takes the bowl while she sprinkles the pungent spice over the dough. They make a great team, so I go to Dahlia and lift her onto my hip so she can watch her sister pour an ungodly amount of cinnamon into the dough.

"Watch it with the cinnamon. That can bother your skin," I say. Jasper takes hold of the jar to temper Daisy's enthusiastic shaking.

I can't help but smile as Jasper struggles to mix in the spices.

"It's probably time to knead it by hand," I say.

Jasper hesitates only a second. Then he's plopping the lump onto sprinkled flour and folding it over with his palms. Watching his hands work is mesmerizing.

"Have you kneaded dough before?"

He shrugs. "I may have been watching sourdough videos online. Like where they decorate them all fancy."

"Impressive," I say, my eyes following his rhythmic folding and stretching.

Baby Dahlia tugs sharply on a lock of my hair, pulling me from my stupor. Wincing, I extract my hair and begin bouncing on the balls of my feet to keep her happy. She's getting too big for this.

"How does that look?" Jasper asks, his expression vulnerable.

"Great. Can you toss it in that plastic bag?" He complies and zips the edge closed. I grasp the bowl and take it to the sink with my free hand.

"Why don't you guys go play and I'll clean up," Jasper suggests. But Daisy growls her disagreement and seizes his hand.

"Go," I say. "I've got this, and you could do with some fun." He takes Dahlia from me and follows Daisy. She drags him toward the bathroom. While I wipe down the counter, Daisy brushes his pale hair and begins to wrap tiny rubber bands around tufts of it.

When Jasper walks out again, I can hardly breathe for the laughter shaking my entire body.

"Glad you're amused," he growls.

"You're so pretty," Daisy coos, her hands holding Dahlia's to help her sister bumble across the wood floor.

Jasper comes up behind me, hands hugging my waist. "Don't you think I'm pretty too?"

"Very much," I say, twisting to face him. Fingers linked behind his neck, I admire Daisy's styling. "And you smell amazing," I say, leaning closer to smell the sprinkle of nutmeg and ginger across his chest.

"Careful," he rumbles. My heart jumps into my throat at the sly smirk on his handsome face.

Feeling flustered, I turn back to the girls. "You guys want to paint? We've got to go outside, and we need to put on extra shirts." Daisy claps and Dahlia squeals. I can feel Jasper's eyes on me, but he stays quiet.

It doesn't take long to outfit the girls with smocks and fingerpaints. I lay a stretch of butcher paper across the ground. The girls happily draw rainbow lines and dots across the paper.

Exhausted, I drop into the closest hammock. I don't mean for my eyes to close, but I can monitor them with my inhuman hearing.

"Oh, this looks good," Jasper says. Sitting up, I look from him to the girls. My mouth falls open. The girls have moved from their canvas to the exterior wall of the cabin. So much for monitoring them.

"I'm so sorry," I stutter, rushing to grab their hands and peel them away from their defacement. "Daisy, you know better."

"I was serious, I think it looks great," Jasper says, chuckling.

Hawthorne and Crickett pick that moment to arrive as I'm still staring at the girls' artwork. Leaning in, I hiss, "I'll clean this up." We rush back to the porch to present the girls to their parents, tugging their smocks off as we go.

"We painted the house!" Daisy blurts, looking proud. Crickett's mouth tightens into a concerned frown.

"Don't worry about it. Just a little finger paint. It washes off easily," I assure her.

"I want my playdough!" Daisy whines.

Crouching, I look into her eyes. "We talked about how that playdough is for the classroom. You can play with it tomorrow with your friends. Remember?"

"Oh, right," she says. Hawthorne rolls his eyes at his daughter's antics and leads his little family away.

"Thank you, Marigold. You are the best!" Crickett hollers over her shoulder.

Once they're gone, I unfurl the hose and begin to spray the log siding. The paint runs down, making puddles swirling with pink and blue. As I'm stepping closer to concentrate on a particularly stubborn area, the snap of a branch startles me. Swinging toward the noise, the hose comes with me.

The water is still pressurized from my hold on the hose, and the spray soaks Jasper from chest to knees in a split second.

His surprised expression is so cute and my nerves so frayed, that I can't help but burst into a fit of giggles. For a moment, he blinks at me, mouth slightly open. The hose sprays into the dirt at my feet.

"I'm so sorry," I say, fighting back another fit of giggles. Spell broken, he stalks forward, reaching for the hose in my hands, but I twist away.

"Marigold, give that to me," he says, his low voice caressing my skin. He sounds far too calm for someone scrambling to take something out of my grasp.

"No way!" I say, backing up a few steps and grinning like a maniac. But Jasper is incredibly quick, and when he darts forward, I cannot react in time. His arms clamp around mine, and in the struggle, water shoots straight up and covers us like rain.

"Happy now?" he asks, water dripping off his nose and eyelashes.

"Yeah, I am," I snicker, trudging over to turn off the hose he's now pointing at the ground.

We stretch out on the wooden floor of the patio, letting ourselves dry before we traipse across the cabin's wood floors.

Stretching my neck to look at Jasper, I say, "I forgot to ask, how goes the Alpha Counsel prep?"

"Fine. We spent ages going over everyone we know from each pack that might be there. And I know a lot of them, but it's still a lot of new names to learn."

He looks up at the beams above us, the fading evening light haloing his profile. He's breathtaking.

"So your parents will be there," I say quietly, "And maybe your sister?"

"Maybe. I'm not sure how much they're training her, since she's their heir now and everything. They won't bring her if she isn't ready to make a good showing."

"Have you talked to her at all?"

He turns his head, aqua eyes meeting mine. "The two times I texted her, she sent back a picture of her middle finger."

"That gets the point across, I guess."

His lips curl in amusement.

"Would you try to talk to her if she comes?"

"If I can. But I doubt I'll get a chance."

"Are you okay with that?" I probe, my tone gentle.

He sighs, turning his head back and staring at the ceiling. "No, but it's her choice. It's a two way street. And to be realistic, she'd probably try to gut me given the chance."

"That serious?" I ask, my brows furrowing.

"That's just a Tuesday for Ember," he says, fondness in his voice.

"How did you turn out so normal?" I joke.

He sits up, one eyebrow raised in challenge. "Maybe I'm not that normal, after all."

"Normal is overrated," I mutter, climbing to my feet. The dripping has mostly stopped, and I'm ready for a fresh set of clothes.

Jasper

The week slips by, a blur of planning and training drills. Slate takes his anxiety out on all of us during training, and Fisher is ecstatic to let us sweat.

Friday is the worst. Setting up tables and chairs on a remote corner of our territory is not a pleasant task. But the entire team pulls together and we get the job done. Once it's finished, I'm covered in dirt and sweat. We hike back as humans. Everyone is getting hungry and hungry wolves are usually grumpy.

Brushing my hands together, I cross the clearing back toward home. If I hurry, I should have enough time to shower before dinner.

Marigold's voice filters around the training building, and I can't help but detour. Coming around the back of the building, my feet slow when I see her. Her glorious hair is pulled into a high ponytail and her hands grip a crossbow. She looks like a warrior goddess.

Cassia, Fern, and Hazel watch her, giving out tips and encouragement. Cassia and Fern are both accomplished fighters, and Hazel has taken to the training like she's been here her entire life. I couldn't have put together a better group for Marigold to train with.

With a vicious grin, Marigold levels the barrel of the crossbow at the plywood target. Narrowing her eyes, she fires. The arrow embeds dead center. Pride wells in my chest.

She resets and shoots again, another perfect shot. After the third time, I realize she's more than proficient, she's incredible with a crossbow. It's wildly sexy and terrifying at the same time.

Cassia, Fern, and Hazel all whoop and cheer her on, covering up the sounds of my approach.

Marigold hops on the balls of her feet, looking pleased with herself. As she turns toward her friends, she catches sight of me. The last thing I want is to interrupt her training, so I simply raise an eyebrow and smirk.

As I'm turning away, Fern spots me. "Jasper, come see if you can challenge Marigold. None of the rest of us can best her."

Marigold's smile is apologetic. "He spent the whole day setting up for the counsel tomorrow. I'm sure he doesn't want to."

"Are you scared to go up against me?" I dare.

"You're going to regret that," Hazel says with a dark laugh.

Marigold loads the crossbow and hands it over. "Are you familiar with this style?"

"Yeah, it looks about the same," I murmur, brushing her hand with mine before she steps back, looking expectant.

With a slow breath, I level the muzzle at the target, already a pincushion for her bolts. One more breath, focus on steadying my hands, and I shoot.

It hits the target on the outside edge. But at least it doesn't fly off into the trees.

"That was really good," Marigold says. If I didn't know her so well, I wouldn't catch the patronizing undertones.

"Thank you," I say, stepping closer than necessary to hand the weapon back. She reloads and with practiced motions, shoots a bolt within a millimeter of mine.

"Show off," I huff. She grins, warmth and sunshine flooding my blood, and the embarrassment is entirely worth it.

"Go relax. I'll stop by before it's time for dinner," she says quietly. The sudden urge to kiss her, maybe on the forehead, pushes me a half-step forward before I catch myself.

She's already passing the crossbow off to Hazel and giving her tips as I stiffly walk away.

After my shower, I come out of my bedroom in clean clothes with my hair still damp. Marigold sits on the sofa with her feet tucked up. It looks like she's waiting for me.

"You look kinda tired," she says sweetly.

Shrugging, I plop down next to her. "Thanks," I say with a sarcastic smirk. "Though I can't say the same about you. Beautiful as always."

Her smile turns shy. "Hazel invited us to hang out after dinner."

"Campfire?"

"No, apparently there's some meteor shower. I guess they usually watch it together, but she thought we might like to join them." Reading between the lines - no Cedar or Onyx. Just the two of us hanging out with another couple.

"I like the sound of that. But do you want to?" I ask cautiously.

"Yeah, it sounds fun. We should bring a couple of blankets though." She pops up and takes my hand, pulling me toward dinner.

I don't let go of her hand until the trees part to reveal the rest of our pack chattering away.

Plate full, I settle at our group's favorite table. Benches creak as friends join us, eating and laughing. The stories and jokes wash over me. I'm happy to soak up the warm familiarity. The light slowly fades and my thoughts center around the girl beside me and our plans for what sounds suspiciously like a double date.

Marigold

"This is the Lyrid meteor shower. It'll be better the later it gets, heading toward morning. But I know tomorrow is a big day, so I didn't want to keep us up too late," Hazel says, squeezing Slate's hand.

We hike toward the cliffside, enjoying the sounds of the woods after dark. Bugs chirp and little nocturnal animals rustle as they start their days.

Jasper walks beside me, glancing over every few steps. My heart jolts as his hand brushes against mine. It must be a mistake. But when it happens again, like electricity zinging through me, I start to doubt.

Instead of making a fool of myself, I wrap my arm around his bicep. It allows me to touch him and eliminates the awkward brush of our hands. This is how friends walk together. Right?

From the smug look on his face, I'm not so sure.

The trees open up to a million stars. I've lived here my entire life, but it still fills me with a sense of wonder.

The sounds of the river below are louder in the night. Without speaking, the boys spread the blankets out a few feet away from each other and we all settle.

I should not feel this nervous, but my heart races as I unfold our second blanket and drape it over our legs.

Already the air is turning icy, but that isn't what causes me to shiver. It's the heavy silence and the heat of the man next to me.

Jasper misreads my shiver and pulls me down against his side so his arm cushions my head. His other hand draws the blanket up to cover all of me. Luckily, Hazel and Slate are too wrapped up in each other to pay us any attention. It's still silent, but now the blood rushing in my ears drowns out even the sounds of the water.

"So we're looking for shooting stars coming from the south and we should get to see one every five minutes or so. But maybe less because the moon is fairly full." Hazel's voice cuts through my haze.

The moon drenches the sky around it, washing out the stars' lesser light. It's almost entirely full, and I know that phase means our instinctual urges are stronger. That must be what's happening, because the heat of Jasper's body is burning me, branding my soul.

"You need to relax," he whispers, turning so his lips brush the shell of my ear. Flinching, I stiffen further. "What's wrong?"

Deep breath, slow exhale. "I guess I'm feeling jumpy," I whisper back.

Jasper nods, a hardly perceptible motion. Instead of letting it go, he runs his free hand down my arm and takes my hand. His thumb digs into the pressure point between my thumb and index finger and it takes all my self-control to keep my gasp silent. Releasing, he massages my palm until I relax into him.

Limply, I offer my other hand to him, and he repeats the process. He'd probably start on my shoulders too, but we are distracted by the first shooting star streaking across the sky. It fades as quickly as it started. I can't help but let out an excited squeak.

Jasper's head turns again, his breath warm on my cheek. "You're adorable."

"Like in an annoying way?" I bat my eyelashes at him. He chuckles and turns back to the glittering sky.

His answer comes after a long delay, so quiet I almost miss it. "Like perfection."

He rests his hand across my stomach, right above my belly button. It's under the blanket, so our friends can't see how his fingers spread out to touch more of me over my cotton shirt.

Another light catches my attention, followed by another star close behind it. As more meteors cross the sky, the majesty of it captures me. I can't look away, although I am always painfully aware of Jasper beside me. My hands have moved to his bicep, gripping him like he's my emotional support childhood blankie. His muscles ripple as his thumb strokes down my midriff. The motions are lazy, as if he isn't aware of what he is doing.

It seems cheap to interrupt the majesty of stars streaking across the sky, and I can barely keep my breath even, so I don't even attempt speech. Slowly, I melt against him and forget everything but the stars above and his touch.

Jasper wakes me up with a soft touch to my cheek. "Marigold, we better get home. Tomorrow is a big day."

He tucks one of the blankets around me as we walk back, keeping his hands on my waist. Hazel and Slate say their goodbyes and head eastward.

In our cozy cabin, Jasper leads me to his bedroom, takes off my shoes, and trades my blanket for the comforter. I don't even remember him climbing in beside me. My sleep is dreamless.

CHAPTER NINE

ALPHAS & ANXIETY

Jasper

The Alpha Counsel meets along our northern border which serves as a central point between Ironcrest and Granite Ridge. Only the Valley Pack will have to travel far, but Cashel and his team are always welcome in our territory.

The day is clear and the weather mild. The perfect setting for a meeting of the most powerful wolves in the region.

Cashel arrives early, greeting Heath with a hug. Heath's hand stays on his friend's shoulder as they part.

"It's good to see you."

"You as well." Cashel is a stocky man with dark skin and curly hair. "How are you feeling about this meeting? What are we concerned about?"

Heath doesn't hesitate. "Zephyr met with us recently and blamed all of last fall's events on Ferris."

Cashel nods, rubbing his jaw. "Any theories on what's going on between Ironcrest and Granite Ridge?"

"We will see if they have any conflict today," Heath answers darkly.

The Valley Pack's Alpha looks to me. "Jasper, look at you in your new pack."

I shuffle my feet, forcing a polite smile.

"Jasper has settled in well. He orchestrated today's event, actually. I'm sure you won't be surprised to hear that the other packs took quite a few letters to convince them to participate," Heath says. The pride in his voice warms me. My weeks of effort did not go unnoticed.

"Let's see how it goes," Cashel says, his voice thick with apprehension I find mirrored in my grim smile. Determination and dread swirl in my chest.

Slate seizes the Alpha's attention and I relax, watching as Cashel takes Hazel's hand and introduces her to the Valley Pack Beta, Malachite. He looks like a younger version of his father.

Hawthorne wanders over after exchanging pleasantries with Zinnia, Cashel's third. She's a slim woman with her dark hair shaved into a pixie cut. His expression shifts from amused to concerned as he looks me up and down. "You doing okay?"

"Honestly?" I ask. He nods. "I feel like I'm going to throw up."

Clearing his throat, Hawthorne steps closer, his eyes commanding my attention. "It's going to be fine. We're prepared for this. You, more so than anyone else. Trust yourself."

"I'm not sure I see how a meeting with Ferris is going to go well."

"Ah." Hawthorne tips his chin down to meet my gaze. "Your father is outnumbered and outmatched. He'll be forced to play nice."

"That's what I'm afraid of," I admit. "He's not going to take kindly to the pressure." He squeezes my shoulder reassuringly.

Sounds of wolves drift through the trees, followed by rustling and then footsteps. My fists clench as the Granite Ridge Pack comes into view. It's a bigger group than I expected. My parents have brought more than a handful of guards, including Aries, a great brute with long black hair, and Flint, a wiry and pocked wolf who I've wanted to disembowel since childhood.

Ferris wears his favorite leather jacket over designer jeans. He'll take any chance to show status or wealth. Beside him, Sienna wears a lacy red camisole and black leather pants. For someone who ran through the woods and then shifted from wolf to human, she looks ridiculously glamorous. Her eyes flicker to me, though she shows no emotion. My father is stone with not a single twitch in my direction.

"Ferris." Heath greets him, noticeably cold in comparison to how he greeted Cashel.

"Heath," my father answers, a grim smile on his face. Heath doesn't greet Sienna, and she raises her nose in the air, clearly offended, but my dad does nothing to appease her. Theoretically, they should be equals, but he's never given her that respect in these types of official meetings.

Slate stands beside Heath, his arm tight around Hazel's waist. Her claim mark scars are highlighted by the wide-neck top she wears. Sienna's lip curls as she regards them.

To her credit, Hazel's political smile never wavers, but I can sense her anger through the pack bond. Slate's as well. It's understandable. Sienna isn't only my mother, she's Slate's mother too, though we have different fathers. She left when he was an infant, and if that wasn't enough reason for his disdain, she's had it out for Hazel since she arrived last year. Slate may not care about Sienna's lack of a role in his life, but any offense against his mate is unforgivable in his eyes.

Heath breaks the tension. "Ferris, you remember my heirs, my niece Hazel and her mate, Slate."

"So nice of you to bring them," Ferris replies cooly.

Sienna gives a cat-like smile. "Unfortunately, our Ember had to stay home, but I would like to introduce you to Hawk."

A slender young man steps forward. His reddish hair is brushed back into a bun and freckles cover his skin. "He joined us from the Alpine Pack, son of the Alpha. He is Ember's Intended."

Heath nods curtly. "Congratulations."

"Thank you," Hawk says, his voice rough, like he doesn't speak often. His posture squares off, like he is striking a practiced pose to hide discomfort. I can't help but study him. I've never met anyone from the large pack a day's drive north of us.

My sister has an Intended, a mate for someone not yet an adult. She won't turn eighteen for a few more months. Did she pick this wolf, or did our mother arrange it? Does she even like him? Nausea churns my stomach. It's not the kind of news I expected, and it shouldn't bother me as much as it does.

Cashel shakes Ferris's hand and Hawk's, sharing his own congratulations.

Finally, Ironcrest arrives. Zephyr strides forward, flanked by his Beta, a fierce woman named Beryl, and his Gamma, Dell. A collection of guards follows silently.

His cold gaze sweeping the group, Zephyr says, "No Nyx, I see."

Heath shakes his head. "No, she couldn't be persuaded."

"Typical." Zephyr shakes hands with each of the other Alphas.

The leaders settle around the table. Between Alphas, Heirs, and Betas, all seats are full. I stand beside Hawthorne, keeping my posture rigid and my eyes on our enemies.

Aries and Flint stand opposite us, glowering from the other side of the table. Despite six months apart, their hatred of me burns bright.

"I'd like to thank all of you for making the trip and contributing to the first Alpha Counsel in eight years." Heath starts, his deep voice commanding attention. "Preceding this counsel, Ironcrest met with us. Zephyr, would you like to share what we've discussed?"

I'm not the only one watching Ferris and Sienna for their reaction.

Zephyr threads his fingers behind his short hair and leans back. "Yes, I let the Bracken Creek Pack know that I recently expelled several wolves after discovering they contributed to the abduction of the Bracken Creek heir last fall."

The air crackles with tension. I suspect everyone is thinking the same thing. Beryl's eyes are on Ferris, making her thoughts perfectly clear.

"I don't think we have to address those dramatics again," Sienna says, her smile thinning.

"It wasn't discussed originally, so I'm not sure why you are saying 'again'," Slate says, his words like ice.

Cashel sits forward. "Considering it was a major conflict between two of the four packs represented here, I think it should be addressed."

Ferris's arrogance soaks into his every word. "Considering our valid claim on the female was challenged and you schemed to take one of my children from my pack, I think the matter is best left in the past."

My nails dig into my palms, but I give no other outward sign of my pounding heart or the blood rushing in my ears.

"Our challenge was more than you deserved when you had committed a crime against us," Hazel says. Zephyr smirks.

"Peace." Heath holds up a hand. "My pack is willing to move past the incident, as long as Granite Ridge upholds the peace measures we are working to pass here today. But we will not be forgiving again." Sienna scoffs. From Slate's tense posture, I can tell he is struggling to accept our Alpha's words. But Heath has made his decision. "Before we discuss them, does anyone else have any other grievances?"

"I do," Zephyr says, "Ironcrest has been having some issues with the Raven Pack crossing our borders."

Malachite leans his forearms on the table, mimicking his father's pose. "That's a serious accusation."

"Unfortunately, it's true. So far it seems to be just scouts. I believe they're testing our security for weaknesses. A condition of our participation is support in addressing this problem."

"Noted. What support are you requesting?" Heath says.

"I simply need to get in touch with Nyx. She's surprisingly difficult to reach."

"Not a problem." Heath turns to the other two Alphas.

"Granite Ridge has no grievances," Ferris says, his face lacking its typical intensity. It makes the hair on my arms stand up.

"Neither does the Valley Pack," Cashel confirms.

"Excellent," Heath says, though his tone is flat. "Then we can proceed to some of the measures we'd like to propose."

"Let's hear it," Zephyr says.

"I think it's time we renewed our commitment to not take wolves from each other's pack, particularly against their will."

"Agreed," Cashel says. Zephyr nods.

Ferris smirks - actually smirks. "Granite Ridge agrees." As if they hadn't actively been taking wolves captive. My teeth grind together hard enough my jaw clicks.

"Secondly, we feel it would be wise if all Alphas maintain a phone line where we can contact each other."

"I'm not going to carry around a cell phone so you can call me whenever you want," Zephyr drawls.

"I'm sure your Gamma could handle it," Cashel says, his smile not reaching his eyes.

"We will see about it," Ferris says.

"Fine." Zephyr rolls his eyes.

"Lastly, in addition to a regular Alpha Counsel, I recommend our representatives, such as our Gammas and their apprentices, begin to meet regularly with the goal of greater pack cooperation."

"How regularly are you thinking?" Cashel asks.

Ferris looks away as if the table isn't worthy of his attention, "Waste of time."

"Would you prefer we meet without you?" Zephyr says with a sneer. Ferris crosses his arms and sits back.

"How about bi-monthly? Or quarterly," Heath suggests.

"Quarterly sounds good to me," Zephyr says.

"Quarterly, it is." Cashel folds his hands.

"In the future, we should consider inter-pack gatherings," Heath suggests, "but for now, our Gammas can meet regularly and we can reconvene the Counsel in six months."

Ferris frowns. "The Counsel meets annually."

"In the past, the bonds between packs were stronger. Perhaps if we had maintained those relationships with regular meetings, we could have avoided some of the conflicts of recent years."

Cashel nods. If I remember my history, Zephyr became an Alpha only five years ago when he challenged for his position.

Nyx is younger as well, but the remaining three packs were led by the same Alphas for much longer. They know the history because much of it was caused by their hands.

"Anything else?" Ferris asks.

"Do *you* have anything else?" Cashel asks him. Ferris scowls at him.

"I'm sure you're all eager to get home. I have no more agenda items," Heath says.

They make small talk for a few more minutes, though it's obvious Ferris believes he is above such things. Zephyr's words feel insincere and make my skin prickle. Cashel and Heath make little effort to continue the conversation, and soon everyone is looking to their teams.

Ferris stands, Sienna rising gracefully after him. Without a word, they walk away, falling into a practiced formation.

Hawk walks behind Sienna, in the place I would have occupied. As their forms retreat, my lungs relax and I can draw a full breath again.

"I'll be off too," Zephyr announces, snapping his fingers to call his wolves forward.

Finally it was just our team and the Valley Pack's representatives. "Come sit down," orders Heath.

Hawthorne takes the empty seat on Heath's other side, and I join him. Dell sits across from me.

"Would you like to stay and debrief, my friend?" Heath asks Cashel with a genuine smile.

"As I said earlier, what is going on with those two?" Cashel says, gesturing toward the empty seats across from him.

Slate rests his forehead in his palm, elbow propped on the table. "The thing that concerns me the most is how quiet Sienna was."

Exhaling harshly, I look up to meet Slate's gaze. "And the fact Ferris was so calm. Aside from that outrageous version of events he spewed, he went along with everything peacefully."

Cashel's Gamma, Dell, tips his chair back. "What about Zephyr's accusations about Nyx?"

"That doesn't sound like Nyx. She doesn't like to leave her community. Why would she invade Ironcrest territory? She has more land than she needs already," Dell says.

Hawthorne nods. "We'll talk to her and see what's really going on."

"Sounds good. Keep me updated." Cashel stands. "Have a good afternoon, friends."

As we folded up chairs and prepare to leave, Slate finds me and says, "We agree that was suspicious as fuck right?"

"Yeah, but I have no idea what they're playing at." He shakes his head, walking back to Hazel and kissing her cheek while she chats with Heath. Her warm smile seems to soothe him, reminding me that I have Marigold at home, and I'd like nothing more than to go wrap my arms around her and kiss her, if she'd let me.

CHAPTER TEN

BREAKFAST & BORDER DISPUTES

Marigold

All the knots came back to my fingers easily, and in the last two days I've made a handful of plant hangers. Jasper has a collection of little houseplants in his bedroom, but the light is much better in the living room.

Humming to myself, I screw hooks into the wood planked ceiling and link the loops up. Carefully, I nestle the pots into each, leaving a line of hanging plants along

the sunniest window. They should grow much faster now.

I step back and smile. It looks great. What else can I do?

Digging around, I find a pair of sunflower-print throw pillows in the back of the linen closet. They look perfect on the sofa.

Dishes washed, my bed re-made (though I have no intention of returning to it), and books organized by color, I finally sprawl across the sofa and enjoy the late afternoon sunlight pouring in, filtered by the plants.

"That looks great," Jasper says, stepping in. He holds two dinner plates in his hands. "Hungry?"

I smile contentedly up at him, accepting my plate. His smile is warm, but the tightness around his eyes betrays his worry.

"I hope you don't mind, I installed the decor you requested as payment," I say. Jasper rotates one of the plants to inspect the macrame encircling the pot.

"You decided on plant hangers instead of a big wall piece?" he asks.

"You can't afford a big wall hanging from me," I say. Sitting up, I reach for his hand and pull him down beside me. His arm goes around my waist automatically and my stomach flips. There's something in his touch, the way his fingers dig into my skin, that is more possessive than normal. Either he's more upset than I realized, or we've taken our relationship to a new level.

"How was the counsel?" I ask, taking a bite of the lasagna. It's delicious.

He takes a few bites of his dinner before he shares, "Overall, it went well. But, I don't know, Ironcrest and Granite Ridge were acting strange."

I grip the top of his leg, a few inches above the knee. "What do you mean?"

He sighs, sinking back into the cushion and pulling me closer with the motion. Concern over the counsel isn't enough to keep me from losing myself in the comforting cocoon of his arms.

Eventually, Jasper pulls me out of my reverie. "Well, my parents were really quiet. Didn't argue at all when Heath brought up an agreement to not steal wolves from other packs."

"That's always been against our rules," I say.

"That hasn't exactly stopped them in the past." His grip around me tightens.

"They won't get away with it again."

I can feel the expansion of his chest as he takes a slow, deep breath. "And then Zephyr was saying that Nyx is invading their boundaries. Wants sanctions against her. So we agreed to attempt to arrange communications between them."

Pulling back, I frown. "Nyx wouldn't do something like that."

"That's what I thought."

"Why would they say that?" I twist to face him, pulling my legs up to sit cross-legged. Our dinner plates sit forgotten on the coffee table.

He rubs at his jaw, thinking. "What if something has changed with Nyx's leadership?"

"I can ask my dad," I say. From the blank look on Jasper's face, I realize he doesn't know, "My mom was from the Raven Pack. My grandparents live there."

His eyebrows shoot up. "Really. You're the connection Heath mentioned." My shoulders tense in a quick shrug.

"Yeah, we visit them maybe twice a year. The Raven Pack is tiny. They can't keep watch over all that land effectively. I've always wondered why Ironcrest or Granite Ridge don't try and buy some of that acreage."

He stares at me.

"What?"

"That's it," he says. I can see thoughts flying behind his eyes.

"What's it?" I prod when he falls silent.

"That's what Zephyr wants. If he says Nyx is the aggressor, he can set them up to take her territory without consequences. Or at least without full consequences. He has an excuse."

Winding a lock of hair through my fingers, I consider his theory. Logically, it makes sense. But the idea that a pack would attack another pack unprovoked is barbaric. Shifters don't go to war without a serious reason.

"Are you going to tell Heath about your idea?" I ask.

"Definitely." He chews his lip. "I'll see him in the morning. That'll give me time to think it through."

"Do you think Granite Ridge is in on it?"

"That's the thing, I can't tell. Ferris knows now that the other packs know what they did to Hazel. He should be defensive or at least angry. He was so calm, it felt unnatural to me. And Sienna hardly said a word." His voice begins to wobble. Sensing his need for support, I scoot closer.

"You'll figure it out."

"I can't shake this feeling they're after me. Or after Slate and Hazel. I'm not sure. It's like they're so carefully not looking our way, the absence of any snide remarks or threats feels wrong. Sneaky, I guess."

There's real fear in his eyes. Cautiously, I reach out and brush his mussed hair behind his ear. "They can't do anything. We won't let them. And we have allies to help if they really do throw everything they've got at us."

He has no answer and instead studies the floor, his worry a heavy thing clinging to him. The droop of his shoulders, the tightness around his mouth. I can't stand it.

"Hey!" I say, squeezing him tighter. "No more of this. We are a badass pack, and we have the most incredible leaders protecting us, including you. And I know you'll keep us safe."

Remembering our deal from a week prior, my hands find their way to his shoulders and I dig in, thumbs kneading his muscles. He lets out a long exhale and his eyes close. I urge him to turn away from me, giving me more access to his back

Working my way down, the heels of my hands press along the line of muscle on either side of his spine. His head falls forward. The tension starts to ease once I begin long strokes down the line of his shoulder blades.

"Better?" I ask.

He turns those soulful eyes on me and I can't breathe. I couldn't move if I wanted to. The depth of adoration mingling with sadness paralyzes me.

"I don't deserve you," he murmurs, twisting toward me. My hands glide from his shoulders up to hook around his neck. His blonde hair slips over my fingers.

Feeling dizzy, I suck in a ragged breath, trying to keep my head. But his hands are on my hips, pulling me into his lap.

Suddenly the only thing I want in the universe is to get as close to him as physically possible. Maybe that's always been what I wanted and my walls are too brittle to stop me any longer. Our faces are inches apart, hands gripping, abdomens pressing.

"I was thinking about last week," he says, his voice vibrating through me. "And if I had known that was your first kiss, I would have done things differently."

"I…" I have no idea how to respond to that.

He keeps one hand on the small of my back, but the other skims my jaw. His skin might be flames, the way it burns me, but it feels so good as his thumb strokes down the column of my throat. I can't look away. He's a cobra, toying with his prey, and I desperately want to feel his fangs.

"If you don't want me, please tell me or just walk away." His voice is hoarse, none of the soothing rich tones he usually has.

Swallowing, I press my hips forward, aligning more of our bodies together. That will have to be answer enough, because there's no way coherent words are coming out of my mouth right now.

He holds me in place, eyes searching for something. Is he deciding if *he* wants this? When I'm about to melt into a puddle in his lap, he tilts my jaw, fingers tightening around my jaw and throat. A thrill runs through me.

Pulling me to him, he uses his grip to hold me still as our lips collide.

While our first kiss was heavenly, this one feels different. It's intentional. Methodical. Sparks shimmer from every place we connect, pooling low in my core.

My lips part and his tongue tentatively teases me, coaxing my mouth open for him. It's a jolt in my gut, the lush feeling of his tongue against mine.

He overwhelms me, and I sink backwards on the sofa, his legs hemming me in. The weight of him presses me into the cushion, solid and reassuring.

We kiss over and over, firm, soft, sweet. I'm addicted and I don't want it to end. But when I slip my hands under his shirt and start to pull it upwards, he hesitates. I can feel his smile against my lips as he whispers, "This is your first kiss re-do, so let's not go from zero to a hundred."

That makes me giggle, despite the fact I also want to lick him and bite him and drag him to bed. He kisses me once more, and then stands up and offers his hand.

We get ready for bed, and I step into his bedroom, feeling jittery. He pulls me against him, my head tucked under his chin.

"Better first kiss?" he asks, barely above a whisper.

Blushing, I nestle in closer. "No complaints about the first one. But I think that might have been the best kiss in the history of the universe."

"I can't disagree."

"So is that a one-time redo, or is this something we do now?" My attempt at casual fails, the lilt in my tone giving away my insecurity.

"If you like."

"So we're friends who kiss?" I ask, hoping he will demand more.

"Is that what we are?" he asks, the hesitation in his voice triggering a flash of panic that constricts my lungs.

"I think I'd like to do that again," I say carefully, looking for a reaction. "And I think it's safe to say you're basically my best friend, so at the very least..."

"If that's what you want," he says, pressing his face into my hair..

"It sounds good to me," I say. I'm too frightened he will pull away.

His heart beats through his skin against my cheek. He's anything but calm. The moment feels fragile.

Nervously, I say, "I think I like kissing you. And with how stressful everything has been, it's probably good for your stress, too." Maybe I mean it as a joke, but it just comes out breathy. All my emotions are layering and muddying my happiness. I need to shut up.

"Okay," he says, his thumb stroking my ribs.

Despite the unease churning in my gut, the shock of emotions has exhausted me, and I can't keep my eyes open. His warmth soaks into every fiber of my being, relaxing me. If this is all we have, it's enough for now. And with time, surely I can convince him he wants more.

Jasper

"Wake up! It's getting late and I miss your face," Marigold calls, breaking through my sleepy fog. Had I slept so late that I missed my morning run?

The bed is empty and a flash of disappointment needles me.

Best friends who kiss. Good for stress.

So this was an outlet for her. A safe way to explore what she likes. I'm a test dummy.

I should break this off, tell her it's real or it's nothing. But she's scared, flighty, unsure of herself. She'd choose nothing and I would lose her.

Damn it.

I drag myself out of bed and throw on fresh clothes. The house smells of butter and sugar, so I'm not surprised to find Marigold in the kitchen, polka dotted oven mitts on her hands and a tray of steaming blueberry muffins on the stovetop.

The real issue is Marigold's clothing or lack thereof. Under the vintage ruffled apron, she's wearing a pair of boxers that look like the ones I typically sleep in, slung low on her hips, along with the world's tiniest tank top. Where's the loose shirt she slept in? A mile of midriff stretches between her top and bottoms. If she takes the apron off, I may collapse where I stand.

She turns those blue-green eyes on me, and I jerk forward, trying to act passably normal despite my heart pounding.

"Good morning, Sunshine," I say, kissing her cheek. It's Sunday, a whole day to relax - once the leadership debrief is finished.

Reaching for plates in the cabinet, I startle as she swats at me. "Go sit down," she commands.

I prop my fists on my hips. "If you think you're going to serve me while I sit there and do nothing, you're damn wrong. You do everything for everyone else, but in this house, I get to take care of you." She blinks at my declaration while I grab two plates and select the biggest muffin for her. I can't help but smirk at her wide-eyed surprise as I cut open the muffins and slather them with butter.

The fridge is devoid of fruit, but at least we have milk, and I set two glasses of it on the table beside our plates, before settling in a chair and pulling her down into my lap.

"Really? I'm eating my breakfast from here?" she quips, slinging an arm around my neck.

"Yeah," I say, grinning up at her, far too pleased with myself for the little that I did. "I like you right where I can keep an eye on you."

Rolling her eyes, she takes her first bite. I'm captivated as her tongue swipes her lip to get the small crumbs.

With my free hand, I lift my breakfast and take a bite. But the hints of cleavage under that apron are wildly distracting. After my second bite nearly misses my mouth, I admit, "I think it would be easier for me to eat if you were wearing a bit more clothing."

She scowls at me. "That's ridiculous." And then, proving a point, she unties the apron and tosses it over the empty chair.

I try to keep my eyes on her face, but that lasts about half a second, before I'm hungrily surveying the way her breasts stretch the thin, black fabric, barely contained.

"Fuck," I mutter.

My fingers skim the waistband of the boxers on her hips. I can't help dipping a finger under the edge, biting back a groan when I feel nothing but smooth skin. Suddenly, I'm not hungry for breakfast. In fact, I might starve to death if I don't get my mouth on her skin..

Marigold tilts her head, her smile turning sly. "Sorry, I'd better go get dressed," she teases before popping to her feet and taking a step toward her bedroom. My hand shoots out and grabs her wrist, pulling her back into my lap. "Oh, did I get it wrong? Am I wearing too much?" She's too sassy for her own good.

The most beautiful flush stains her cheeks, spreading down her neck. I close my mouth over her inner wrist still constrained in my hand, biting the skin gently. The contented sigh slipping from her mouth is intoxicating.

She reaches for the hem of her shirt, and I band an arm across her stomach to stop her. "If you take anything off, I'll miss my meeting."

"We can't have that." She squirms against me. Rose gold hair cascades against my cheek.

"Not only the meeting. I probably wouldn't let you leave this cabin for days."

"Oh, no." She draws out the words, her voice dripping with honeyed sarcasm while her hand comes up and she slowly slides the spaghetti strap over the edge of her shoulder.

A low growl escapes me, my control slipping. "Marigold, I'm serious." I can't peel my eyes away from that stretch of bare skin from neck to shoulder and the way it dips above her clavicle.

"So am I," she whispers, temptation in her eyes.

That's all it takes.

Shoving our breakfast dishes back, I lift her onto the table. Her blue-green eyes glow from within, and those pillowy lips part in surprise. Her knees separate as I stand and press into her.

She lets out a giggle that sounds like pure light as I press a hand to the small of her back to keep her from falling back into our plates. Through the rush of need, I'm barely aware of her hands going to my neck and jaw, before she's kissing me and I'm devouring her.

Her tongue runs along my lips, urging them open. My heart stutters at the way she nips her teeth over my bottom lip for a second before delving into a deep kiss that leaves me starved for oxygen.

With a cute little snarl, her nails press into my skin, spurring me on. I break off from her mouth, kissing her jaw and then the hollow right under it.

I'd like to take my time, but it's too much of a frenzy as I'm kissing and licking along her neck, looking for a spot that will make her moan. Knowing that no one else has ever done this makes me illogically possessive.

As my tongue teases the skin right at the base of her throat, she lets out a little choked sound. I suck softly, loving the way her nails dig in and her thighs squeeze my hips. I could spend all day doing this.

"More," she whimpers.

Her hand closes over mine and drags it up to her breasts. She follows it by pulling at her tank top, but somehow I stop her. I'm not sure where the willpower comes from. "Keep your clothes on, woman," I say through clenched teeth. However, I can't help myself from running my thumb down the line of her breast, between them, and then over her nipple. The thin fabric does nothing to hide the shape of her.

She takes advantage of my fixation, pressing her own mouth to my neck. The feel of her tongue running along my throat makes me bend, pushing into her, my hand tightening over the softness of her breast. The minx responds by tipping her hips up, so I'm pushing against the warm center of her. I'm grateful in that moment for the thick black sweatpants between us, because those boxers are not enough of a barrier. She compounds it with a nibble of her teeth on my neck.

Too much.

I step back, gasping for air or anything that can calm the inferno burning me alive.

Marigold is flushed, her eyes glowing despite her pupils eating up the irises. Her chest heaves while she regains her breath, and then she throws back her head and laughs.

Dumbfounded, I stare at her. My brain struggles to restart rational thought. When she looks back at me, she says, "That was fucking amazing." All I can do is shake my head and gawk at her. "Do you really have to leave?" she asks, biting her lip as she stares boldly into my eyes.

The challenge of her tone gives me something to focus on other than the scent of her skin. Slowly, I lean in, letting my breath feather across her neck, keeping my lips a millimeter above hers. She arches, desperate to resume devouring each other, but I stay barely out of reach. "I really do."

Walking away, I have to adjust myself. Her disappointed growl follows me out of the house. Closing the door behind me, I lean back against it, heart beating frenetically.

What the hell was that? Friends that kiss, my ass. That was a full-blown seduction.

It takes all my self-control to not race back into the cabin. If that is her idea of friends with benefits, I cannot imagine her feelings about being mates. Shoving my hand through my hair, I tug at the roots aimlessly.

With great effort, I force myself away from the door. There will be time later to figure out what Marigold is thinking. I have a feeling that whatever she wants, she'll get. This woman will be my undoing.

Heath paces, making all of us terribly uncomfortable seated around the table while our Alpha stands. The emotions pulsing through the room are suffocating.

Slate rests his forehead in his hand, looking more than a little stressed. Leaning in, I ask, "Where's Hazel?"

"Running patrol," he answers quietly. "She wanted to check the Granite Ridge border this morning."

Hawthorne's hands are folded in his lap, his ankle propped up on the opposite knee. He's had a decade plus of experience over Slate and I, and it shows in how calmly he faces everything.

After what seems like hours, Heath speaks. "I've been thinking about Ferris and Zephyr's alliance. They were meeting regularly for a long time, and now Zephyr seems to have truly renounced him."

"Like he said, he could have realized it was better for his pack if he was aligned closer to us and the Valley Pack," Hawthorne offers, though he looks unconvinced.

Slate drags his hand through his long hair. "Do we think it's a farce?"

Heath sinks into a chair, opposite Slate. "That's my intuition, yes."

"That would explain Ferris's lack of reaction. Not protesting our statements, not trying to place blame on anyone else," I say.

"But why?" Slate asks. "What are they playing at?"

Gripping the edge of the table, I swallow and share my theory. "My mind keeps going to the Raven Pack. It seems unlikely that Nyx has been aggressive toward Ironcrest."

"I agree," Hawthorne says, "I asked Elm last night, and he feels the same. He is contacting his relatives there for us."

"Thank you," Heath says. "So what about the Raven Pack, Jasper?"

I exhale stiffly. "If Zephyr paints Nyx as the aggressor, he has grounds to retaliate. And who knows how far that retaliation could go."

The entire room goes still. Slate's dark forest eyes connect with mine, his gaze intense.

"He wants to take over the Raven Pack," Heath concludes.

Hawthorne curses. "Do we think Granite Ridge supports the plan? Maybe they are working together."

"That would explain their show of standing apart, so no one would suspect their alliance in the matter," Hawthorne muses.

"Diffusing suspicion," I conclude.

"We need to talk with Nyx," Heath says.

Slate sighs. "If she'll see us."

"We'll head up there if we have to," Heath answers.

Hawthorne pinches the bridge of his nose. "That will be an uphill battle."

"Hopefully Marigold's grandparent's come through for us, then," I mutter without thinking. Slate glances at me briefly as I say Marigold's name. Clearing my throat, I say, "We need to watch those cameras we installed, and I think we should consider drones."

"Drones?" Hawthorne echoes, his eyebrows rising. Heath's mouth turns downwards, but he looks to Slate.

"If we have any evidence to support our suspicions, it's more than warranted. But ideally, Nyx would agree and we could stay on her side of the border to block anything from happening," Slate says.

Hawthorne nods. "We really need to talk to her. I'll see what else I can do."

Heath looks to Slate. "Set up a special patrol to run the borders along Granite Ridge, Raven, and Ironcrest." The Beta nods. "Jasper, send me the information on drones. Cost, how long it'll take to get them up and running, all of that."

"Yes, Alpha."

"I'm going to call Cashel and see what he thinks. Let's check back in the morning, or come find me sooner if you have anything notable."

With that, we are dismissed. Slate trails after Heath, and Hawthorne claps me on the back as we head toward the door. "That's clever thinking. I hope you're wrong, but I suspect you aren't."

"Thank you, me too," I say grimly. We walk together toward the training building, but as he steps through the metal door, I turn south toward my cabin and the gorgeous girl waiting inside.

CHAPTER ELEVEN

PiCKLES & BRAKE PEDALS

Marigold

i've barely finished cleaning the kitchen when Jasper arrives home from his meeting.

"What have you been doing?"

I spin and take a step back, pressing my back into the edge of the kitchen counter.

"Did you seriously clean while I was gone?"

I scowl at him. "What did you expect? That I'd be lying in bed pining after you the entire time you're gone?"

He's all tension and bright aqua eyes as he closes the distance between us, wasting no time as his mouth presses to the spot on my neck that makes me shiver.

"Is this supposed to be a reward or punishment?" I ask, breathy.

Jasper growls, scraping my skin with his teeth. "It's a hello. If I was rewarding or punishing you, you'd know it." I could melt into a puddle in the middle of the kitchen from the heat in his eyes.

"Did the meeting go well?" I ask, the words spread out as my brain turns to sludge.

He halts his work and leans back to look me in the eyes. The glow of them shows how turned on he is, and suddenly I'm doubting if we will do anything else besides ravage each other today. That would be absolutely fine with me.

"They agreed with my assessment. We're putting together a plan. Everything is going to be fine."

Relief washes through me, relaxing my muscles and giving way to a burning desire to touch every bit of him that I can. With the stress lifted, I can keep him all to myself without any guilt. At least for a few hours.

"So what do you want to do today?" I ask, hoping he says stay in bed.

"I'd like to take you on a date," he says.

"Wow," I say, my grin widening until my cheeks hurt. "What's the plan?"

"You'll find out. Nothing too crazy, but I think we'll have fun," he answers.

Resisting the urge to squeal, I kiss his cheek and head toward my bedroom to put on real clothes. "But we have to be back in time for dinner. I invited everyone over for a game night. I hope you don't mind," I say over my shoulder.

His eyes go wide. "You did?"

"Um, yeah. They all know about our living situation now, so why not? I can cancel if you like or ask Hazel to host."

A slow smile breaks out across his face. "No, it sounds great. Just unexpected."

After some deliberation, I pick a yellow sundress with tiny white daisies all over it. It might clash with my hair, but I don't care. The dress makes me happy, and Jasper must like it too because his lips part silently when I walk out of the bedroom.

He's wearing jeans for once, though they are black like most of his clothing, paired with a black Henley. It might be casual, but damn if he doesn't look scrumptious.

It's a quick walk to the parking lot, and we don't see any of our packmates.

Jasper's car is a sleek and sporty SUV. Black of course. It's shorter than the trucks the pack owns, and somehow much fancier. He opens the door for me and I slide onto the leather bucket seat.

"Wow, that's a lot of buttons," I mutter as Jasper settles into the driver's seat and pushes another button to start the car. The steering wheel has a little shield in the center with a tiny stallion. I have no idea what brand it signifies.

He grins at me, throwing the car into reverse and smoothly pulling onto the winding road to take us to town.

"This is a nice car," I say, peering at the central flat-screen display. Jasper hums, smiling as I continue, "Do you like it better than the one you had to leave behind?"

He shrugs. "It's a newer model of the same thing. I like what I like."

"Oh, cool," I say. He turns from the dirt road onto the highway and I admire the trees whipping by.

He glances at me. "Do you want to get your own car at some point?"

"Probably not," I admit. "I don't even drive." That gets his attention.

Frowning, he asks, "Do you know *how* to drive?"

I shrug. "Never learned. It didn't seem important." He shakes his head, and his hand goes to my leg, sliding higher until my entire body is tingling. He stops, fingers gripping high on my thigh, the hem of my dress pushed up. I have half a mind to grab his wrist and shove his hand higher, but that's a bad idea while he's driving.

His hand lifts as we exit the freeway for the tiny mountain town that sits about twenty-five miles from the pack. I've been in town a few times, but it's so small, there isn't much reason to visit.

Jasper parks on the curb in front of a brick building. I tug my dress back down before he opens my door and helps me out. Our fingers weave together and he leads

"This is my favorite coffee shop. Well, the only coffee shop within a hundred miles, but it's still great. I finished my degree online right here," he rambles, pushing the heavy wooden door open. Is he nervous?

The smell of caramel, cream, and coffee swirl around us. The steam wand on the espresso machine hisses as a barista with green hair froths some milk. The sounds of country-folk music resonates softly.

"What would you like?" he asks, squeezing my hand gently.

"Tea, please."

"Something fruity or something creamy and spicy?"

"Spicy sounds lovely," I say, unable to resist breathing in his scent. It somehow fits in this coffee shop with the acidic coffee and sugary syrups.

Jasper orders a fancy cold-brew coffee for himself and a hot honey chai latte for me, before pulling me by the hand over to a couple of leather armchairs in the corner.

He strokes the inside of my palm with his thumb while we wait, making my whole arm prickle, until he has to release me to stand to get our drinks. I accept the warm cup and take a sip. The spices remind me of Jasper. Delicious. I should not be turned on by a chai latte.

"So I know the last school day was kinda rough. But tell me about good days," he asks, lounging back in his seat. If I had come into this coffee shop and seen him for the first time, I'd be too intimidated to speak with him. He's magnificent with early afternoon light hitting his pale hair and highlighting his straight nose and full lips. I'm convinced he is prettier than I am.

"Marigold?" he prompts, and I snap out of it.

"Okay, you want wholesome and cute, or funny?" I ask.

"Funny," he says, eyes gleaming.

"This happened before you came, so I don't think you've heard the story yet." Sitting forward in my seat, I drop my voice. "So this one is actually my brother's fault. Last year, when Cobalt was nine," I pause, my hand covering my mouth as I try to stay in control long enough to tell the story.

"Yeah?" he asks.

"Okay, when you were like ten or eleven, did you ever go through a phrase where you were drawing..." I choke back a laugh at his confused expression. "Male parts?'

Jasper snorts, shaking his head. "I don't think so, but I've seen kids do that."

Taking a deep breath, I nod. "So Cobalt was doodling peens on his notebook. Not the stuff he turned in, just the notes I wasn't supposed to see." Jasper shakes his head, his lips pressed together to suppress his grin. "Well, of course the other kids got in on it."

"So what happened?"

"Daisy turned a page in."

"Oh, no."

I nod. "I asked her what was drawn on the corner of her math quiz." I pause, enjoying his eyes going wide. "And she said it was a pickle."

Another rough laugh escapes him.

"So I had to go through everyone's notebooks."

"Of course."

"And I find a lot of these drawings. But everyone is claiming they're pickles with eyeballs"

"Naturally."

"So I sit them down, and ask why they think these are pickles. And Starling looks me dead in the face and says, 'Because Cobalt drew a stick figure eating one. So they must be pickles.'"

He drops his head, body shaking with laughter. "Seriously?"

"Yes. A stick figuring *eating a pickle*."

"Stick figure…" he says between laughs. I nod, reaching out and running my hand down his back as he calms down. "What did you do about your brother?"

Shaking my head, I cross my arms. "Let my dad deal with it. Honestly, it was probably Indie's fault as much as Cobalt's."

"He seems like a trouble-maker when he wants to be," he says, and I have to agree. I love my brothers, but they are a lot to handle.

"You're a great teacher. And you're funny," he praises, taking my hand, flipping it, and kissing my wrist. I can't help but be disappointed I'm in my own chair and not in his lap. Public space and all.

Back in his car, he pulls out of town, but then slows and parks on the side of the road.

"Whatcha doing?" I ask, fidgeting with the leather seam of my seat.

Jasper smirks. "I think you should drive."

Spluttering, I shake my head. "No thank you. This is a really nice car. I'd rather learn on a junker so if I screw something up, it's not a huge deal."

"It's fine," he insists, running his hands over the steering wheel.

"Bad idea."

He opens his door and slides one leg out. "I'll be right here. We can go slow."

"Seriously, what if I bust your car?" I say, reaching over to grab his sleeve and keep him from climbing out of the vehicle.

"Marigold, you can do this." The command in his voice silences me.

The driver's seat is overwhelming, with so many indicators and knobs. Jasper points out the speed and how to change from Park to Drive to Reverse. I know the basic mechanics, but I've never tried to use them.

"Foot on the brake, and take it from Park to Drive," he instructs. I hold down the brake so hard, I expect to snap the pedal.

"Now ease off the brake, and it'll start rolling forward, and you can steer us off the shoulder into the road."

Gritting my teeth, I lift my foot, only to slam it back down when the car lurches forward a few inches.

"Try again," he orders, his hand coming up under my hair to massage the nape of my neck.

On the second attempt, I manage to roll along the side of the road. Slowly, I pull the wheel to the left until we're drifting onto the pavement.

"Okay, you'll need to add a bit of gas before another car comes along and gets pissed we're going five miles per hour." I shoot him an alarmed look and he laughs, his hand squeezing the base of my neck, thumb rubbing circles. Tentatively, I press down on the gas pedal. The second we surge forward, I yank my foot back and he smiles at me. "It's okay, Sunshine, try again."

Soon enough we're hurtling down the road at an impressive twenty miles-per-hour. But once another car pulls up and swings around us with a honk, I lose my nerve.

"Can that be enough?" I ask, my knuckles white on the steering wheel.

"If that's what you want," he agrees and then jerks forward when I tap the break harder than I meant to. Somehow I manage to slow and pull off into the grassy shoulder. A bush scrapes along the side of his car and I cringe, but Jasper seems unbothered. I reach for the door handle to get out, but he grabs my forearm and pushes the button to turn the car off. "Where are you going?"

"Swapping back," I say, frowning at him.

"You can climb right across," he says with a cocky tilt of his head.

Rolling my eyes, a reach for the door. "Yeah, I don't think so. I'm too clumsy for that." The center console is fairly low and flush, but I still don't like my odds of not kneeing him in the groin.

His eyes spark. Oh, crap, I know what that look means.

Before I can open the glossy black door handle, hands grab my waist and I'm hauled over the center console into his lap. I want to be angry, but I'd spent our coffee date wishing I was here, so it seems hypocritical to put up a fuss.

For a moment, he holds me, his brassy grin softening while he inspects me. Unable to help myself, I reach up and drag my fingers through his hair. He leans into my touch, eyelids drooping as he enjoys my nails against his scalp.

I love him like this. He's still charming, but the polished edges are washed away to show something real and genuine underneath.

Leveraging against the door and the dash, I lift one leg across until I'm straddling him.

"You make me crazy," he murmurs, his hands falling to my hips and slowly stroking over the fabric of my dress.

"I think you were already crazy," I tease.

With a growl, his hands slide up to run across my ribs, causing me to jerk away. He pauses and his eyes flick up to study my face, understanding dawning. If he starts to tickle me, I really will knee him in the groin.

A few heartbeats pass as he decides what to do, but then he's pressing against my back and urging me closer. Heat and spice envelops me.

After last night, I'd like to think I'm an expert at kissing Jasper. It's been my new favorite hobby, so when he scatters light, tormenting kisses across my cheeks and the edges of my mouth, I want to grab him and shake him. He's being a tease.

Instead, I grip the sides of his face and cover his mouth with mine. He tastes like coffee and vanilla and I'm lost in the blissful sensation. His tongue, his teeth tugging my lip, his hands roving. It's everything.

My dress has ridden up, exposing the length of my thighs. His hands track upwards, teasing the hem of my dress. I let out a frustrated groan and can feel his mouth curve into a smile.

Softly, he uses his hand to tip my jaw up and give him easier access to my neck. I arch my back and throw my head back. It's a display of trust and vulnerability, and from the hitch in his breathing, one he finds appealing. He kisses down my neck, nipping the skin and then smoothing over the sting.

At the base of my throat, his sharper canine teeth scrape my skin, causing me to gasp. He repeats the action, momentarily taking up all space in my consciousness. All I can do is hold on to his shoulders. His lips close around the spot and he sucks, following with a lick that sends sparks down to my toes.

He leans back enough to look at the spot, a wicked smile forming. I don't need a mirror to know he left a hickey. The possessive curl of his fingers on my hips and the growl he lets out is pure wolf shifter.

His next kiss is demanding, aggressive, and I love it, from the way he forces my lips apart to the unyielding pressure. Tension builds in my body as he slides his palms up my legs again, pausing at the top with the barest brush before descending. I can't take it anymore.

Blood pounds through my veins, beating so hard I'm sure he can feel my pulse everywhere our skin touches.

"Jasper," I rasp, my words choppy, "if you don't start touching me, I'm going to have to do it myself, because otherwise I'm going to die."

His laugh is evil. "Not sure what you're talking about, Sunshine." My nails dig into the skin on his biceps. He knows exactly what I mean.

My forehead falls against his shoulder, my eyes squeezed shut. Releasing my hold on his arms, I reach down between us and under the hem of my dress. Before I can touch where I need, his hand grabs my wrist with a guttural "Mine."

I'd love to make some clever comeback to that, but the second he says mine, all rational thought drops out of my head. I'm burning, about to break.

"You need it that badly?" he teases, his whisper almost inaudible. "Let me hear you beg."

"I did," I whine, the shake in my voice betraying my failing composure. My free hand slides under the collar of his shirt, loving the heat of his skin.

His chuckle makes my stomach clench. "You didn't."

Scowling, I open my mouth to argue, but the feel of his lips against my skin short-circuits my brain. He kisses further down my chest, tugging the neckline of my dress down. His mouth across the sensitive skin on my breast is enough to break down my resolve entirely. "Jasper, please. I need you."

Grinning, he releases my wrist and runs his palms up my thighs. Tentatively, he brushes his fingers across my panties. Light, teasing. On the second pass, he's firmer, and my body squirms in reaction.

"Hold still," he says softly, authority in his voice causing me to stiffen.

His teeth close on my breast, marking me again, as his fingers hone in right where I need him, swirling and pressing. The sharp pain punctuates the pleasure. My vision goes spotty, touch overwhelming the rest of my senses. His voice sounds far away as he says, "Good girl." I come so hard I think I might actually die.

Jasper gathers me up in his lap with my head against his chest. "You okay?" His words are sweet, but his tone is wicked.

"I didn't realize," I say, gathering up my scattered thoughts. "When it's just me, it doesn't quite hit that hard."

"You're saying I'm the best you've ever had?" I can hear the pride in his voice. My laugh is dry.

The weight of his arms around me is comforting, like an anchor holding me together. Finally he breaks the silence. "What do you imagine when you touch yourself?"

Closing my eyes, I say, "You want to hear that I think about you?"

"I think about *you*. Even before you moved in," he confesses, his cocky tone replaced with vulnerability. Nuzzling his nose into my hair, right behind my ear, he sends a shiver through my body. "So what about you?"

"Really, before?" I ask, a flush rising up my neck. He nods and I feel it more than see it. "Okay fine, I think about you, but only recently."

"As long as I'm it from now on," he says possessively, "In fact, you don't even need to do anything. Come to me and I'll take care of you."

Rolling my eyes, I tip my chin up and place a soft kiss on the edge of his jaw. "Sure." No girl would turn down an orgasm like that one. Talk about some amazing benefits with this friendship.

"I feel like I should return the favor," I say, shifting on his lap so I can cup his erection through his jeans. That can't be comfortable.

He kisses my cheek and then opens the car door. "As nice as that sounds, we should get going. We don't want to miss dinner."

"I'm fine with missing dinner," I say, reaching for his belt buckle.

Scowling, he shakes his head. "No missing meals."

With that, he slides out from under me, and heads around to the driver's seat, leaving me to fumble with my seatbelt like I've forgotten how my limbs work.

RENEGADES & RECKONING

Jasper

Marigold eats with her dad and brothers, and I eat with Slate and Hazel. If they notice that every inch of my skin smells like Marigold, they don't say anything. If she was at the table, they'd definitely notice her flushed skin and the glances she keeps giving me, even across the meadow. Being roommates doesn't excuse eyeing each other like that.

I head directly home, but Marigold lingers, walking with Hazel. The girls are giggling and my stomach flips. It's not that I don't want anyone to know we're involved,

but they will all assume we are well on our way to being mates and Marigold isn't ready for that label, if she wants it at all.

"Okay, what are we playing?" Onyx hollers the moment he's through the door. Cedar follows him quietly.

"I've got a new game for us," Marigold chimes, following them in.

"Hey guys," I say from the kitchen, pulling a 12-pack of IPAs from the fridge.

"I nabbed a few snacks from Crickett," Marigold says. She holds out a plate to me, grinning. It's stacked with cheese and salami, beside an impressive array of pickle spears.

"You got pickles?" I ask incredulously.

Marigold shrugs. "Just in the mood, I guess," she says with a wink. Using two fingers, she raises a pickle to her mouth and takes a bite. At my grimace, she breaks into silent laughter.

Hazel joins me in the kitchen, her dark brown hair loose around her shoulders. She hands me a casserole dish while giving Marigold a strange look.

"What did you make?" I ask, peeling back the tin-foil.

"S'mores bars," she says.

Onyx leans over her shoulder. "Wow, those look fantastic." He swipes a bar before I can even set them down.

Hazel's eyes crinkle as she smiles at him. "I added caramel between the graham crackers and chocolate. You're welcome."

"I love you," Onyx says before taking a huge bite and groaning.

Slate shoves him away and grabs Hazel around the waist from behind, kissing behind her ear as she cackles.

My eyes go to Marigold to find she's already looking at me. She smiles, showing her teeth, and slowly runs her tongue over her top teeth. Fuck. This is going to be a long night not touching her if she keeps taunting me.

"What's the game?" Cedar asks, opening a beer with a crack and a hiss.

Marigold pulls a card game out of her bag and waves it back and forth. The brown and gold cover says, "Sheriffs and Outlaws," with a little sheriff's badge over an old fashioned pistol.

We load up plates and lay out the cards. Slate sits on the sofa and Hazel sits on the floor between his legs. Cedar grabs the armchair and Onyx stretches out on the floor, leaving one seat open. Marigold sits beside Slate, tucking her feet up under her, and motions for me to sit beside Hazel with my back against the sofa right below her shins.

The game isn't terribly complicated and Marigold explains the basics. Everyone draws a card to assign their roles, but keeps them secret. Only the Sheriff has to turn over his card to reveal his role - it's Slate. He flips the card over with a sigh.

I lift my card and peek. Outlaw. To win the game, my task is to eliminate the Sheriff. There are two Outlaws so I'll have some help, though I'll have to figure out who. Anyone who fires at the Sheriff is likely the other Outlaw. But the moment we do so, the people assigned as Deputies will attack us and defend Slate. They win if the game ends with the Sheriff alive.

The last person is assigned Renegade. "The Renegade wins if they're the last person alive in the game," Marigold explains. I turn that over in my mind, trying to predict how that may play out.

Marigold hands me a stack of cards, a mixture of actions for shooting others or blocking their shots, along with a few random bonus cards to give special abilities.

"Any questions?" Marigold asks.

"How are we supposed to know who is what and who to shoot?" Onyx asks, a whine in his voice. He shakes his dirty blonde hair out of his eyes and squints at the cards in his hand.

Marigold winks. "You'll have to figure it out based on what everyone does. Most likely a Deputy won't shoot at the Sheriff, right?"

"Great," Slate says sarcastically.

"Aw, you'll be a great Sheriff," Hazel coos, ending with a dark laugh.

Shaking his head, Slate lays down a horse card, making it harder for us to shoot him. Hazel goes next, and with a flourish, she tries to shoot Cedar.

"Do you even know who I am?" Cedar asks, tilting his head with a curious look.

Hazel scrunches up her nose. "If I'm the Deputy, then there's a seventy-five percent chance that you're an enemy, right?" I almost miss it, but Marigold reaches out and pinches Hazel on the back of her arm.

"Alright." Cedar frowns, moving his marker down one life. We each get five hits before we are eliminated. Hazel looks up at Marigold, an innocent flutter of her lashes the only sign of silent communication between the friends.

Marigold cranes her neck and smiles sweetly at me. "Sorry Jasper." And she lays down a card to shoot at me.

"What the hell?" I cry out, just dramatic enough she knows I'm teasing. "Well, guess what? Too bad!" I say, setting down a card to block her shot. All five lives still intact. She pouts, crossing her arms and leaning back into the cushion. She's adorable.

I lay down a gun card before me so I can shoot people further away. Onyx lays down his own gun and Cedar fires back at Hazel.

"Watch it," Slate says menacingly.

"She could be the Renegade, out to trick you." Cedar points out.

"I would never!" Hazel rests her chin on Slate's knee, wrapping her arm around his calf.

Back to the Sheriff, and Slate lays down a gun so he can shoot further. "You're strategic," I note. He shrugs.

Hazel takes another shot at Cedar, and then Marigold takes a shot at me. With a glare, I send one back at her and she gasps. We both move our markers down one life.

While everyone's eyes are on Onyx's hemming and hawing over his next move, Marigold bends down low, leaning over my shoulder with her hair curtaining her, and murmurs, "I'm going to get you back for that."

My hand moves to her calf and I squeeze it lightly. Her smile is devious.

Onyx decides to lay a specialty card that shoots at everyone including himself, and only Slate and Onyx come out unscathed with blocking cards. Down to three lives.

In the next round, Cedar is eliminated. He flips his card to reveal the role of Deputy.

"Whoops!" Hazel says. "Sorry, Cedar. Thought you were an Outlaw."

Marigold studies Onyx, her lip between her teeth. She decides he is the next target, and over the next two rounds, both she and Hazel work to eliminate him.

This gives me a chance to shoot at Slate. Unfortunately, it proves to be a mistake, because he still has plenty of blocking cards and all five of his lives. Sliding my marker down to zero lives, I groan and flip the card over to reveal Outlaw, a twin to Onyx's role card in front of him.

"I knew it!" Marigold says. She grins at Hazel who is looking far too pleased with herself. Slate who is looking suspicious of both women.

"One of them has to be the Renegade, and the other is your Deputy," Cedar explains the obvious, resting his chin on his fist and studying the pair. Slate lays down another bonus card which gives him an unnecessary ability to shoot further, effectively buying himself time to figure out which girl is which role.

"She's the Renegade," Hazel accuses. Marigold narrows her eyes at her. Hazel's next shot is at Marigold, and Marigold fires back.

"I'm the Deputy," Marigold says, pressing her lips together as Slate looks between them.

"Sorry," he says, shrugging and laying down a card to shoot Marigold.

"Thank you, honey," Hazel says, kissing his outstretched arm.

"How could you do that?" Marigold says. She slaps her hand over her role card and slowly slides her palm back to reveal her designation as Deputy.

Slate grimaces, looking at his mate. She laughs and thumps down a final card to shoot Slate and win the game.

"Sorry, babe, I'm the only winner this round!" She lets out a whoop, and Slate grabs her and hauls her up into his lap, scolding her while kissing whatever he can reach.

I flip Hazel's role card to confirm - Renegade.

Marigold's fingertips skim the nape of my neck before she stands to get a drink.

Cedar says his goodbyes and then heads out, mentioning something about a long day tomorrow transplanting something in his garden.

Marigold folds her legs under her, settling back on the sofa behind me. She holds a little plate with some chips and another pickle spear. It crunches as she takes a bite.

"Want some?" she offers, leaning forward.

"I don't actually like them," I say quietly, causing her to shake with silent laughter.

Onyx takes his seat and we all sit around the coffee table enjoying the remaining snacks and beer. It gets quiet, but it's the heavy quiet that makes my lungs constrict a bit. Slate and Hazel are both watching Marigold and me.

Hazel lets out a sigh. "Guys, we need to talk."

Nausea rolls in my gut. I'm not usually an anxious person, but nobody can hear "we need to talk" and not react.

"What's up?" Marigold says brightly, though the pitch is too high.

"It kinda seems like things have changed a bit. Did you guys start dating?" Slate asks.

Marigold startles in her seat, and I work to keep my face calm.

"We're roommates," I answer evenly. "And even if we did get involved, I would hope everyone would respect our privacy. I'm not sure why this keeps getting questioned." Hazel cocks her head and raises one eyebrow. She knows me too well.

"Hold on, what did I miss?" Onyx says, sitting back with a frown.

Marigold's mouth gapes, looking between Onyx and Hazel, her cheeks getting pinker by the second. "Okay, we kissed."

Slate bites back a smile, but Hazel narrows her eyes at me. "Just roommates?"

"Oh, no, it's not Jasper's fault. It just kinda happened. Like an accident," Marigold stutters. My muscles tense, a headache starting behind my eyes.

Onyx interrupts, "Are you fucking kidding me? Accident my ass. You become roommates and then decide to go at it? Easy access, I guess."

"How about you watch your mouth," I growl.

"How about you stop taking advantage of your roommate," Onyx says, venom in every syllable.

"You don't get a say-" I snap back, but Onyx stands, leaning into my space.

"Do you have feelings for her, or are you enjoying toying with her?" he asks, a deadly calm in every syllable that I've never heard from Onyx before.

"She's my friend," I say, standing to face him.

"Then knock it the fuck off." His eyes flash electric blue, and I know we are seconds from a fight. Wolf shifters losing control is dangerous for everybody.

I'm sure my own eyes are glowing a similar shade. I can feel my wolf answering his challenge. Because of my higher position in the pack, I'm driven to react to disrespect or challenges, like the bold stare Onyx is currently giving me.

Marigold's hands go to my arm, but Hazel tugs her back.

"Onyx, back off" Slate warns, the authority in his voice breaking through the tension.

Onyx turns and storms out, slamming the door behind him. Finally I can turn, and Slate's eyes are lit up green as he regards me. I take a deep breath and push down the instinct to fight and defend.

"He's really upset," Marigold squeaks, shell-shocked.

Hazel pinches the bridge of her nose. "I get the feeling friends with benefits isn't a thing for wolf shifters?" Slate nods, his shoulders sagging.

"Look, you guys know why we don't do this kind of thing. Your wolf instincts don't know the difference. You're going to start acting like mates and end up hurt because you don't mean it." Slate squeezes Hazel's shoulders.

"You'll ruin your friendship," she adds.

Nodding, Marigold wipes at her eyes and lets out a sniffle. I can't stand when she cries; it hits me like a punch to the chest.

"I appreciate your concern, but at the end of the day it's not your business and I think you've overstepped," I say firmly. Before Hazel can argue, I add, "You've upset Marigold, so let's circle back to this once we've all had time to calm down and think."

Slate takes Hazel's hand and leads her toward the door, giving me a sympathetic bro nod. Before the door shuts, Hazel calls out, "I love you Marigold. I'm here for you." I can't even be angry that she's already Team Marigold if this becomes a conflict.

"Well that went downhill fast," I grumble, walking back to the sofa. Marigold is curled up like a hedgehog, legs drawn up and cheek against her knees.

Taking a deep breath, I sink down onto my knees in front of her and slowly pry her hands apart. Once I get her to release her grip, her legs fall and she straightens into a seated position, though she's still hunched over. Her beautiful face is blotchy and her eyes are red.

"I didn't mean it like that," she whispers.

"I know," I say. That doesn't change that what they said was true.

She throws her arms around me, laying her head on my shoulder, so I loop my arms under her legs and lift her. She clings to me as I walk her back to our bedroom. We might be in trouble, but I can't sleep without her.

Gently, I lay her down on our bed and then walk around to the other side, pulling my shirt off as I go. She props herself up on her elbows, watching me. The tears on her cheeks are drying.

At the edge of the bed, I hesitate. What's best for her? To continue this physical relationship when she has no idea how to handle the emotional side? This is all becoming a mess faster than I realized, and we have to figure it out.

Sliding under the covers, I roll onto my side and prop my head up, mirroring her pose.

"I'm sorry," she says, reaching out to tentatively touch my chest, like she needs the contact. "I didn't know what to do with how upset he got."

"It's fine," I say, resting my hand on the hollow of her waist. "But I need to know what you want. We weren't clear before. Am I an experiment for you?"

Long, wet lashes frame those blue-green eyes. "No."

"So, what am I?" My voice betrays how desperate I am. I would give anything to hear that she loves me, because I am falling for her and I can't slow it down.

She takes a shuddering breath and sits up. "I don't know. It's still so new, and I feel... confused, I guess."

Confused is better than friends with benefits. A step forward she isn't ready to label.

"Do you want some space until you're not confused?"

Her strawberry-blonde waves sway over her bare arms as she shakes her head. "I don't want space, but are you okay with giving me time to figure it out?"

Without waiting for an answer, she slides her leg over me and pushes my shoulder so I land flat on my back. Leaning down, she lowers her voice. "Space is the last thing I want. I'm always thinking about you. I don't want to be apart. Is that bad?"

Her words are irresistible. She might not be ready to recognize her feelings toward me, but they're there. Clear in the shine of her eyes and the way her hands spread over my skin.

I answer by pulling her face down and covering her mouth with mine for a long, slow kiss.

Her breathing shudders. My thumbs wipe away the last of her tears as I frame her face with my hands. Unease shines in her eyes. This undefined connection between us weighs heavily across her and I want to take some pressure off of her.

Words tumble out before I can think better. "I'll be whatever you want me to be. I'm not going anywhere. Boyfriend, hook up, I'll take anything you give me. I just want you." I know how stupid it is, but it's the only way I know how to make things easier for her in this situation.

Marigold searches my face, as if she can sense the struggle raging in my heart and head. "Okay."

She gathers the fabric of her dress in both hands and pulls it over her head in one smooth motion. The world could have stopped spinning and I wouldn't have noticed.

My hands graze over her ribs and lightly skim the swell of her breasts. She leans forward, one hand on my chest, pushing herself into my hands.

"If you made me come that hard with your fingers, I'm a little scared of what you can do with your cock." Her voice is husky.

This girl is unbelievable.

My fingers dig into her skin. It takes two steadying breaths before I can speak. "That's the thing," I say, wincing at her parted lips and vulnerable expression. "I don't want to do *that* until I'm claiming my mate."

Swallowing, Marigold's face falls. "That makes sense." She rolls off me and stretches out, arms crossed over her bare breasts. A blush colors her cheeks.

"Where are you going?" I murmur, brushing her hair over her shoulder to expose that glorious bare skin. Her mouth curves into a hopeful smile.

She runs a hand down my side, thumb stroking my abs. Leaning in, I kiss her sweet mouth, putting all my longing and devotion into my slow, deliberate movements. We kiss and let our hands rove, until she lays her head down on my pillow and nestles under my chin. It feels incredible to wrap my arms around her and feel her breathing even out. She's addicting, and I have no guarantee she's mine.

Chapter Thirteen

CONFESSIONS & INVESTIGATIONS

Marigold

Slate knocks on our door the next morning. Jasper invites him in. "What's up? Do we have a change of plans for the day?"

Shaking his head, Slate turns toward me. "Actually, I was hoping Marigold would visit the Raven Pack with Elm today. Scope things out and get a feel for what's going on up there."

Jasper's words about the Raven Pack and Ironcrest echo in my thoughts. "Sure, sounds like a plan."

Slate leaves me with a nod. When I return to the table, Jasper tugs me into his lap and kisses me soundly.

"I need to go," I say.

"No," Jasper argues between kisses peppered down my throat.

Sighing, I sink into him. "A long run will give me time to think about us." He hums in response, his hold loosening so I can pull back. I give him one more lingering kiss and force myself to walk away.

My dad is waiting for me, sitting on a bench in the big steel training building. "Hey, Dad." He gives me a hug.

"Ready to see Heron and Breeze?" he asks, referring to my maternal grandparents.

"Let's go," I say, opening the door to my dad's faded green pickup truck. Once we're on the road, I ask, "So, what are we looking for exactly?"

"Mainly a temperature check. Is Nyx still the reclusive Alpha we all love, or is she possibly leading raids? Is there any sign of Granite Ridge or Ironcrest pushing in?" he says grimly.

"Alright, that sounds manageable."

"So what's new with you, kiddo?" he asks with a smile. Our last family dinner was dominated by Cobalt's stories of his recent adventures, and Indigo sharing about the new healing techniques he's learned during his apprenticeship with our grandmother, Sable.

"Had a fun game night with everyone last night. Oh and I went into town with Jasper and checked out the coffee shop there. It was cool."

"Just you and Jasper?" he says.

"Yeah," I say, trying to sound casual. My dad nods. Would he approve of me and Jasper? Silence stretches between us and I finally give in to the impulse to ask. "So, after working with him a while, what do you think of him?"

"Jasper?" His lips thin while he considers. "He's talented, that's for sure. Seems loyal, but it's only been a few months. Considering his parents, I don't think I'll trust him until it's been a few years."

That's not ideal.

"He's gotten really close with all my friends. I don't think he had friends or supportive leaders in Granite Ridge. He seems happy, so I don't think we need to worry about his loyalty," I argue.

"That makes sense." His tone ends the discussion.

Pulling down the Raven Pack's access road, I keep waiting for a guard to stop us, but no one greets us until we've reached their compound. While our buildings form a loose circle, the Raven Pack's buildings are huddled together in a tight block.

We approach the larger pack house and a pair of female Thetas stop us.

"I'm here to see my grandparents, Heron and Breeze," I say. "I'm Marigold, Ivy's daughter. And this is my father, Elm, her mate."

"We remember you," the taller woman says. Her black hair reaches to her waist in a glossy curtain. She's familiar, but not anyone I clearly recall from our last visit a few months ago. She nods to her partner, who disappears inside.

A few minutes later, the younger woman reappears and motions for us to follow her inside. The side entrance leads into a hallway, and our guide brings us past various meeting rooms and recreation rooms until we reach the foyer.

Breeze ambles from another hallway, a smile creasing her face. She holds her arms open, and I gladly hug her. It's been too long. "My sweet Marigold, you look so much like your mother," she coos. When she sees my father, her face chills. "Elm."

"Hello, Breeze. You look lovely," my dad says. She brushes him away and takes my hand to lead us down the hallway until we reach a door left open.

The studio apartment opens into a small sitting room with a bed tucked around a corner. Heron hugs me as well and then shakes my dad's hand. We sit in armchairs and sip bottled water.

"It's always good to see you. But this is unexpected," Breeze says. Her curly blonde hair is streaked with silver. Heron reaches over and takes her hand. They've been mates for fifty years.

"I wish this was simply a visit to see you. But there have been some recent events we need to discuss with you" my father says. "A few days ago, there was an Alpha Counsel. Your Alpha was the only one who refused to attend. But Ironcrest made some accusations against your pack."

Their faces become solemn. Asking them to speak about pack business without their Alpha is uncouth. But they know as well as we do that Nyx wouldn't speak with us.

I fiddle with my hands. "Zephyr claims that you are crossing his borders and testing their defenses. We know that's not possible, but we need to know what is happening. How have things been with Ironcrest and Granite Ridge in the last few months?"

"Oh, I see," Breeze says, looking to her mate. He rubs his thumb across her hand comfortingly.

Heron clears his throat. "What they're saying, the opposite is true. Ironcrest has been raiding our borders, testing our patrols, even taking supplies from our storage houses."

"Why haven't you guys brought this to the other packs?" I ask.

"You know how Nyx is. She feels we can handle it." Breeze says, giving me a pointed look. "So there's nothing you can do."

"We think Ironcrest means to fully invade, perhaps with Granite Ridge's assistance," my dad says, getting to the point.

"I can't see that happening. They're badgering us, not starting a war," Heron says mildly.

"Do you have defenses prepared if they do?"

"It doesn't matter. They're just causing trouble." Breeze turns her face away from us.

Grimacing, I lean forward, inserting myself into their argument. "But why would they make those accusations in the Alpha Counsel then?"

"To shift the blame, I suppose." Heron answers.

"Our leaders are concerned about a possible attack," my dad says.

"You don't need to worry. Your help will not be accepted anyway."

"Heron, you have to talk to Nyx," I beg, "Our help could mean the difference of victory or being wiped out."

"They wouldn't dare," Breeze sniffs.

"But what if they do?" I press.

Breeze stands, puttering into the kitchenette. "I don't want to talk about this any longer."

My dad focuses on Heron. "Would you let us inspect your borders?"

"Absolutely not," he snaps, "You won't find anything other than the disturbances I've mentioned."

"Can I speak with Nyx?" I ask.

"I don't think that's a good idea."

"I don't understand why you guys would reject someone wanting to help you," I say, frustration getting the better of me.

"We don't need anyone's help," Heron says, crossing his arms.

As sweetly as I can muster, I ask, "Can you at least tell us everything in more detail? In case Ironcrest starts to harass us as well? So we know what to watch for."

With some coaxing, my grandparents go over every detail they can think of, which, unfortunately, is not a lot. We leave disappointed and nervous.

Jasper

It's hard to focus on Hazel's report about patrols when my mind only wants to replay Marigold's words, *I'm always thinking about you. I don't want to be apart.*

It feels foolish to hope she'll decide she wants something permanent. Unfortunately, I'm so far gone, I don't think I could ever move on. This is my fault. I'm the one who decided to kiss her again.

"The strangest part is the lack of new markings along Granite Ridge," Hazel continues. "Ironcrest has maintained their borders, but it's not like Ferris to neglect his."

Heath leans back in his seat. "I think we can all agree they're acting strangely."

"Perhaps because they are also potentially preparing to invade the Raven Pack, they are focusing their forces along that border," Hazel says.

"It makes sense, if Ironcrest is accusing Nyx of aggression to justify their moves, Granite Ridge might choose a different tactic. In this case, keeping a low profile," Hawthorne suggests.

Heath nods, but my stomach is in knots. I can't tell if that edgy feeling is general anxiety about my parents' pack, or if there's something I'm missing.

A whiff of Marigold's scent drifts in, and I twist to see her approaching the meeting room, Elm behind her.

"How was it?" Hazel asks, standing to pull out chairs for them. Marigold sits next to her and squeezes her friend's hand.

Elm frowns. "Nyx refused to see us, but we were able to confirm that Ironcrest has been raiding the Raven Pack for the last six months."

"That's a long time," Slate says, brows drawing together in alarm.

"This isn't a reactionary plan. It's a long term strategy," Heath agrees.

"This proves Jasper's theory," Marigold declares. My heart jumps. "They're definitely manufacturing an excuse to take the Raven Pack over."

Hawthorne locks eyes with Elm and asks, "Are you totally sure about what they said?"

"Yes. Heron and Breeze might be prickly, but they are honest."

Hazel sighs. "So what do we do about it?" Slate grasps her hand, threading their fingers together, and she gives him a tired smile.

"They don't want our help," Elm says.

"So we do nothing?" Hazel protests.

Slate lifts her hand and presses a kiss to the back of it. "It definitely limits how much we can help."

"We may be jumping ahead," Heath says. "I should go up to see Nyx myself. She's not unreasonable."

"Thank you," Elm says quietly, looking down at the table.

"We can go tomorrow. Hawthorne, please leave messages so they have a chance of expecting us. I'd like to bring this whole team. Lazuli and Cassia can manage for a morning."

My heart rate picks up. It's unheard of to travel without leaving a Beta behind. Heath is more concerned about this threat than I realized.

"Alpha, may I come?" Marigold asks, her voice timid. Heath nods.

Protectiveness surges in me. If she's coming, I need her by my side. But only Slate and Hazel know about us, and Hazel isn't exactly supportive. As if feeling my tension, Marigold glances up and meets my gaze.

Once Heath dismisses us, I follow her out of the room. I'm done pretending to be indifferent to her when we are around the rest of our pack. Taking her arm, I lean in. "I missed you this morning. You looked stunning walking into that meeting and saying my name." At least I keep my voice low.

She runs her tongue over her lips but stays quiet.

Once inside our cabin, she halts, posture rigid. Her breath is shallow and her hands clench and unclench. I wrap my arms around her, waiting until she's ready to tell me.

Slowly she relaxes. "I didn't realize how serious this was. This could turn into a battle and people are going to get hurt. And I don't think Nyx will do what it takes to stop it." She spirals. "And I'm over here pretending you're some hookup. Like it means nothing to me. That's the furthest thing from the truth."

My muscles go taut, like I'm afraid to move and spook her.

She draws a slow breath. "Unless you're going to decide you're done with me, I don't see this ending. Because I don't want to live without you."

"I don't either. I'll never be done with you," I say, the words tumbling out before my brain catches up.

"What's wrong with me?" she says with a laugh. "We were supposed to be friends. Now I can't function without touching you. You're all I think about."

Every word is what I've been dreaming of.

Her back hits the door as I crowd into her space. I press a hand on either side of her head so she's trapped. "We could never have just been friends." Her mouth opens in surprise, but I can't stop. "I've been trying to resist you since I arrived. You're my sun. You're what I see when I close my eyes. You've worked your way into my soul."

Her eyes glow a glorious shade of warm blue and her expression is hungry. All the things I've been imagining doing to her flood my thoughts at once.

She's faster than I am. Hands grabbing my shoulders, she jumps on me and wraps her legs around my waist. I'm lost in her kisses. They're urgent and needy and everything I've always wanted. Fire burns across my skin, maybe coming from her touch, or maybe from inside of me. I'm consumed.

Every sense falls away except her skin on mine and the sound of her breathing, the little noises she makes.

Her fingers tug at my hair and her thighs tighten as I push her back into the door. I can't get close enough.

My heart races and I can feel her's doing the same. Every inch of skin is soft and warm as my hands rove across the swell of her breasts and down her ribs. Finally I grip her ass and pull us away from the door. She clings to me, her mouth moving to the side of my neck, her tongue licking behind my ear and then her teeth nipping my ear lobe.

As I stride toward my bedroom, she whispers, "Just to be completely clear, I'm all in. I want to see where this can go."

Gently, I lay her down across my comforter and lean over her, my hands resting on either side of her head. "Good to know I'm not alone in this. That you feel the same."

Her eyes meet mine for a moment. The only movement is our chests rising and falling in a chaotic rhythm. Neither of us are willing to break the spell.

Slowly, her hand comes up and brushes the hair from my eyes. Gentle fingertips skim down my cheek and jaw. I turn to kiss her palm, and her eyes flutter closed. Taking her hand, my mouth closes over her pulse point, and then down the tender, pale skin of her inner arm. Her scent is warm and sweet, like sunshine and wildflowers.

"If you told me a month ago that we would be here, doing this, I would have never believed you," she murmurs.

"I would have," I say, grinning as her hands pull my shirt up to expose my torso. She licks her lips as her hands trail over the ridges of my abdomen muscles. I've never been so grateful for athletic shifter genetics. "Like what you see?"

Her teeth sink into her bottom lip. "You don't need *me* to tell you how gorgeous you are."

"It couldn't hurt."

She rolls her eyes. "You smug asshole."

"But I'm *your* smug asshole." My low laugh rumbles out of me as I lower over her. "For example, you are stunning."

She is. Her tan skin is flushed, her constellation of freckles standing out. Brightness sparkles in her lit eyes, her lips parted as a slow smile spreads across her heart-shaped face. That wavy reddish-blonde hair spreads around her in a halo. She looks like a goddess. And she's mine.

The quilt bunches under her hands as she squirms. I could stay here with her forever like this. Well, maybe not exactly like this. I want to touch and taste all of her. Right now.

Her hands ease my shirt up and I tug it over my head, tossing it away. She lets out an appreciative hum. I bury my smile in the smooth skin of her stomach, pressing kisses across her hips to below her belly button. Quiet giggles tighten her muscles under my lips. My hands move to her hips, loving her shiver as I hold her down.

Delicately, my teeth pull her waistband down, exposing more bare skin. Maybe I forget to breathe, because I'm dizzy. Spiraling. Or perhaps it's the sparks of electricity coming off her fingers cutting grooves through my hair. Nails scratching my scalp.

She tugs impatiently, the urgency returning to her motions. Her heels push against my lower back, pushing my hips down against her and my chest against her bust. She's lush and fits against me perfectly.

Our mouths crash together again. The difference between our first kiss and now is startling. Her tongue delves into my mouth. Bold. Demanding. I'll give her whatever she wants.

My hand slips under her shirt. Like most shifters, she doesn't wear a bra. There are no barriers to cup one breast and run my thumb over her nipple. She shutters and I do it again, her teeth closing down on my bottom lip in a quick bite.

"Don't start biting unless you want me to bite back," I warn. The words float between us like smoke. They represent everything we haven't discussed and what could come next. If this works and she wants to make this relationship permanent, I would gladly mark her as my mate. It chains my heart to hers, keeping us together forever. Not all couples take that step. It's shifters' version of marriage, without the option of divorce.

She doesn't respond. If she was nervous or scared, she'd say so. Marigold is never short on words. Her silence is confident, broken only by a moan as I draw her shirt higher and lower my mouth over her other breast.

With an insistent tug, she pulls my face back to hers. Our lips brush, press, drag, over and over until I've lost all sense of time. Her hands explore, but we don't take it any further. There's a seriousness underlying each touch. We are finally on the same page. This isn't for fun. It's devotion, and we both know what comes next isn't something done on a whim.

CHAPTER FOURTEEN

DRONES & DEVIL'S SPAWN

Marigold

Heath calls the team together in the morning. He drives the first truck with my dad and Hawthorne. Slate drives the second truck with Hazel, Jasper, and me. I'm grateful. In the back seat, I can distract myself by holding his hand and tracing the lines on his palm.

Thunder clouds approach from the south, their rolling gray matching my anxious heart.

Nyx's guard has tripled since yesterday, with six wolves standing around the pack house. My blood goes

cold. Is this for us? Or have things escalated with Ironcrest?

Hawthorne climbs out and speaks with them. When it's clear he's being turned away, Heath joins the discussion. Two guards go inside, and after a long wait, they return and allow us entrance.

The meeting room is dusty. Heath sits and we all settle around him at the dated conference table. Hazel clicks her nails together anxiously.

"Nyx, " Heath says, rising as the Raven Pack Alpha joins us. She's younger than I expected, with olive skin and dark hair in a short bob.

"Sit down and tell me what you want," she says curtly. My hands grip the arms of my chair. Through our pack bond, I can feel a spike of irritation, but everyone's face stays calm and neutral. Heath begins, "Thank you for seeing us. I won't waste your time. We have reason to believe Ironcrest and Granite Ridge are planning a full-blown attack against your pack and we want to help you."

Nyx stays quiet for a long moment. "Why?"

"At the Alpha Counsel," Heath says, ignoring Nyx's snort, "Zephyr claimed your pack has been violating their borders and that you are the aggressors."

"So I've heard," Nyx replies dryly. "Not sure what his lies have to do with me."

Heath takes a slow breath, his hands loosening as he calms himself. If it was my father, he would have attacked Nyx for that tone.

"Ironcrest has the numbers, paired with Granite Ridge, they have close to one hundred wolves who can fight. I would prefer it if my ally was not wiped off the map."

Nyx's lip curls. "You don't need to worry about us. We've got things well in hand."

Heath's control starts to slip. "What is your plan if they invade? If one hundred wolves descend on your compound?"

She shrugs, and I don't expect an answer, but she finally says, "Lockdown."

"And all your packmates out of this building?"

"I'm sure they'll manage."

"Why are you refusing help?" he asks, anger seeping into his words.

"Because I don't need it," she says. "I think you should take your wolves and go. I don't want that devil's spawn in my house."

Jasper stiffens, and Slate leans forward menacingly. Even Hazel bristles. Heath's voice drops. "Jasper is a valued member of my team."

"Just get him out of here," Nyx says, looking down her nose at us.

Still reeling, I reach over to grasp his thigh, trying to give him whatever support I can. Heath pushes his chair back. "Thank you for your time, Nyx. We can see ourselves out."

Before she disappears, my dad abruptly stands. "Alpha Nyx, I would like to stay with my relatives. Let me see that my mate's parents are safe."

Her eyes narrow, but she says, "For Ivy's sake, I'll allow it. That one too, if she wishes." Her long black nails point at me, before she spins on her heel and walks out.

The idea of hateful, judgmental Nyx abandoning her pack and hunkering down is not something I can tolerate. If I have a chance to help, I have to take it. I look to my Alpha. "I would like to stay too."

Heath nods. "If that's your choice, please be safe. And we will figure out what else we can do to help."

My throat is thick, but I take deep breaths and stand with my father. I'll miss Jasper, but it's temporary. Heath leads us out and climbs in the truck with Hawthorne.

Jasper grabs my elbow and pulls me close. "I don't want you to stay. It's an unnecessary risk."

"I'm sorry about what she said. But I want to help."

"If this all goes sideways, you'll be trapped," he hisses, his platinum hair falling forward as he leans over me. "You can help from home."

"I'm sorry, I already decided. I'll be back soon."

"I need you," Jasper says, brows furrowing. The pain in his expression cuts away at my resolve.

Squeezing his hand, I remove it from my elbow and step back. "It'll be okay. I'll miss you." My eyes burn as I fight tears.

"What did he say?" he dad asks, frowning as he looks over at Jasper speaking with Slate.

"He doesn't want me to stay. He thinks it's too dangerous."

My dad crosses his arms. "That's not his business. He isn't your Alpha or your family." My heart twinges. "You're doing the right thing."

"I'm not sure, Dad."

He huffs and walks back inside the pack house. I'm going to follow, but I can't help but linger for one more goodbye with Jasper.

Instead, Slate goes from speaking to Heath to approaching me. "Marigold, we need you back at Bracken Creek with us."

I blink at him. "What? Heath said I could stay."

Slate's expression softens. "Jasper brought up some good points. We need your knowledge of the Raven Pack to advise us. And it'll be easier for Jasper to contribute if he isn't panicked about your safety."

Are you kidding me? The prickle of tears burns as anger fuels them. I could go to Heath and protest, but I already know he will back up his Beta. I hold no ranking, so I have no grounds to argue against him.

Numb, I climb into the truck. Jasper slides into the seat beside me, and Slate steers us back onto the road.

"I'm sorry," Jasper says quietly.

All my anger overflows, and I'm not even quite sure what I'm so upset about. Flashes of Nyx calling Jasper demon spawn, Jasper going behind my back, the idea of those Raven Pack members trapped outside the pack house and left for dead, it all swirls in my mind.

"I can't believe you did that," I mutter, feeling hollow.

Jasper reaches for my hand, but I pull away. "I'd rather you're angry with me and safe, than putting yourself in harm's way."

"That's not your call to make," I blurt, my heart rate accelerating. "I never thought you would be that controlling."

Slate looks over his shoulder. "Marigold-"

"Shut up, Slate, you're in trouble too," I snap. Hazel pats his knee and stays quiet.

"I don't want to control you, I want you alive," Jasper says, his voice dropping to a dangerous growl.

"That's not your job. You're not my mate, not my boyfriend," I say, my vision blurring slightly. It feels like stabbing myself with a knife, saying those things to him, but I'm so angry and scared, I want him to hurt the way I am. Even if I'll hate myself for it later.

Jasper looks straight ahead, his jaw tight. "Last night, you wanted to commit to me because of how serious everything was. And now you're pushing me away for the same reason."

Snarling, I hit the back of my head against the headrest. "I'm not scared, I'm angry that you're trying to make decisions for me that aren't yours to make, and you're going behind my back to manipulate the situation. If that's how you operate, I clearly don't know you well at all."

His chest rises in shallow breaths, but he has no response. The entire car stays silent, seeped in heavy emotion, until we reach the parking lot.

Heath calls Jasper and Slate away for a meeting to discuss our new tech surveillance, and I throw my arms around Hazel and cry into her shoulder until I am gasping for air.

Hazel rubs my back and holds me steady.

When I finally get ahold of myself, she squeezes my hands and says, "Okay babe, what do you want to do about the situation?"

My eyes feel gritty and my throat is thick, my chest aches. But under it, I feel so disrespected. He didn't trust me to make my own decisions. Is that how every major conflict is going to go? Because that's a deal breaker for me.

"I'm not sure," I say, tucking my forehead against her shoulder. Her hands run up and down my back, soothing me.

"You have any and all options. I'll beat his ass for you. We can trash his cabin or key his car. Anything you want."

Through the ache, I can't help but smile. She's loyal to the end and I've neglected our friendship during this whirlwind with Jasper. When she was falling for Slate, she never pushed me aside.

My hands tighten around her in a hug. "Thank you."

Her nails run through my hair, brushing it off my cheek. "You deserve to be treated the best. If that's Jasper, great. But if he is being a dick to you, I don't care if he is my brother-in-law. I'll neuter him without a second thought."

Jasper

Trudging after Heath, my heart thumps in my throat. Marigold was far more devastated than I expected, and now I'm walking away from her.

"Give her a little time, man," Slate says. "Hazel will help."

Will she, though? I love my brother's mate, but she is emotional.

"I've never seen her that upset." I scrub my face with my hands.

"Neither have I." I flinch at his words.

"I should have found another way. Or stayed with her."

"You know that's not reasonable. What you did was fucked up, but I would have done the same thing." He shakes his head.

"No, you would have dragged your woman off like a caveman."

Slate shrugs, a small smile lifting his mouth. "Maybe."

In his office, Heath pulls up the security feeds. We sit and watch the records on fast forward, slowing the feed whenever a group of wolves runs by. It's our patrols.

"Let's set a second patrol along that northern border," Heath says.

Slate nods. "I'll arrange it. Any specifics you had in mind?"

"Run it twenty-four seven. And I think it's time to use those drones," he says, leaning back in his office chair.

"Agreed." Slate looks at me expectantly.

Two drones arrived yesterday. "It might take a while to get them set up, and then I'll need to train a few people on using them."

Heath nods. "Maybe Vale, Aven, or Onyx."

"Onyx would be great at it," Slate says.

"Alright, I'd better get started. Can you send Onyx my way? I'll let you know when we are up and running."

The drones are fairly easy to set up, and within an hour, Onyx and I are flying them across our compound, trying to get the hang of it. Visibility would be better if it wasn't so cloudy, but overall I'm impressed with the little machines.

However, the light is fading and while they have night vision capabilities, I can already tell it will be tricky to fly them after dark. We are not experienced enough yet.

Heath observes us. "Looks good. Go ahead and run one in along the borders around the Raven Pack tomorrow, and see if we can spot anything."

"Anything else tonight?" I ask.

Already striding away, Heath shakes his head. "Go get some rest. I have a feeling tomorrow is going to be rough."

We stow the drones away and leave the offices. Darkness has fallen. Onyx grips my arm and nods resolutely before we part ways.

For once, I'm glad my cabin is close to the training building and offices. My jog slows on the porch, and as I step in, I breathe in her scent. It's faded like she isn't here. Frowning, I push open the door to my room, empty. The door to her room, empty.

My stomach clenches as I realize the bag she brought her things in is now missing from its spot hanging on the footboard. Striding across the room, I pull open the closet and reveal empty hangers.

No.

She's taken her belongings and left. My chest feels like I've been struck. I stumble and slump onto her bed. Where would she go? Back to the Raven Pack? No, she has no way to get there unless she runs, and she wouldn't disobey Slate. She's got to be with her brothers or maybe Hazel.

My gut roils and my shifter instincts surge. But I can't have this discussion in wolf form. Gritting my teeth, I head toward Slate and Hazel's cabin, trying to contain my pace to a fast walk when all I want to do is sprint.

Warm light glows from the windows, diffused by linen curtains I helped hang. Hazel picked a dark green paint for the front door, with brass hardware. I have to pause a moment before knocking. It won't help to start this conversation angry.

My knuckles rap on the glossy wood and my sensitive hearing picks up hushed female voices. Finally the hinges rasp as Hazel cracks the door.

Her body fills the opening, blocking my entrance and my view into their living room. "Jasper," she says.

"Is she here?" My voice is harsher than I intend.

"She doesn't want to see you." Hazel tucks her hair behind her ears, the only tell that she feels guilty.

My hand grips the door frame. "We need to work through this."

Hazel's brown eyes meet mine and I see resolution in her unwavering gaze. I won't be getting past her. "She'll come talk to you when she's ready. Not before."

"I want her to come home," I plea.

Slate steps onto the porch behind me and rests his hand on my shoulder. "It's okay. She needs some space."

Her safe space should be with me. She needs to be home. In our home. My mouth opens and closes but I have no response.

"I'll talk to her," Slate offers. Hazel's eyes narrow at him, but he shrugs. "Go home. We'll see you tomorrow."

My throat is thick. Slate takes one last look at me and steps past his mate. I can hear Marigold murmur a greeting to him, and it's like knives cutting into me.

"Good night, Jasper," Hazel says softly, closing the door in my face.

I can't seem to move my legs. Each breath is jagged. My wolf surges forward, overtaking my human form. My ripped shirt falls to the ground and I scramble out of my sweats, not caring if Hazel or Slate sees the evidence of my shift.

The anxiety buzzing under my skin slowly fades away. In this form, worries are dull, but the grief of potential loss still chokes me. My four paws stumble and regain balance as I lope into the forest.

Every step further from Marigold feels like a mistake. My path curves, bringing me back toward my brother's cabin. Snarling, I pick up speed and run past.

Needing to feel anything else, I increase my speed until there's nothing but the ache in my lungs and the burn in my muscles. Our endurance is for moderately paced runs, not full out sprints. Soon, I am spent.

I intend to return to my own home, but I finally slow outside of that same damn cabin. It's silent now, with all the lights dark. Panting, I stand outside of the window of their second bedroom. It's an art studio with a day bed pushed against the far wall.

Exhaustion strips away the remaining fear, until only sadness lingers. I curl up, white tail over my nose.

Those few hours of sleep do nothing to refresh me. Sunrise curls through the forest. With a shake, I force myself to trot away from Marigold so I can shower and change before getting to work protecting my pack. I'll be back as soon as I can.

The morning is filled with video surveillance. Additional volunteers need to be trained in using the monitors while our Thetas and Zetas are all busy preparing for the fight we all hope is not coming.

I miss lunch, and perhaps some part of me hopes that Marigold will notice and bring me food. But she doesn't. Why would she?

"Are you ready to use those drones?" Heath asks.

I glance over my shoulder. The lines of his face seem deeper, as if he hasn't slept either. "Yes, Alpha."

"Take Onyx and get going."

We drive around to the highway north of the Raven Pack. The drone's range is only about twenty miles, so we pull onto the pack's access road to stretch our reach. Not deep into their territory, still in the border region where we don't risk offending them.

The drone whirs as it lifts off the ground. I study the screen and navigate it higher as Onyx settles back into his seat and closes the car door. "I'm sorry about the other night," Onyx says after a stretch of silent concentration.

Shrugging, I say, "It's okay, no big deal."

"You guys get in a fight?"

I grind my teeth, trying to not imagine how upset Marigold is right now, while I'm miles away working to keep her safe. "I'd rather not talk about it right now."

Onyx looks out the window, respecting my request. "Do you think we'll find anything? I can't imagine Ironcrest actually making a move."

"Oh, they will. I hope I'm wrong, but I don't think I am. My dad wouldn't hesitate to invade another pack, and Zephyr is a narcissist."

We pilot the drones along the border between the two packs, following the coordinates Heath and Slate maintain. Just empty trees. Sweeping back north, we see a lone scout, but it's not clear which pack he is from. It's impossible to tell if the apprehension I feel is from the scout, the overall situation, or my fight with Marigold. Onyx seems unconcerned, so we continue our sweep.

The sun dips lower, but we still have at least an hour of light. I want to pack it up and leave, but Onyx has taken over piloting and he squints at the screen. "What's that?"

His mouth turns downwards as he slows the drone. "Shit."

A dozen wolves weave through the trees, headed directly west. I fumble my phone and type out a warning to Heath and Slate.

Onyx hands me the control and I circle around, trying to stay far enough away that they don't notice the drone. But as I push further into Ironcrest territory, I see another group of a dozen wolves, and then a third.

"Shit!" I say louder. "If they're making their move, they'll follow up with drivers. We need to get out of here."

Onyx's eyes widen. He knows as well as I do that if Ironcrest is attacking and they catch us on this access road, we are dead. Pebbles crunch under our tires as he turns the truck and hits the gas.

It's not until we lurch back onto the highway that either of us breathes. His knuckles are white on the steering wheel as we build up speed. Mile markers zip past.

As we pass the turn-off for Ironcrest's compound, we see a line of silver and white SUVs. We are safe, but it's a punch to the gut to know Ironcrest is fully moving against the Raven Pack.

Despite my best efforts, our drone can't keep up and we lose the connection. It drops into the trees somewhere along Ironcrest's southern border. Hopefully I can retrieve it in a few days with its tracker, if it's still in one piece.

Throwing the controller down, I type out messages to Heath, detailing everything we were seeing and answering his rapid questions.

In record time, we pull into Bracken Creek's dirt lot.

Pack members jog in and out of our training building. Heath stands in the middle, giving out directions.

"What's the plan?" I ask.

"We're going up there. Gear up for a full assault."

Onyx follows me to the storage lockers, and we pull on chest rigs and grab handguns and wolfsbane bullets.

The guns are a relatively new addition to Bracken Creek's defenses. After Heath learned of the weapons Granite Ridge keeps on hand, he agreed to upgrade our options as well. The wolfsbane bullets will knock a shifter out for half a day or longer, and a second bullet can be fatal.

"Are you ready for this?" I ask Onyx.

He narrows his eyes. "Those motherfuckers shot me last year. I'm about to get my revenge." He tugs the neckline of his shirt down to reveal a scar high on his chest.

"Sorry about that," I mutter, tightening the straps of my harness.

Onyx shakes his head. "It wasn't you."

It's kind of him, considering I was on the wrong side of the conflict when he was shot.

"Fifteen minutes and we roll out!" Heath shouts.

CHAPTER FIFTEEN

BRAIDS & BATTLES

Marigold

Hazel drags her nails along my scalp, combing out my hair down my back as I lounge on her couch. "I'm sorry," she murmurs. Her empathy does little to soothe the tension in every cell of my body. This waiting game is torture with my heart is cut from my chest.

The door bangs open and Slate walks in. "Ladies, it's time to fight."

"They're moving?" Hazel yelps. "Already?"

"Yeah." His apologetic frown is a thin line.

Hazel stands, offering her hand to me. "Okay, let's do this."

I roll to my feet, adrenaline flooding my system. Panic over Jasper's safety nearly overwhelms me, and my regret over leaving him doubles.

"Sure I can't convince you to stay back?" Slate asks Hazel, closing the distance between them and pinching her chin with his hand. When she scrunches up her nose at him, he leans in and kisses her.

The rolling thunder clouds loom darker than this morning, the ominous gray promising mud and an early nightfall.

With shaking hands, I pull on shoes and grab the tight athletic jackets we wear during winter training.

"Ready?" Hazel asks, her eyes blazing.

We jog across the meadow and into the training building. The pack is buzzing around us, both those who are going and those staying to defend suiting up and grabbing weapons.

Slate tosses a chest rig to Hazel, and I tighten down the nylon straps to fit her snugly. She loads her gear before turning to help others.

"Marigold?" Jasper's voice resounds, and I whip around to see him standing among the trees, staring at me like I am his salvation. It takes all my willpower to keep my feet planted and not race to him. As he approaches, I bite the inside of my cheek.

"Don't worry, I'm not going to the Raven Pack. Your meddling has me stuck on defense," I growl.

"Thank you," he says, relief stark in every sound.

"I'm not yours to worry about," I reply, bristling.

Jasper reaches out and touches my hair, braided in one thick braid down my back. It slips through his hand like rope. "Please tie this up."

"What?"

His expression hardens, lines forming near his mouth. "Pin your braid up. So no one can grab you by your hair."

The fight leaves me. "Okay."

"Be safe. We can talk when this is over," he says, walking away before I can gather my thoughts.

"Marigold," a low voice says. I turn toward Hawthorne. "Ready?"

The small group of adults staying behind gather around him. We are all that's guarding the rest of the pack while our fighters are busy rescuing our reluctant allies.

With a sigh, I join the circle and duck my head while Linden reads out assignments.

We watch the warriors of the pack load into vehicles to leave. Hazel jogs toward me, holding a pair of wicked looking daggers. "Jasper wants you to have these," she says. "Don't argue. He has good taste in daggers and I want you to have all the protection possible." She forces them in my hands and turns away before I can thank her.

My heart is in my throat as Slate's truck peels out, throwing up pebbles under the tires. Jasper rides shotgun. Hazel is right behind them with Onyx beside her. I have to hope they keep each other safe.

Jasper

The car wobbles over the uneven road as we exit our territory and pull onto the highway. With a crack, the clouds let loose and rain splatters across the windshield.

"What's the strategy you guys finalized while I was handling the drones?" I ask Slate. They were still debating when I had left for surveillance.

His eyes flick between the road and the mirrors, his knuckles white. We're going as fast as we dare with a wet road. "Hazel wants to lead your squad into the building to clear a path for evacuations. Heath's team will take care of them once they're outside."

"Sounds good," I say, hands gripping the car door as we pick up speed.

"My team will be going after Ironcrest leadership, and Fisher will be looking for stragglers," he rattles off, his voice surprisingly steady.

"Who are you taking with you?" I ask. Slate's team will be at risk as they seek out the most dangerous of our enemies.

"Onyx, Cassia, and Fern." It's a good team. Cassia is a vicious fighter, and Fern can match her. They will cut through the Ironcrest wolves without hesitation. Onyx worries me, but after everything he went through last year, I'm not surprised he sought out such a placement.

My stomach tenses up in knots while Slate parks the truck along the side of the main road. It means a longer trip on our way out, but prevents the vehicles from being bottlenecked or trapped in the trees.

Hazel leaps from the truck ahead, her eyes blazing like a war goddess. Beside me, Slate adjusts his weapons post-driving, his eyes on his mate. I can't quite tell if the heat in his gaze is protectiveness or reverence.

Our teams take up positions. There are around two dozen of us. Against an estimated fifty Ironcrest fighters and up to seventy Granite Ridge members- we won't know until we see them.

Hazel leads our group of four straight toward the pack house. Lazuli creeps long silently, his dishwater blonde hair looking like ash in the dimming light. Clove takes up the rear. She's the oldest in our group, but as

Fisher's mate and the twin's mother, I don't question her capabilities.

Slate's squad stays close to us. Cassia and Fern stalk behind their leader while Onyx scans for danger at their back.

Through the trees, the last of the day's light illuminates chaos. The exterior doors stand wide open, the handles bent. Nearby windows are shattered, glass sparkling in the dirt. They've broken into the pack house. So much for Nyx's defensive plan.

Only a few Ironcrest Zetas stand guard, ready to assist their teammates as the Raven Pack wolves are pulled out of the building. Five younger men and women are led out. The frightened packmates cling together, Ironcrest warriors shoving them along.

A woman with dark hair stumbles and falls, landing on her hands and knees in the mud. Her captor yells, the words unintelligible in the havoc. She cringes as he pulls her upright by her arm, twisting it viciously. I see Hazel's hand go to her own arm. Cold fear settles in my gut.

Our team halts, allowing Slate's team to surge forward, guns drawn. Rapid shots announce our arrival, and the first of the Ironcrest wolves hit the dirt.

Heath's team bands around the Raven pack members, directing them toward the rendezvous location. Moving as one, Slate breaches the door and his team slips in. Hazel nods us forward and we follow the same path.

Inside the pack house, Ironcrest seems to be destroying as much property as possible while they take captives.

Shouts of enemies drown out my thoughts. Slate's team raises guns and opens fire. Shock paints every face. Ironcrest seems entirely unprepared for any sort of resistance.

Hazel motions us forward and draws her own weapon. Now it's our turn.

I level my gun at a large man running toward us and fire my first shot. His feet slip out from under him and he falls backwards. It's the first of many.

Slate's team disappears ahead of us, hunting for Zephyr. Hazel drives us forward, clearing a path through the central hallway while looking for Raven wolves.

Everything blurs. We clear the way and I make sure to stay at Hazel's shoulder, defending her back. The Ironcrest fighters are not armed like we are. Screams ring out down the hallways, and Ironcrest members shift into their four-legged bodies. Lazuli hands his two handguns over to Clove and shifts into his wolf form, leaping to meet the first enemy that sneaks past our gunfire.

My lungs ache and I drop at least a dozen bodies before we reach a larger communal space filled with frightened Raven pack members. The trail of bodies behind us makes my stomach sour, but they will recover in a few days. But this poison lingers so they'll be weak for months. We are crippling their pack in one night.

Hazel ushers the Raven wolves out, sending them down the hallway we arrived through, to where Heath works with Cedar, Vale, and Ewan to get them to safety.

Something heavy slams into me, sending me sprawling. Pain shoots up my hip and ribs. Clove leaps over me, swinging her fist toward a bulky Ironcrest man with black hair. Scrambling to get up, I draw my second gun, but I'm too slow. The man slashes at Clove and opens up a gash on her arm. She glares at the knife in his hand as he jerks backwards. Most shifters don't bother with blades when we have built-in claws and fangs, but I've always liked a good dagger.

Stepping past Clove, I aim and fire, watching his body collapse as the wolfsbane pollutes his veins. Clove snarls, gripping her forearms as blood streams between her fingers.

Hazel directs Clove toward Heath, and Lazuli goes with her, using his snapping jaws to attack any enemy we missed on the way in. As I step over the man who slashed Clove, I reach down and pluck the blade from his hand, tucking it into my tactical gear.

"Are you good?" Hazel yells, looking at me for a moment before she focuses back on our fight.

"Great," I shout. We move forward, seeking out victims and destroying their attackers as we go.

With a kick, Hazel snaps open a door to reveal a dozen Raven pack members surrounded by four Ironcrest wolves, two already shifted. Aiming, I drop the black wolf easily, but the gray wolf leaps at Hazel before I can react. Its jaws close around her arm, over her protective gear, as she's slammed to the ground.

A two-legged Ironcrest guard rushes me, yelling unimaginative profane threats as he collides into me. Pulling my third gun free, I shoot up into his gut. Wolfsbane splatters back at me, stinging the exposed skin on my hand.

Scrambling up, I witness Elm pulling the black wolf off of Hazel as she fires directly into its chest. The fourth Ironcrest man drags Elm back, hooking his arm around Elm's neck to choke him. Throwing myself forward, I twist as my shoulder hits the floor and fire directly into the enemy's back to avoid hitting Elm.

As his attacker falls sideways, Elm's knees hit the floor. We're all on the ground for a moment as the Raven wolves swarm around us, helping us up. Hazel directs the hostages toward Heath's team with hoarse instructions and hand movements.

Elm's eyes connect with mine. His expression is hard, but so is mine. A battle is no time for reconciliation, and frankly I don't care if he likes me or not. He's still pack, and I would defend him even if he wasn't the father of the woman I love.

The hallway quiets as we draw closer to the main gathering space. Elm leads the way and I cover Hazel's back. She stops suddenly as we enter the larger space.

Several enemies lay sprawled across the floor. Slate has Zephyr at gunpoint. Nyx sits primly with her hands zip-tied on a leather armchair, watching with a vicious curl of her lips.

Have we won?

There are still dozens of Ironcrest wolves unaccounted for, and when my thoughts are able to slow down long enough to process, I realize I have not seen a single Granite Ridge fighter.

Ice floods my chest, down my arms and swirling in my stomach. Granite Ridge is not here.

Hazel grabs my arm, frowning as she studies my face. "What's wrong?" I blink at her. "Jasper!" She gives me a shake.

"Granite Ridge," I manage to say, my voice breaking. "Not here."

Hazel's eyes go wide and she spins, striding toward Zephyr. Her hands draw her dagger from a back sheath - I recognize it as the one that I gave her. Despite Slate's shout, she storms up to the Alpha and shoves the blade against his throat.

"Where is Granite Ridge?" she snarls.

Zephyr looks away, his face a mimicry of boredom. The uneven flutter of his breathing and his blotchy face gives him away.

Hazel presses the blade into his skin with a snarl. Sneering, he finally answers her. "At home, I assume, since they couldn't be bothered to hold up their end of the deal."

Slate steps closer, demanding, "What deal?"

Zephyr stares defiantly into Slate's face. "They were going to split the Raven pack with us. They wanted the wolves. We were keeping most of the land."

"I need to get home," I say, almost doubling over as nausea rolls through me.

Slate's eyebrows shoot up, though his focus never wavers from his prisoner. Fluidly, Hazel withdraws, leaning close to her mate. "Granite Ridge may have used this as a distraction and decided to make a move on us."

"No," Slate says. "That's not.."

I don't want to hear his reasoning. There's nothing he could say that would stop me. It's everything I can do to keep my wolf from bursting through my skin as I sprint toward the exit.

As night air washes over me, I pull my gear over my head and toss it toward a wide-eyed Cedar. Clothes only half off, white fur bursts over my skin as my wolf instincts take over.

I barely register Hazel shouting to Heath as my powerful lupine form plunges forward, vaulting over bodies and foliage alike.

Racing downhill, I barely slow as I wade into the creek. It's not too deep here. Water slides across my back, but the chill is nothing compared to the fear slicing into me. My claws scrape on the rocks as I pull myself upward. I shake my fur instinctively, barely slowing as I cross the shallows and reach the shore. I'm back in our territory. Muscles coiling, I leap forward and up the slope.

It's miles back to our pack's commune and Hazel races behind me the entire distance. There's no time to thank her, but I'm fiercely grateful. When it comes down to it, she's my sister, more so than Ember ever was.

My ears strain to hear any hint of noise from our home, though there is still at least a mile to go. Wolves can run fast and far, but as a shifter, I am even faster. Pushing myself all-out, the distance goes by in a blur.

Adrenaline spikes as the scent of smoke reaches me. Past the outlying cabins, orange and gold light glows from the inner circle of buildings. Keeping out of sight, I stalk in a wide circle, creeping closer.

Flames lick around the diner, melting the linoleum and pulling the roof down over the ashes. Crickett will be devastated. I hope she is far from the fire with her two daughters. Hawthorne was tasked with protecting our home. If Granite Ridge has attacked, where is he?

Hazel creeps up beside me, a low whine echoing the feelings of shock and grief flooding our pack bond. Anger, too. So close to her, I can sense her emotions stronger than the others, but if I focus, I can feel a sense of grim resolution from others nearby. Aside from general proximity, it tells me nothing of their location, only that they aren't in too much pain.

The two of us circle around toward the south, past the burning building. Through the smoke, we watch unfamiliar wolves move in groups between buildings. The activity seems to center around our training building. I'm not surprised they've chosen it for their headquarters.

A dozen Granite Ridge pack members on two legs march in and out of the steel structure, removing some of our supplies and distributing our remaining weapons. My hackles rise.

Lined up along the edge of the picnic tables lay several bodies. None of them look familiar, and more than one has a crossbow bolt sticking up from their chests. I hope they are all enemies and none of our own packmates. There's no sign of Hawthorne, Marigold, Linden, or any others that stayed behind.

We move further south, trying to pick up any trail. With the shouts of our enemy and the crackle of flames, it's overwhelming. Smoke blots out my sense of smell. But Marigold is here somewhere. I have to find her.

Marigold

Smoke blocks the moonlight and panic rises up, choking me. My students huddle in Cobalt's room - the one with the window facing the forest. As far away from the front door as possible without risking being trapped if the building gets torched.

I pace the living room, all the lights off, waiting to be found. Sending these children into the forest with enemy wolves circling would be a death sentence, but it's only a matter of time until we are discovered. Thank the goddess my family's cabin is one of the further buildings from the center clearing.

The sound of soft crying drifts down the hall. Peeking in, I see Briar holding Willow as she softly cries. Elwood is curled against her arm, with Cobalt beside him, doing his best to look brave. A fierce pride rears up. "It's going to be fine. Alpha Heath will be back for us any minute," I murmur.

I have to believe it. Heath will come charging back, leading all of our packmates in a rescue mission. Surely, Jasper is safe and sound.

My knuckles are white around two daggers. My gun is empty, drained during the first wave of Granite Ridge wolves. Hawthorne threw himself in their path so I could lead the children to safety. I have to hope Crickett and his daughters are still safe in their home's basement. Even worse, I have no idea where my brother Indigo is. He was with Linden when they attacked, and the older wolf would have gotten him to safety if possible. All I can do is trust and focus on the children in my care.

Taking a steadying breath, I pace back toward the door, around the sofa. The shouts of our enemies grow louder.

Blood rushing in my ears, I crouch and shuffle toward the front window. Dark figures block the moonlight momentarily, causing my heart to leap into my throat.

The door blows in with a bang. My teeth clench. I will not scream.

Three Granite Ridge wolves dart in, two humans and one shifted. No time to hesitate. Without waiting for them to spot me, I strike from my position beside the door. My dagger slices into the upper back of the taller man with all of my strength behind it. He drops with the blade embedded into his back, blood gushing in a way I've never seen before. His scream turns to a gurgle.

The second man grabs my arm, squeezing until I drop the second knife meant for him. My cry of pain is drowned out by his angry shout. His grip never lets up as he shoves me backwards and onto the sofa.

He looms over me. My nails dig into my palms, my panic bleeding into my muscles and weakening me. I will not give away the children's location - although the wolf will discover them in seconds anyway. With any luck, they'll be out the window already.

"What a pretty little thing," the man says, one hand grasping the back of the sofa beside my head while his grip moves from my wrist to my hair. With an ugly smile, he twists a chunk around his hand. I want to gag.

Gritting my teeth, I kick up, striking him between the legs. He grunts and doubles over, his breath on my face. The hold he has on my hair drags me sideways and tears spring into my eyes at the pain.

Wolf jaws close over his arm, causing him to drop his hold on my hair. A white wolf drags him backwards and to the ground. Shocked, I push myself up and scramble over the back of the sofa to gain some distance.

Another wolf snarls and stalks closer to me while the man across the sofa screams. Spit drips from his bared teeth.

Weapon. I need a weapon.

There's nothing. I'll have to shift. My hands grapple with the tactical gear. I have to get it off or I'll be tangled up.

The dark wolf growls, its hackles rising, making it look huge. Another step, and my vision narrows as my heart races so fast my chest aches. My hand slips on the buckle, fear numbing my fingers.

The wolf lowers, its haunches bunching, preparing to leap. This time I can't help the shriek that tears from my mouth.

With a dull thud, one of my daggers embeds into the wolf's ribcage, throwing him back against the wall. The body slides down to the wood floor, leaving a slick of blood on the old wallpaper.

"Don't fucking touch my mate," a voice growls. Slowly, I tear my eyes off the dying wolf and turn toward the gravelly voice.

Jasper stands on the other side of the sofa, naked with blood smeared across his mouth.

CHAPTER SIXTEEN

STRATEGIES & SCHEMES

Marigold

Cashel meets us at the edge of his territory. His mouth is a grim line, but he doesn't hesitate to help us.

"I'm sorry to be coming to you like this," Hazel says, head high despite the child in her arms and the exhaustion weighing her down. "Until we can regather our forces to take back our home, we don't have many other choices."

"We have the resources and the space. Isn't this what allies are for?" Cashel reaches out to grip her

shoulders. "They will regret every second they dared to spend in your territory."

Jasper's hand tightens over mine. Under his sweats and t-shirt, bruises cover his hip and ribs, causing him to limp. He's wiped his face the best he can, but blood spots his clothes and hair - and mine too.

The Valley Pack opens up a handful of cabins for us while their team puts together a second dinner that we share in a large meeting space. Like the Raven Pack, they have one central pack house, but with more individual cabins surrounding it.

Jasper eats with one hand, his other hand gripping my thigh possessively. Hazel eats across from us until our team from the Raven Pack returns. As the door opens to reveal more of our packmates, she launches herself across the room into Slate's arms with a cry.

Heath limps in, his arm over Cedar's shoulders. Fisher follows, his mouth a grim line.

They should be returning home victorious, but Granite Ridge swept that out from under us.

Jasper leans over and kisses my cheek before rising to follow Heath, Slate, and Hazel. Suddenly alone, I curl my arms around my knees.

A shadow blocks out the overhead light for a moment before my father sits beside me.

"You're okay!" I squeak, squeezing my arms around his shoulders. Tears prick in my eyes for the millionth time in the last few hours. "What happened up there?"

The gray streaks glint in his reddish hair as he shakes his head. "They surrounded the pack buildings and Nyx was so sure that all the security doors would hold. But in less than an hour, they broke windows and simply unlocked the doors from the inside."

"They weren't reinforced?"

"Most of them were."

"How could she be this stupid?"

Sighing, my dad picks up his bowl. "She's stayed so far away from everyone else, I don't think she had any idea what they were capable of. Maybe she believed they would never actually attack." He takes a bite of his dinner and I make no attempt to fill the gap in our conversation.

"How'd it go back home? I didn't get much information," he finally says. The tremor in his voice tells me how deeply he feels this, even if his words are casual.

Rubbing my hands over my face, I slowly exhale. "Within minutes of everyone's departure, Granite Ridge arrived. They were everywhere. I gathered the kids I was watching into your cabin. So it's a bit damaged, I'm sorry."

He cocks his head. "What do you mean a bit damaged?"

"I may have stabbed someone in the living room." His mouth twitches, prompting a grin to spread across my own face. "Three guys came in, so I stabbed one, and then Jasper took the other two out."

"Jasper," he says, more contemplative than questioning. "I saw him in Raven. He went back?"

Swallowing, I nod. "He's the reason most of us made it out. He realized Granite Ridge wasn't with Ironcrest in the attack and guessed what they were doing. He reached me just in time, and Hazel rescued a few others."

"Who was left behind?" His voice drops.

"I don't know for sure. I think Hazel was trying to account for everyone. They captured Hawthorne, and a few others. Crickett and the two girls are locked away, I think. Not sure who is with them. But they won't last long down there."

"We will get them back," he growls. I nod. "I'm so glad you're safe."

My head rests on his shoulder. "You too, Dad."

Jasper

"This is my fault. They wouldn't have come after us otherwise," I say, hanging my head.

Hazel's eyes blaze. "Absolutely not. If anything, it was revenge for what I did."

A low chuckle emits from Heath's reclined form. Marigold's grandmother Sable has cut away the pants below his knee and is wiping down the gash across his shin. "Unfortunately, this grudge extends far past your recent offenses."

"Worth burning buildings?" Hazel asks, her mouth downturned.

Heath nods. "As a child, Sienna thought she deserved to be the Alpha someday, but she was rejected over and over. She's wanted revenge since before you were born."

"The Granite Ridge Pack has always been in conflict with us, although it used to be friendlier. More rivals than enemies. But when Sienna went to Ferris, it got worse. And it's been twenty years of that festering."

Too many eyes watch me. Gritting my teeth, I slowly nod. "She's always been unpredictable and vengeful. I'm not sure why I ever thought this day wasn't coming. But you're right, when it comes down to it, I don't think this has to do with me or Hazel. It's always been her obsession."

"You more than most know what she's capable of," Sable says without looking at Hazel. Slate responds with a growl. It's a testament to Heath's poor condition that he does nothing to curb Slate.

"So what happened after we left?" I ask.

"We shot Zephyr to take him out for the day, and left him tied up in Nyx's care. A group of Ironcrest wolves retreated, but Nyx has plenty of prisoners to deal with. We got your call right around the time we were finishing off the stragglers that didn't retreat when they had the chance," Slate says, anger curling around every sound.

"Well, we were able to pull most of the pack out. From what I can gather, most of our elders are still there, along with Hawthorne's entire family, and Starling is with her grandmother. The rest of the kids aside from those three are all here safe."

"Glad to hear it," Heath says.

"My biggest concern is Hawthorne. And we don't know about Linden either, but we know for sure that Hawthorne took the brunt of their attack."

The room is solemn. Heath grips his chair arms with white knuckles, and it's impossible to tell if it's over his Gamma or the pain of the wound Sable is treating.

"So what are we going to do?" Slate asks.

"Get our home back," Hazel answers viciously, reaching over and threading her fingers through his. My lungs tighten. I don't want to be here in a meeting, I want to be with Marigold. But this is for her.

"Jasper, what do you think they'll do now? How will they fortify their position?" Fisher asks.

My teeth roll over my bottom lip as I try to force my thoughts in order. "They'll centralize. Hostages, leadership, resources, everything."

"What about defenses?" Heath wonders.

"Maybe cameras, but I think it's too early for them to have hacked into any of our tech so they're probably relying on patrols. And they like bigger patrol groups, so it's easier to hear them coming."

"We need a way to get inside and get our people out before it turns into an all-out fight and they can be used against us," Hazel says.

"Focusing our assault on wherever the hostages are held," Fisher begins. Slate holds up a hand, silencing him.

"The easiest way would be through the front door." Slate's voice drops, the determination bright in his mossy eyes. Something about his tone pushes away my conflicted thoughts. He's right.

And with that, we begin to brainstorm a plan to reclaim our home.

The cabin given to us is a two bedroom. Slate and Hazel take the other bedroom. When I stumble into the building after my brother and his mate, I find Marigold in the bathroom. She stands before the sink and scrubs her hands.

Closing the door behind me, I approach her cautiously. Her eyes are red but dry as if she's run out of tears.

"I have blood on me," she whispers. I see droplets drying to brown across her shirt and joggers. The skin on her hands is raw as she continues to scrub. I remember the enemy with my dagger sticking out of his back. It's the first time she had to kill someone.

"Hey, it's okay," I say. Leaning past her to the shower, I crank the handle over to red. "Nothing a hot shower can't fix."

Sniffling, she nods and allows me to pull her shirt over her head. "Thank you," she says. Her hands go to the hem of my shirt, and she gently peels it off me. My hands go to her waist, pulling her closer.

"You were amazing today," I praise her, "You saved them." It's true. Her students would likely be dead now without her bravery and quick thinking.

Her hands skim up my chest and stop at my neck as her thumbs stroke along my jaw.

"You took down two guys," she murmurs. "You threw that dagger right into that wolf before he could hurt me."

"I would do it again in a heartbeat to protect you."

Her alluring lips don't answer, instead, she presses a kiss to my mouth. There's more discussion to be had, but I won't rush her.

Hooking my thumbs into her waistband, I ease her pants down and then turn her toward the shower. Her grip on me tightens, pulling me with her. "You want company?" I ask, smiling wryly. She answers by tugging my hand under the water spray. "Anything for you."

Shedding my pants, I step into the tub and allow the shower spray to coat me. The tempered glass door slides closed with a dull thud. Water streaks down her stomach as she faces the stream and allows it to strike her face and front. My fingers work through her hair, untangling the remnants of her braid and massaging her scalp.

Finding some soap, I run my palms down her arms and then across her chest. She melts into me. The last of the soap rinses away and I'm drawing leisurely circles across the skin on her ribs.

"See? All better." I murmur into her neck. At the sound of my voice, she twists in my arms and resumes kissing me, this time fiercer and wilder. Her nails prick the skin on my back as she pulls me flush against her. Water drips from her closed eyelashes, hiding any tears she might shed.

She nips along my jaw, eliciting a shudder and causing my hands to clench in her hair. "Take me to bed." Blinking at me, she amends, "I need you to hold me and know we're okay."

"Alright, Sunshine."

We borrow towels and wrap ourselves up before creeping across the hall to our designated bedroom. Leaving her hair damp, she climbs under the blankets completely bare. Her wide blue-green eyes watch me, wide and vulnerable.

"So are we okay?" I ask cautiously, crawling across the bedspread toward her. Her tongue swipes her bottom lip and I'm tempted to forgo my questions so I can kiss her senseless. But we need to discuss us. I'm not going back into battle without knowing she's mine.

"Yes, I think so," she says.

Drawn to her warmth, I hover over her and nuzzle against her neck. She arches and presents her throat to me. I can't help the groan that rumbles from my chest. The wolf part of me loves when she's submissive.

"I'm sorry for going behind your back. I couldn't stand the thought of you being directly in the path of our enemies," I say before licking the skin in the hollow under her throat. She rewards me with a soft sigh.

"I should have talked with you first. I should have listened to you," she says, her hands sliding over my shoulders and pulling me down.

Breathing in her scent, I gather my courage. "So about what I said in your family's cabin?"

Her breathing halts and her eyes trail over my face while she gathers her thoughts.

"I'm sorry, you don't need to say anything." I murmur, "I just wanted you to know I'm ready to commit, whenever you are. And it's okay if you need time. Months or even years. I'm not going anywhere," I trail off.

"I want to," Marigold says. "There's no point in denying what we are." Her hand skims down my side. "This is forever."

Her words blaze across my skin, leaving a trail of heat and need. She wants me in that all-consuming and permanent way. The need to possess and mark surges in my chest.

"You are my mate." Her lips form the words that I'm desperate to hear. Everything I've wanted. My vision blurs for a moment and I have to suck in air to steady myself.

Marigold

Jasper's eyes glow so brightly, I suspect they'll leave spots on my retina. His aqua eyes are incredible at all times, but when he's angry or aroused, they're spellbinding.

"Little mate, I want to make you mine," he says, that velvety voice deep and raw. My stomach swoops.

"Good. Make me yours." I nip his bottom lip, smiling back at him as his eyes widen. His surprised expression melts away to the cocky smirk I love so much.

He exhales, eyes narrowing. His lips skim over my skin again. "I want to claim you so badly. Are you ready for that?"

"Yes, mark me," I urge boldly.

His growl rolls into a groan. "I don't want to rush this because we're in this situation with tomorrow being dangerous."

"I don't care the situation, I want you," I argue, suddenly impatient.

"Are you sure?" he asks.

"Yes, please, baby," I beg, knowing how much he loves it. To emphasize my point, I hook my legs around his.

"I love you," he says, kissing me before I can answer. When he breaks away, I echo him. Reaching up, I thread my fingers through his damp hair.

His eyes are so dark, the aqua is a glowing rim. Hesitating, he bites that full bottom lip. "This might be uncomfortable for you."

"Worth it," I say, trying to reassure him even though I'm quite sure it'll be worse if we don't, considering the throbbing between my legs has me on the verge of humping him.

Keeping his gaze locked on mine, he slides his hand between us, teasing across my entrance and dipping one finger inside of me. My eyes flutter closed at his touch. Grazing upwards, he circles my clit, and my back arches against my will.

My nails dig into his side. "Jasper," I whimper. When I open my eyes, his focus is still on my face. "Next time I come, I want it to be on your cock."

He stiffens, the muscles along his back tensing under my hands. "You're making it hard to stay calm and be gentle," he says, his voice hoarse.

The joke is so easy, I can't resist. "Yeah, I make it real hard," I say with a grin. Snorting, his forehead falls to my chest.

"I can take it. I'm not made of glass."

"No, you're much more precious," he says, pressing a soft kiss to my sternum.

I'm out of patience. My heels dig into his ass as I whisper in his ear, "Then you better fuck me or I'm going to burst into flames."

His smile is wicked and my blood sings at the glint in his eyes. "If that's what my mate wants." Carefully, he lines himself up and nudges my entrance.

As he pushes in, my eyes squeeze shut. The stretch is blissful despite the discomfort, but as he reaches a certain spot, moderate pain jolts me. Gasping, I cling to him.

"Breathe, Sunshine," his soft voice commands. "Breathe." I obey. After a couple of breaths, my muscles relax.

"Doing okay?" he asks.

"Fucking fantastic," I reply, my words choppy.

He brushes his lips across mine and then begins to move.

"Oh," I blurt. "Oh!"

A growl rumbles from his chest. "You feel incredible."

I could say the same, but words won't form in my brain. Instead, I reach one arm above me and push against the headboard to hold my body steady.

"I love you," I murmur, saying it over again.

His smile is genuine. "I love you too." He slows and I let out a low whine in protest. "Patience," he whispers. Sliding a hand under my knee, he adjusts our angle. A little gasp escapes my mouth as he rolls his hips, the angle deeper.

My core clenches around him as I twist under him, trying desperately not to scream. But the feeling of his slow movements inside of me while I shatter is overpowering. He bends over me, stifling my cry with his mouth and tongue.

My pleasure comes in waves, flooding every cell in my body as he begins to move again. These aren't the smooth thrusts we started with, they're urgent. He drives into me and then he's slowing and pushing in harder. I watch his look of concentration as his composure splinters.

His breath is hot on my neck, and my instincts vibrate with the desire to bite and be bitten. He licks down my neck to the juncture of my shoulder. I want to beg, but I stay silent, knowing the instinct must be riding him hard as well. Sharp teeth press against my skin and I can't breathe. The cut into my skin is exquisite.

He moves back, his mouth slightly open and my blood on his lips. I push up, reaching for him, and he tips his head to offer himself to me. Reverently, I kiss and then bite into the muscle.

The tang of his blood barely registers as a swell of emotion washes over me. Warm affection, passion, the desire to protect, admiration. Everything he's feeling echoes in me, and for a moment I can't distinguish my emotions from his.

The bond between us settles and I return to myself. He is like a glowing presence and I suspect I will be able to sense when he walks into a room without needing sight nor scent.

"That's kind of a lot," I murmur. Jasper's answer is pressing his lips to mine, traces of our blood mixing as he presses me back down into the pillow.

The stroke of his tongue is now paired with a wave of his enjoyment alongside my own. I know he feels the same.

Finally he breaks away. "You've ruined me," he rasps.

"Good thing we can do that whenever we like," I purr into his ear. His answering growl makes my toes curl, as he withdraws and reaches for one of our discarded towels.

A blush heats my cheeks as he cleans me up. And somehow that leads to him touching me again until I'm whimpering his name into the pillow.

CHAPTER SEVENTEEN

HOSTAGES & HEISTS

Jasper

"Good morning, Sunshine," I say, loving how her weight feels against me. Her head lays across my chest, an arm and leg thrown across me.

With a deep breath, she rolls off of me and rubs her eyes. "Where?" she starts to say before going quiet. I grip her waist and pull her against me, pressing a kiss to her temple. For a moment she stares at the ceiling.

"I think this is the happiest and saddest I've ever been at the same time," she says.

"What do you mean?" I ask carefully.

Marigold sighs and turns her face toward me. She tips her chin up to kiss me briefly before answering. "I've lost my home but I found my mate." She draws out the last word, testing it out with a tentative smile. It wavers, like she's unsure if it's okay to be happy when our friends and family are preparing to do battle.

"Tonight, after we've reclaimed our territory, you can just be happy," I murmur.

"Supremely happy." Her palm skims my chest, her lips touching my skin. She works her way down to the ring of pink scars from last night. A permanent marker of our commitment.

"Mate," I say, "As much as I would like to repeat last night right now, we have a lot of preparations to complete today. Are you feeling good?" Reaching up, I run my thumb over the matching circle of tiny pale scars that mark her as mine. Her happiness buzzes between us.

She nods. "Let's do it," I smirk and she rolls her eyes at me. "You know what I mean."

We dress in borrowed clothing. Coming out of our bedroom, we see Hazel and Slate eating granola bars and fruit in the kitchen. Marigold pads toward them without any hesitation. A flush creeps up my neck as I follow her.

"So what's the plan?" Marigold asks.

"We'll have a debrief on everyone's roles, and then it's time to kick some ass," Hazel says. Her eyes flick up to me for a moment.

"It's a good plan," I say, feeling uneasy with Hazel's full attention on me. Her eyes narrow. She doesn't like how much risk Slate and I are taking on ourselves.

"Alright, let's go," Slate says, pushing off from the counter. Marigold turns to follow him.

Glancing back at Hazel, I pause. One eyebrow is raised. Silently, she raises one hand to her own claim mark where it peeks out from her loose shirt. Unconsciously, I mirror her, adjusting the neckline of my shirt to make sure my mark is covered. The instant she sees my motion, her eyes widen.

Giving a slight shake of my head, I silently beg her to stay quiet. It's Marigold's news to share when she is ready, and this morning isn't exactly ideal timing for a celebration. Hazel's nod is subtle, and I let out my breath.

"Are you guys coming?" Marigold says, holding the front door open for us.

"Yeah, sorry," Hazel says, sliding past me and jogging to the door. I follow with deliberate steps, letting my mind turn over the details of our strategy as we walk to the debrief.

The sun has begun to dip below the tree line by the time Slate and I are trudging across Bracken Creek territory. Slate walks stiffly, his nerves showing in the clench of his jaw.

"How's Hazel feeling?" I ask.

He jerks as I shake him from his thoughts. "She's okay. Physically fine. Eager to take on Granite Ridge."

"Good."

"So," he says, hesitating, "you and Marigold?"

Pine needles crunch under my feet. "Fine."

"Sounded like you guys made up," he says lightly.

"We are not having this discussion," I reply with a dry laugh.

"Did you ask her to be your mate officially?" he asks.

There's no way I can lie to him. He would see through it instantly.

"You did, didn't you," he says, a wide smile spreading across his face. He chuckles, running his fingers through his dark hair to sweep it away from his forehead.

"I don't think she's ready to tell anyone," I say softly.

"So how'd you ask?

Shrugging, I rub at my arm. "Well, it wasn't so much asking, as it was calling her my mate as I killed a wolf who was about to attack her."

"Ah." Slate nods, as if this makes perfect sense.

"Last night she said she's all in," I finish my story.

After a few more steps, Slate asks, "Did you claim each other?"

My guilty smile is answer enough. Slate turns, his hand gripping my shoulder. "I'm really happy for you guys."

Coming from my older brother, it means a lot, and the emotion rising in my chest surprises me.

"Wolves ahead," I warn, tracking them by sound. Slate sighs. I know he'll hate this part. But it's necessary, and it was his idea. Even Hazel agrees that it's our best shot.

We continue to walk forward, unbothered as Granite Ridge wolves surround us. Snarls and barks echo through the trees.

"We're here to negotiate," Slate says, raising his hands in surrender. Our captors drive us forward, though Slate refuses to increase his speed despite the jaws snapping at our legs.

The circle of buildings surrounding the meadow looks mostly untouched, with the exception of the blackened diner. A few structural beams stand leaning against one another in the rubble. But at least it's the only destroyed building. I try to ignore the bodies, still uncovered a day later.

Sienna and Ferris have set up court in the training building. It's the largest space in our community and it's full of weapons. Two-legged guards take us from the patrol. Rough hands grip my biceps and tighten zip-ties around my wrists. I don't recognize many of them, and the ones that are familiar keep their eyes on the ground. Slate lets out a low growl as he's restrained and we are led forcibly toward the enemy's command center.

Inside is surprisingly quiet. Chairs have been brought in for the Alphas and benches dragged forward into a loose circle for subordinates to sit at during meetings.

"Isn't this a nice family reunion?" Sienna says, rising from her seat. She's in head-to-toe scarlet, standing out from the grays and blues around her. Her waist-length dark hair falls in dramatic waves and her eyeliner is sharp as a dagger.

"Hello, Mother," I say, the words painful as I force myself to meet her gaze.

She strokes my face. "It's so good to see you again. And both of you together! I never imagined this day would come."

Slate leans away from her touch when she tries the same motion with him. Clicking her tongue, she turns back toward Ferris.

"So what brings you back to me?" Her mate stands, resting a hand on her shoulder. Her lip curls at the contact but she covers it with a sly smile.

Clearing his throat, Slate says, "We are here to negotiate a surrender under terms that protect the lives of our packmates."

Ferris's cold eyes narrow as he stalks toward us. "I have everything I want, and we will get your wolves eventually. Why should I make any concessions?"

"When you negotiate with us, you'll find out," I say, meeting his stare boldly. I'm baiting him. He will make mistakes if he's angry. Maybe.

"Where are our wolves that you are holding hostage? I'd like to verify their safety," Slate demands.

"Don't worry, they're all settled in some cabin," Sienna says with a dismissive wave, her irritation sharpening her words.

My eyes flicker to the doorway, tracking the fading light. It's our only signal for when our teammates will move.

The red-headed wolf called Hawk stands at the doorway, gripping the frame as if he doesn't want to be forced any closer. His eyebrows arch at the sight of us with our hands shackled behind us. "Alphas, the Zetas have been unable to break into the supply shed. What would you like us to do?"

Behind Hawk, a slim girl with dark eyes and shoulder-length navy hair stalks forward. My sister. Unlike her Intended, she shows nothing but delight at my vulnerable position.

"Burn it," Ferris says without hesitation. Ember's mouth curves into a smile.

Sienna whirls, glaring at him. "Absolutely not. Use the captives. Surely one of them knows how to unlock it." She turns toward Hawk. "Use whatever force is necessary to persuade them."

Hawk looks between them, lines creasing his forehead.

"It's fine," Ferris says, dismissing him by turning his back.

Ember scoffs, crossing her arms petulantly. Still scowling, she moves away from her future mate to stand behind her mother. Those glittering dark eyes regard us as something vile yet interesting, like exotic roadkill.

With a smile that shows fangs, Sienna advances on us. "So what are you able to offer us?"

I raise my chin. "We need some assurances first. Like where is Hawthorne?"

"Oh the Gamma?" Sienna asks. "Somewhere around here." I wish I could read the thoughts behind her cold eyes, but she's as veiled as ever.

"Is he alive?" Slate asks.

"For now," Ferris growls.

Sienna sighs as if this is all tedious. I adjust my stance, trying to take the pressure off my injuries. Her eyes snap to the movement.

"What is this?" Her voice finally sounds surprised. She tugs my shirt aside, revealing the claim mark Marigold left last night. Even with two decades of experience dealing with her, I'm unable to read the expressions crossing her face.

"Well?" she demands.

"I guess that information can be a part of our bargain," Slate says. My hands clench into fists at the idea, but I trust him.

"Fine," Sienna huffs, turning back toward Ferris. "Why don't we sit down and have a talk."

Without looking at her, Ferris sinks back into his seat. "Whatever my mate desires." Sarcasm stretches his words. My mother does not appreciate being patronized. Her shoulders tighten as she sits delicately beside him.

Awkwardly, we perch on benches a few feet away from our mother, further from Ferris. Ember stands behind her father, her stance deceivingly relaxed. It's impossible to miss her hand drifting to the blade she wears concealed at her hip. If Ferris was to say the word, she would likely murder Slate without a second thought, and perhaps me as well.

"Now, tell us what you had in mind," Sienna says.

Marigold

"They're in the training building like we expected," Onyx says, studying the battered drone controller in his hands. Muscles tense, he stands like a soldier and not the irreverent friend I grew up with.

"Can you see how many wolves are surrounding them?" Hazel asks in clipped tones, her eyes peering through the trees although we are too far to see our targets.

He shakes his head, his dirty blonde hair falling over his forehead. "No, I can't get any closer without tipping them off. Sorry."

"Thank you for being cautious," I say. Worry knots my gut. My mate is in the enemy's hands, and I have to trust they won't hurt him before we can free them.

"Let's go," Hazel commands. Down the line, our teammates shift into their wolf forms. Shucking off my shirt, I allow my light reddish-gold coat to ripple down my arms. The cloud of anxiety lifts as my instincts surge forward, loosening my chest so I can breathe.

The scent of damp wood, rotting pine needles, and lingering smoke envelops me. With a shake, my ruff shivers down my back, softening some of my excess energy.

Cassia brushes up against me, Fern beyond her. The pack bond is a light burning in my chest. I draw strength from the hopeful determination and the protectiveness that drives us forward.

No matter what, we will be successful and do whatever it takes to get my mate and our pack back safely. There is no alternative.

The group is quiet while a select few, including Vale and Ewan, move northwards. Hazel slinks forward, stepping carefully to stay silent. We follow.

Onyx stays back with Heath, eyes on the training facility as he flies the drone in cautious circles. I don't glance back at them, but their low voices are comforting.

A howl cuts through the twilight. A second voice lifts to join it. Low barks and shouts from our enemies respond, and within minutes, the Granite Ridge patrol turns north. They are noisy and it's easy to track their progress. With any luck, they'll be chasing our fastest runners far from the community, buying us precious minutes.

Hazel breaks into a run and I fall into step at her flank without thought. Our packmates follow, racing in groups of threes and fours. We weave through the trees as the sunset turns the pale green boughs into gold. This land is familiar. I could navigate with my eyes closed this close to the center of our territory.

The scent of the destroyed diner clouds my senses, the acrid melted plastic and charred metal burning my nose. The offensive smell of a rival pack thickens as we approach the largest cabins we believe hold hostages. Underneath, fresher scents of our family members and friends confirm our guess.

Swift and silent, we surround the first cabin. The moment the door opens with a creak, Fern leaps. Her paws hit a guard and throw him onto his back with a jarring thud. His hands flail, but he's unable to reach a weapon before Fern's teeth close over his neck. She dispatches him with little concern if he can recover or not. I can't fault her, not when her daughter and mother are held captive inside and this man would kill her given the chance.

Her black wolf disappears inside. I follow, pausing to grab the ankle of the downed guard and tug him away, shoulders heaving. We need a clear exit. Disgusted, I drop his limb and cross the porch to push through the ajar door.

The snarls of approaching enemies pull Hazel away, and most of our team follows her lead. They will face the larger threat while we retrieve our packmates.

Fern stands over another Granite Ridge guard, leaving a third one for me. The anger of the last day narrows my focus until I am a missile of fangs and fur. He attempts to draw a weapon, but my teeth sink into his arm before he can get his hand around the gun tucked into his belt. Claw, rip, tear. Blood pools across my tongue and I open my mouth to let it drip onto the floor.

Stepping off my victim, I look up as slim arms fling themselves around me. Fern stands in human form, supporting one of our elderly packmates while her daughter, Starling, squeezes my neck as her tears soak into my ruff.

"Well done, my dears," Starling's grandmother says.

"We're not close to done yet. Cedar and Clove have a rescue team ready to evacuate you. Let's go," Fern orders, her last words turning to a bark. She plants a kiss on her daughter's forehead and pushes her toward her grandmother before she shifts back.

Ears scanning for our enemies, I trail the rescued hostages until Cedar takes my place. He bumps my shoulder, a silent encouragement, while Clove takes Starling's hand.

The sounds of a battle filter through the trees. Fern and I break into a sprint toward the clearing. We race to reach our teammates as they leap toward the Granite Ridge wolves surrounding the training building.

Fisher wrestles with a brute of a wolf outside of the training building. As the larger black wolf pushes our trainer down, my father joins the fight, ripping it away.

Working in tandem, they take down the wolf and move onto the next one together.

The training building's door is still shut, causing my heart rate to spike. Jasper and Slate are still in there with Sienna, Ferris, and an unknown number of cronies.

Before I can reach them, the Granite Ridge patrol pours into the clearing. A dozen more wolves throw themselves at us, jaws snapping.

With a vicious snarl, Hazel leaps at the wiry dark gray wolf leading the charge, knocking him into the dirt. As another silvery wolf rushes to his defense, my paws dig into the earth to launch myself forward.

The idea of someone hurting my loved ones turns my vision to a haze. My paws meet his unprotected ribs as I knock him to the ground beside the first. Hazel's jaws close over his neck, eliciting a whimper.

Jasper

Sienna's eyes go wide as howls filter through the metal roof.

"That's your pack here to surrender?" Ferris asks caustically, already pulling a knife from his belt. At his hand motions, the guards file to the door with guns raised. The first two open the door and step out.

Slate catches my gaze. I tip my chin down in the barest of nods. I'm ready.

"It's their whole bloody pack attacking," a guard shouts.

"Then we can take them all out at once," Ferris says. Sienna turns her focus from us to him, her lip curling.

"Subdue, not kill. Without spoils, there's no value left to be had," she says, her words too quick to sound confident. I frown at her. It sounds as if she doesn't want our pack entirely destroyed. There's no time to consider the implications as a bang sounds. The wall vibrates as if a body was thrown against the siding. It's followed by a trio of shots fired, a louder snarl, and a muffled scream.

"Get out there," Ferris growls. The remaining guards throw the door open and join the battle.

"Don't move," Sienna growls, taking out her favorite dagger. She looks between her sons and her mate, Ember hovering like a shadow at her shoulder. Ferris approaches the door, his blade raised defensively.

Slate nods, signaling that we cannot wait any longer. As we shift into our wolf forms, the zip-ties slip off.

Sienna lets out a furious shriek, backing away. She bumps into Ember, who looks gleeful at the change of events. She's always been bloodthirsty. Within seconds, she's shifted into her black wolf, her hackles raised to make her look larger than her petite form truly is.

Slate moves toward Ferris, his teeth bared. Sienna is mine, but Ember blocks my path. With a growl, I spring. Ember snaps at my shoulder, seeing if she can get me to back down or weaken my attack. Not a chance. We've been sparring since we were children. Her black wolf stands no chance against my larger white wolf, and I know how her mind works.

Ember crouches, using her smaller size to get below me. Her teeth close on my ruff, too close to my throat for comfort. My paws push back, propelling me away until I can lower my muzzle and force her to the ground.

Paws on her ribcage, I snarl, keeping my sister growling on her side. My message is clear - stay down.

Slate advances past us toward my father, belly low, lips pulled back to display his teeth. Ferris pulls a gun from a holster at his back. That's not a wolfsbane gun, it's real bullets. Fear splinters through me. Slate attempts to leap before Ferris can fire, but even he isn't faster than a bullet. Ferris brings the gun up to aim at him.

The shot gouges the concrete beside Slate's paws. He jolts away, stumbling in his attempt to regain his balance to strike.

Sienna's unintelligible yells echo in the large space, but Ferris pays her no heed. With a snarl, he adjusts his stance. He won't miss a second time.

With a sickening thud, a dagger embeds into his chest. His second shot goes wide and hits the back wall.

For a moment, everything is frozen. Seemingly in slow motion, Ferris tips forward, the gun clattering to the ground, before he covers it with his slumped body.

Ember ceases her struggle, letting out a piercing wine. She scrambles out from under my stunned paws, and shifts back, dropping to her knees beside his body. With frantic hands, she pulls out the blade and presses the heel of her palms against the puncture. Crimson seeps between her fingers.

My gaze searches for the aggressor. Slate is already backing Sienna against the benches along the back wall. Her empty hands are raised.

Tentatively, I step toward Ember and Ferris, toward the blade on the concrete floor. It's Sienna's. My thoughts are slow.

With the slam of metal door against metal siding, Onyx and Cassia scan the scene, weapons raised. Cassia grabs Sienna's wrist and twists her around, injecting her with Rowanberry from a syringe to prevent her from shifting before the woman has a chance to react. She lowers Sienna to the ground as the natural drug floods her veins.

Ember screams, her voice breaking. Under her hands, blood pools around our father. Ferris is terribly pale. Shifting back, I reach for the first aid kit that Fisher keeps on a shelf by the door.

Onyx grabs Ember, attempting to inject her as well. She snarls, yanking her arm away. He clenches his jaw, gripping both of her arms behind her. Like lightning, Ember twists and slashes, Sienna's discarded blade tight in her hand. The dagger swipes along Onyx's gut, slicing his shirt open at the side where his gear fails to protect him.

He lets out a pained noise but refuses to release her. Cassia catches Ember's wrist and knocks the knife away before she injects her. Ember thrashes and screams.

Onyx releases her with shaking hands, letting Cassia shove the girl to the ground to subdue her. Red stains his shirt.

I'm torn between helping my murderous father and my friend. Onyx makes the decision for me. "It's not deep. Don't worry about me." He grunts as he sits on the closest chair and hunches over.

Cassia has covered Ember's body with her discarded dress. With deft movements, she zip-ties the younger girl to a bench and Sienna to her seat before turning to Onyx.

I peel up my father's shirt to reveal the stab wound. It's weeping more blood than I've ever seen. With trembling hands, I press a bandage over it, hoping I can staunch the flow. His eyes are vacant and his breathing slows.

"Dad." My voice cracks and self-loathing surges in my stomach like nausea. I shouldn't care. He's an enemy, and he would have cut me down right after killing my brother.

Slate crouches beside me. "He's gone."

Slowly, I pry my fingers away. I've ripped out throats and sliced open enemies without hesitation, but something about seeing the light leave my father's eyes has shaken me.

"It's okay," Slate murmurs, his hands squeezing my shoulders as he steers me away. "There's nothing you could have done. It hit an artery."

Forcing a deeper breath into my lungs, I straighten. There are still people that need my help. I can't stand here and wallow in my shock.

Cassia pulls Onyx's gear over his head and wipes away the blood.

"Not cool, dude," Onyx mumbles at Ember, his face pallid.

"Don't be dramatic, you're going to be fine. It's barely a papercut," Cassia says. He laughs and then winces.

It's obvious the moment my sister realizes whose dagger sits abandoned and bloody on the floor. "What did you do?" Ember screeches at our mother, straining against the zip-ties.

"Choose my child over my mate?" Sienna asks quietly, her words a little slurred. Ember lets out an anguished scream in response. "You wouldn't be complaining if *you* were the child I saved," Sienna says before turning her face away.

Slate looks between them, his hand coming up to rub the back of his neck. He looks as confused as I feel. For someone who has spent her life attempting to destroy this pack, Sienna didn't hesitate to put her estranged son before her mate, jeopardizing her power in the process.

"You'd better get out there, boys. The fight's not quite over," Cassia growls, looking up from wrapping gauze around Onyx's torso and tightening the bandage in place.

Slate and I pull on our sweats and slip on the gear Cassia hands over. I try to ignore the blood along the side of Onyx's tactical gear as I pull it over my head.

"Ferris is dead, and Sienna is captive. You've lost," Slate shouts, slamming the door open.

The ground is strewn with unfamiliar figures. Our team has dispatched many of our enemies, but small pockets are still fighting.

Hazel whirls, daggers flashing. Fern leaps on a man staggering away from Hazel. A man I recognize as Flint ducks past Hazel's offense and grabs the strap of her harness, attempting to shove her to the ground.

Slate is already across the clearing, seizing the man by the back of his shirt and flinging him to the dirt. His weapon clatters away. He rolls but before he can stand, Slate is on him. Hazel watches her mate as he slams his fist into Flint's ugly face. Three strikes and Flint's lip and cheek are split, his form limp.

Slate staggers up, embracing Hazel as she smashes into him and kisses him roughly.

My eyes scan for my own mate.

The hulking form of Aries blocks my search. He bares his teeth, barreling toward me. Without hesitation, I draw the gun strapped to my chest, praying it still has ammo.

My hand is steady as I point the weapon at Aries. He slows, his grin bloody as if someone has already knocked his teeth loose. "You are too much of a coward to shoot me," he croaks.

"Try me," I say.

His growl is anything but human. I wait until he is a few feet away and shoot into his gut. It's not a fatal shot for a shifter, but enough to take him out of the fight.

Grunting, Aries stumbles, hand pressing to his wound. "I'm going to kill you."

Somehow, he trudges forward, raising a filthy knife. I dance back, readying another shot that never comes. I'm out of bullets. My hands pat over my gear, looking for more.

Aries closes the distance before I realize how fast he's moving. His boots kick my legs out from under me. My ass hits the grass. He looms over me and his face contorts. My lungs scream as if filled with glass as I suck in a rough breath. I need my head clear to survive this brute.

But Aries doesn't move. His eyes stare ahead, and he slowly sways and falls forward. I pull my legs back clear of him as he crumples. A crossbow bolt sticks out of his back.

Across the clearing, Marigold is already reloading and selecting her next target. I'm entranced by the elegant curve of her shoulders as she raises her weapon. She's magnificent.

"Your Alpha is dead, surrender!" Slate yells, firing his gun into the dirt beside a snarling enemy wolf.

There are few opponents still standing.

Marigold advances, her crossbow pointed at a tall figure. Hawk. He raises his hands, dropping his gun on the ground at her feet. Slowly, he kneels, allowing Fern to zip-tie his wrists.

Slate and Hazel similarly restrain the remaining Granite Ridge pack members.

Looking around, I can tell that some escaped. Less than a dozen still stand, and they are battered, heads hanging. Cassia walks Sienna and a sobbing Ember out of the training building, pushing them to the ground at Slate's feet.

Hazel glares at Sienna, advancing slowly with a dagger in her hand. My mother looks up at her, her face passive. It's strange to see her without either a cold sneer or a simpering smile.

A shout rises, a mix of victory and anger. While many are bloody, I see none of our own seriously injured.

A blur of reddish-gold hair and flushed skin streaks toward me. Marigold's weapon lies discarded in the grass. She launches herself, wrapping her legs around my waist as I lift her up. We cling to each other, reveling in the moment of victory. The emotion flowing between us is enough to steal my breath.

"We made it," I say against her neck.

She kisses me recklessly, not caring who sees. I wish the moment could stretch forever, but hesitantly I set my beautiful partner back on her feet and turn to face our pack.

Slate gives me a nod, holding Hazel tight to his side. Heath stands nearby, talking with Fisher. Fern and Cassia wrangle our prisoners into a row. No one seems to have noticed our intimate moment.

Marigold stills. I follow her gaze. Both my mother and sister watch us with haughty expressions. "Jasper, who is that?" Ember demands. She seems to be looking for a distraction. Surprisingly, Sienna stays silent, her expression unreadable.

My mate smiles wearily. "I'm Marigold." She slips out of my grasp and crouches a few feet from Ember. "I hope someday we can be friends, but that's up to you."

Ember glares at her, her mouth opening and closing before she snarls, "Don't count on it." Her sneer is hollow, her eyes haunted.

Marigold shrugs and rises. Pulling her to my side, I lean my temple against her hair. "She hurt Onyx," I say quietly.

"Really?" Marigold says sharply, turning to see our friend leaning against the building. "You doing okay, big guy?"

"Concerned for me, Goldie?" Onyx says flirtatiously.

She laughs. I'm too relieved to mind his tone. A teasing Onyx is fine. It's when he gets serious that we have to worry.

"Thanks, man," I say.

Onyx rolls his eyes. "That sister of yours, she's a piece of work." I have to agree with him.

Ember lets out an angry screeching noise, twisting to bare her teeth at Onyx. The last threads of her composure break away, and she's wild with grief and rage.

Onyx looks unimpressed, his eyes dull with pain. "Give it a rest, psycho."

Across the clearing, Cedar and Lazuli support a bruised and bloody Hawthorne limping toward us. Crickett runs toward him, clutching their toddler between them as she embraces him. Despite his condition, Hawthorne kisses her back and even wraps an arm around her shoulders. Dahlia squeals and clenches his dirty, torn shirt in her tiny fists.

On the ground with a bandage pressed to his shoulder sprawls a vaguely familiar boy with black hair. He's still a teenager. Kneeling, I eye his wounds.

"Get away from me," he growls. Blood mattes his shirt.

"You don't have to go back to Granite Ridge. Life doesn't have to be like that," I say, wishing someone had said the same to me much sooner.

"Piece of shit," he spits, gasping as his muscles seize.

"If you ever decide you want to be free, there are other packs that treat their wolves with respect."

The boy growls until I step away. Marigold runs her fingers up and down my inner forearm, the texture of her skin soothing me. "You can't help someone that doesn't want it."

I know she's right. But it still stings as I look over the injuries of my former packmates. Many of these people would have gladly killed me even when I was still heir of their pack.

My gaze sweeps to the unmoving bodies. It's a pity, but after exhausting our supply of wolfsbane, we were left with little other choice in our methods of attack.

CHAPTER EIGHTEEN

ANSWERS & AFTERMATH

Marigold

It takes hours to gather the bodies into trucks and return them and the remaining Granite Ridge wolves to their territory. They'll have to handle their own burials. It's a relief to get them out of our land.

Sienna stands alone, her face ashen, as she directs her wolves.

"Do you want to stay and help her?" I whisper to Jasper. After everything that has happened, a feeling like pity wells in my stomach.

"Absolutely not. Our pack needs us," he answers immediately. Turning away from his former pack, he

buries his face into my neck. The rise of his chest is comforting against my curves.

He's quiet on the drive home.

The moon peeks over the treetops. Heath stands in the middle of the gathering, leaning on a crutch. His left leg is bound up tight.

Hawthorne holds onto Crickett who is quietly weeping. Perhaps it's the shock of the day or the destruction of her beloved kitchen. My grandmother has already patched Hawthorne. Bandages wrap his torso, one bicep, and the opposite thigh. Despite leaning on his mate, he looks decent with color in his cheeks and a tired smile. Daisy keeps calling him a mummy.

Exhaustion permeates the entire pack. No one is injured worse than Hawthorne, and most only have shallow cuts and bruises. Through the pack bond, I can feel a sense of relief, multiplied by my bond with Jasper. Quiet discussions buzz around us.

My mate's arm wraps my shoulders, holding me against his side. It's comforting.

My hand rubs wide circles across his back, trying to offer as much comfort as I draw from him. He tightens his grip and presses a kiss to the top of my head. The air leaves my lungs in a contented sigh.

His pale hair is silver in the moonlight, a fine highlight outlining his straight nose and high cheekbones. Reaching up, I wipe a spot of blood off his jaw.

Hazel's brown eyes connect with mine. A wry smile curves her lips. It looks like she already knows about our decision.

"Did you tell?" I whisper, frowning at Hazel.

"Slate kinda figured it out." He shrugs, glancing up. "And he told Hazel, looks like."

"If she didn't already know." When I think about it, it's surprising she didn't see through us the moment we walked out of the bedroom this morning.

Our musings are cut short by Heath raising a hand. Silence falls across the clearing instantly Dozens of eager faces watch their leader.

"In all my years as your Alpha, we've never faced a threat this grievous. And despite our injuries, we are all still standing," Heath says, "more or less." He chuckles, motioning at himself.

"We have proven that loyalty and kindness are stronger than greed and revenge." The pride in his voice is unmistakable and it echoes through the emotions of our packmates like warmth spreading from person to person.

Slate takes Hazel's hand where they stand beside her uncle.

Heath glances over at them. "My heirs proved they can lead our pack without me. Their quick thinking and wise decisions saved many of our lives and homes."

Hazel's cheeks flush and her eyes go to the ground.

"That being said, it looks as though the damage to my leg will be permanently disabling. I believe it is best if Hazel and Slate take up the mantle of Alpha in my stead. They are capable and ready, and I know all of us will support them as they grow into the role."

Murmurs of approval echo around us.

Hazel's mouth falls open, but she allows Heath to pull her into a one-armed embrace. He converses quietly with Hazel and Slate.

Jasper's arm around me goes slack. His expression echoes Hazel's. But while Hazel recovers as Heath speaks to her, Jasper continues to blink dumbly at our leaders.

"Are you okay?" I ask. His mouth snaps shut. "What's wrong?"

Like breaking from a trance, he looks down at me. "He just stepped down."

"Yeah, pretty sure we all saw that happen." He frowns at me like I'm missing something. "Jasper, what's upsetting you?"

Clearing his throat, he explains, "My father always said I would never be Alpha until he was cold in the ground. He never would have handed his role over to anyone. The fact Heath would willingly retire and give up his authority."

"Oh," I say, understanding finally. Yet again, our pack has surprised him.

"It's unbelievable," he says, his voice scraping. His happiness for his brother is tinged with sadness, though I would have missed it if we weren't connected with a deeper bond. I know him well enough to be confident it isn't jealousy, but a mourning for a family other than his own. The differences between Heath and Ferris are vast, and I know sometimes those differences feel painfully unfair.

"You've always belonged here," I murmur, tugging him into a tight hug. "Not there. You've always deserved a family like this."

His hands grasp me like I'm his lifeline as he breathes in the smell of my hair until his breathing evens out. By the time we've broken apart, the gathering has dissolved. Hazel stands by Heath, accepting congratulations from various lingering pack members.

"Are you two done?" Slate asks, his fake irritation giving way to a smile.

Jasper smirks and I pinch the skin on his side in a silent warning. "Sorry, yes," Jasper says, "Alpha."

"We'd like to talk with you later. Can we stop by your cabin in a bit?"

"Of course," I say over my shoulder as Jasper pulls me away and spins me to face him.

"I don't think I want to share you once we get home," he whispers in my ear.

"This sounds important."

"So is checking on our cabin," he says. "I have a surprise for you."

"So impatient," I tease, anticipation prickling in my chest.

Before I can protest, he reaches under my knees and scoops me up in a bridal hold. "Hey!" I protest, kicking my legs. My fingers wrinkle his shirt. Striding through the trees, he peppers my forehead, my cheeks, and my nose with kisses.

"Hold on!" he says, tipping me up until I'm hanging over his shoulder, freeing up his other hand to open the door. My shriek turns to a giggle as he slides me back into my original position.

As we step over the threshold, he gives me that cocky grin. "Welcome home."

"Everything looks untouched. We got lucky," I say, surveying our living room.

"Do you like this cabin?" Jasper asks. He lets me slide down his body until my feet hit the ground.

"Yeah, it's great." I look around to see if he made any changes, wondering when he had time to arrange a surprise.

"Really?" he asks quietly.

"Yes, I love it." I laugh, quirking one eyebrow at him.

He takes a deep breath. "Good, because I bought it from the pack. It's not a guest cabin anymore, it's all ours."

The words take a moment to snap into place. "What?"

"We can get something else if you like," he quickly says.

"No, that's amazing." My feet leave the floor once more as he hugs me around the waist and lifts me up. My fingers curl into the back of his hair. "It's perfect, but when did you have time to buy it?"

"Last week."

We settle on the sofa and I grab his hand, my legs across his. Looking at his fingers instead of his eyes, I say, "I feel bad though. I don't have a lot of money, but I can help."

His deep laugh breaks my thoughts.

"What?" I demand, a blush coloring my cheeks.

"I've been putting away money from my family for years, in case I ever had to run. They have more money than sense. You don't even have to work if you don't want to. The cabin barely put a dent in it."

"Are you kidding me?"

It makes sense. I don't know much about cars, but his car seems expensive, and he never seems worried about how much things cost.

"I want to buy you a car too. Something yellow."

Shaking my head, I squeeze his fingers in warning. "No way."

"You can't stop me from getting you gifts." He pulls my hand against his chest so I can feel his heart.

"Yes, I can." My eyes narrow into a glare.

A soft knock interrupts our argument.

"Come in," I say, releasing him and swinging my feet to the floor..

"You deviants better be wearing clothes," Hazel grouches, pushing the door open.

"It would serve you right, after how you and Slate have been," I tease. Jasper buries his face in the crook of my neck and laughs silently.

"Why do I have a feeling you guys will be worse?" Slate sits in the armchair opposite us and pulls Hazel into his lap.

"So what's going on guys? I need to get my mate to bed," Jasper asks, a frown creasing his brows.

Hazel's eyebrows shoot up.

"For sleep," Jasper growls. "It's been a long night."

That's an understatement as the pale morning light begins to filter through the curtains of our cozy living room.

"Well, we are going to be Alphas," Hazel begins, pausing like she isn't sure how to continue.

"Pretty sure that's been the case for like six months," I mutter, trying to not giggle. Exhaustion strips away my filter, making my words goofy and thoughtless.

Slate rolls his eyes. "You know what we mean."

It's too easy to tease him. Hazel's grin mirrors my own in a moment of female solidarity.

"I'm really excited for you guys. You're going to be amazing," I say.

Hazel's blush is back, and Slate's hands tighten around her waist, probably sensing her discomfort. "Thank you. But we are going to need our own second-in-command."

"Yeah?" Jasper says.

"Of course," Slate says.

"We'd like you to be our Beta," Hazel blurts. Jasper freezes, his brows furrowing.

Squeezing his arms looped around me, I reassure him, "Who else would they want?"

He takes a slow breath. "I appreciate that. But I'm going to have to talk with my mate about it." My hand covers my grin.

"Marigold, you don't have to be Beta too if you don't want to. Don't get me wrong, we'd love to have you. But if you'd prefer not to, it's fine. I don't care that it's tradition for mated pairs to take the same position. This pack breaks with tradition all the time. I mean, Crickett isn't Gamma with Hawthorne," Hazel says. She's right. The tension in my shoulders unravels.

"So basically I don't have a choice?" Jasper asks, his smirk softening his words.

"Correct," Hazel teases back.

Jasper huffs. His voice drops, speaking only to me. "Sunshine, how do you feel about it? Should I accept? And we can get back to them about what you want to do."

I can tell he wants to. Despite his calm exterior, excitement bubbles through our bond. I'm excited too. He deserves the position after how hard he's worked to prove himself. Not to mention, his natural ability and dominance dictate that he should be second after Slate.

"Yeah, you should. You're the best man for the job," I say, kissing his cheek.

"Alright," he says.

"Wonderful!" Hazel's smile is genuine. I thought it was Slate's decision to pick Jasper, but seeing Hazel's expression, I realize it was her. I should have known. Slate defers to Hazel as often as possible.

"I'll be happy to talk details tomorrow, but it's extremely late," Jasper says, releasing me to stand. Hazel and Slate both hug him.

I throw my arms around Hazel. "Thank you for supporting him," I murmur in her ear.

"I should thank you for the same thing." Her arms squeeze my ribcage. "Good night," she says, waving as they head out the door. It closes with a click.

"Well, Sunshine?" he purrs, turning away from the front door.

"Honestly, I want to keep teaching. I'm not made for leadership, and I love my students" I say, my heart in my throat.

"Not a problem." He's unruffled.

"Are you okay doing it alone?" I ask.

Jasper chuckles. "It's fine. I want you to be happy, and I think I can handle things. I've got plenty of support. I mean, my brother was Beta for a few years before Hazel joined him."

"You're going to be amazing," I say, completely confident that he will be the best Beta possible.

"And if you change your mind, or get sick of those kids, you have a right to be Beta. The option doesn't go away because you decline right now."

"Thank you." I exhale, tension seeping away.

He stalks forward, closing the distance between us. I step away from the coffee table, toward our bedroom door.

"Marigold, where are you going?" he says, his voice dropping to a rasp that feels like velvet sliding across my ribs.

"Bed?" I ask.

"Come here." His command sends a shiver down my spine. His scent fills my lungs as he reaches me, hands going to my waist.

"No thanks," I say, sliding out of his grasp and pulling my shirt off in one fluid move. He reaches for me again and I shimmy out of range. My hands fold down my waistband, sucking in a breath at the cool air brushing my skin.

"You are really something." He darts forward, catching me around the waist. His body hems me in against the kitchen counter.

"And you are wearing entirely too much clothing." I giggle. To emphasize my point, I tug at his shirt, pleased when he allows me to strip it off. I stop when his shirt is over his biceps and elbows, blocking his face. He has to reach to pull it off the rest of the way.

I don't miss the opportunity to flit away again, luring him into chasing. A predatory smile lights up his face as his eyes begin to glow. I feint left but go right. He's quick on his feet and grabs my hips as I pass him. Hands moving to my waist, he backs me against our dining table.

"Still want to go to bed?" I ask in a breathy whisper.

He lifts me until I'm seated on the smooth wood. "I'm good right here."

"I think you'll need to clean the table after this," I tease.

"I think you need to shut up and kiss me," he quips back.

Leaning in, I tilt my head to kiss him, but instead nip his pouty bottom lip and lean back. "Make me," I purr.

His eyes glitter at my challenge. With deliberate movements, he pushes me back against the table and drags my sweats off, tossing them across the wood floor.

"Jasper," I gasp as he drags me forward until my ass almost tips off the tabletop.

Eyes glowing, he kneels. His hands lift my calf, fingers skimming over the floral tattoo that climbs the back of my leg. "I love this." He sets my leg over his shoulder and I swallow thickly.

Words fall away as his breath warms my sensitive inner thighs.

At the first swipe of his tongue, my back arches and a moan rips out of my throat. A blush warms my skin, but from the way his fingers dig into my legs, it's obvious he loves hearing my reaction.

"My mate," he says against my skin, his words claiming me all over again. It takes me a second to realize the overpowering possessiveness isn't mine. Feeling his emotions sends a thrill through me again. The connection goes both ways. His tongue swirling over me sets off stars behind my eyelids, and he groans at the shared pleasure. He's gentle but relentless, devouring me until I'm breathless and boneless.

"Come on, baby, I don't want to break the table if I get up there too," he says softly, lifting me easily. I sink into his arms, secure in the knowledge that he'll never let me go.

He lays me back across our bed, not breaking our connection for a second. His mouth is soft against mine. This tenderness intoxicates me in a new way.

"You are so perfect. I've never seen anything as magnificent as you with a weapon in your hand destroying our enemies," he says. Glowing aqua eyes pierce my soul.

"Don't ever risk yourself like that again," I say, "I can't lose you."

Jasper frowns. "If I have to, to keep you safe, I'll do it all again."

I open my mouth to argue.

"Sunshine, you would do the same for me. Trust me to not be reckless." The affection in his voice smoothers my spark of outrage. He further soothes me by kissing across my jaw and licking the skin below my ear.

"I trust you," I breathe.

His gaze flicks up to me, halting his progress for a moment. The emotion through our bond is a tangle of gratitude and relief. Didn't he already know I trusted him completely? But after his upbringing and then joining our pack where some wolves still view him with suspicion, I should have realized how much it would mean to him.

His mouth over my breast empties all thoughts from my mind. Nails scoring down his back, I urge his hips against my thighs.

The brilliant smile on his face makes my stomach flip. "Impatient?" he murmurs.

"For you? Yes," I flirt. My hand closes around his length, drawing him against me.

"Whatever my mate desires," he half-teases, half-swears, pushing forward to sink into me. Ecstasy buzzes under my skin.

The softness burns away as a frenzy builds between us. The night before, he was careful and controlled. That's not what I want now. The hard planes of his body press into my curves as we set a brutal pace.

Soft breathy noises escape me, and he answers by lifting my knee against his chest to tilt my hips. My eyes squeeze shut, my body trembling. The feel of his skin against mine is almost too much.

Beautiful tension builds in every fiber of my being until I'm crying out curses. He slows, grinding into me. His release hits me through our shared bond, enough to break me a second time.

Jasper barely separates from me, his arms banding around me like he can't tolerate the thought of not touching me. I listen to his heartbeat as we regain our composure.

I wipe my eyes, surprised to find wetness there.

"Are you okay, Sunshine?" he says, tightening his hold on me.

I nod, sniffling. "More than okay. I'm deliriously happy."

He kisses my hair. "Me too."

As the birds chirp outside our window in the morning light, I sleep deeply, safe at my mate's side.

Spring has finally warmed and the morning air has lost its bite. The river's water flow increases as the snow at higher elevations melts. It's my favorite time of year, as the deer bear their calves and the deciduous trees sprout millions of new leaves.

Marigold stands beside me, her hair gleaming and her eyes bright. I smooth my fingers through my mate's hair, happy she left it loose today. Around us, star-shaped yellow wildflowers bloom - marsh marigolds. Their leaves are glossy green and heart-shaped.

Ahead of us, Hazel and Slate step toward the water's edge, hand in hand. Confidence ripples off them, reassuring the pack members gathered behind them.

Sienna stands on the opposite side of the creek, within her own territory. Beside her stands a towering wolf I recognize as Orion. His clenched jaw shows a measure of anger, but he stays silent. He was a Zeta when I left the pack, but the way he stands beside my mother gives me pause. Sienna prefers to surround herself with the most vicious wolves, but after losing Ferris, maybe she went for brute strength.

Behind Sienna, my sister Ember stands with her hands clasped behind her. Her smile is a poor imitation of our mothers, sly but also full of violent promises that Sienna hides better.

Ember's future mate, Hawk, has his arm around her waist, though there is space between their bodies. She's only six months away from becoming an adult and his claim still stands. I glare at his freckled face. My sister may be unpredictable and dangerous, but saddling her with a mate the moment she becomes an adult won't help anything.

"So what did you want to discuss?" Hazel demands, raising her chin. Slate's hands rest on her hips as he stands slightly behind her, a smug look on his face.

"Peace, of course," Sienna replies.

"That would be at odds with your prior actions, Alpha," Hazel says.

Slate dips his head and places a kiss on the stretch of her exposed shoulder, right over his claim mark. It's a reminder and a challenge.

"I hope you will believe me when I say that Ferris was the driving force behind our grievous assault on your territory," she says. We all know that's bullshit. "I would appreciate it if we could sit down and outline what restitution we can make. I want to move forward as allies."

"It takes time to build trust. And you have many years of deceit," Slate says, his voice low.

Hazel chews on her lip, glancing up at her mate. He nods, ending their silent conversation, and says, "But we will meet with you."

The tension lowers, though no one truly lets down their guard. Hazel leads Sienna toward the shallow end of this stretch of creek so they can stand ankle-deep and discuss matters privately. Sienna looks as if she's smelled something disgusting as she steps into the water and I want to laugh.

As the three Alphas speak quietly, I approach my sister. Stepping off a flat rock, I stop a few feet from her. Ember stands stiffly, her obsidian irises cold as she regards me.

"How are you doing?" I ask. She idolized both of our parents so Ferris's death must be difficult for her. It doesn't surprise me that she sees Sienna's actions as a betrayal, leaving her without a parent she can trust.

Her voice is hoarse and full of malice. "What do you care?"

"He was my father too," I reply, my tone a soft reminder.

Ember's nose wrinkles as she sneers. "I believe he said otherwise after you objectively failed the pack."

"Are you on speaking terms with mom?" I ask, nodding toward Sienna.

She decides not to answer. Instead, her hand goes to Hawk's wrist. "Someday I will be Alpha, and you will only be," she pauses, "what you are now." Her disdain is a physical weight, but I let it slide off of me.

"Happy?" I supply.

"Pathetic." She turns her nose up.

There's no sense in telling her that I'm now Beta. It wouldn't make a difference, and it's not the driving factor in my happiness or my sense of success.

"You are still my sister. If you need me, you can call, and I'll answer," I say, even though she pretends not to hear me.

Hawk regards me, the same indecision on his face as during our fight to reclaim our territory.

"Take care of her. If you hurt her, I will destroy you," I growl. He doesn't flinch, just regards me coolly. It still makes me uneasy to not know this male so close to my sister.

Ember's hand releases Hawk's as she turns away. Her nails are a sharp, black manicure against the white of her fingers as her fists clench.

I hope it's not the last time I see my sister. But just in case, I want to leave nothing unsaid. "Ember, I love you."

"Eat shit," she growls under her breath.

Exhaling sharply, I turn away. Marigold's blue-green eyes are full of concern as I make my way back to her, stepping from rock to rock. "That didn't sound good."

Sighing, I pull her close. "She's angry. She's always angry. But her world is upside down right now." She nods sympathetically. "Honestly, I'm worried what she'll do," I murmur against her ear.

"It'll be okay," she reassures me.

"I hope so. My father controlled her, and now with only my mother... I don't know."

Her hands tighten on my biceps. "You've done everything you can. Nothing that happens is on you." Her words help, but it's her sweet smile that breaks through my worry.

"Jasper," Hazel calls. She signals me to come over. I stride toward them, slowing as the shallow water ripples around my ankles. Sienna's smile thins as I approach. "You know our Beta," Hazel says with a vindictive smile. "Jasper, could you take some notes for us? I'd like your feedback."

"Of course," I say, pulling out my phone. She doesn't need notes from me, but she wants Sienna to see my new position. To show her that she was wrong. I busy myself typing into my notes app, resisting the urge to look up at my mother.

"Sienna, please continue," Hazel says.

She pauses for a moment before continuing to list her proposal. Every time Hazel interrupts her and asks my opinion on something, I can see her seething. After the second polite disagreement, Slate says, "I think we need to revisit this tomorrow. I'm not sure we will get much more accomplished today. It's getting late."

"If you insist," Sienna says, bristling. "I'll expect your call." She addresses only Slate, clearly done with Hazel and I.

"Thank you, have a good evening," Hazel says softly. Sienna tosses her hair and leads her wolves away.

"I think this calls for a celebration. Game night at our house?" Hazel says.

"After pack dinner," Slate adds, taking her hand as we cross back to our side of the boundary.

"Let me check with Marigold, but I'm sure she'll be happy," I say, going to my mate as we reach our companions.

"Alright, let's head home," Slate says, raising his voice for our entire team. With sure steps, he leads the way up the hill and into the trees.

Marigold squeezes my hand, her body brushing against mine as we walk. It'll take at least thirty or forty minutes to walk back, but the company is so pleasant, I wouldn't mind if it was longer. "How'd it go?" Marigold asks.

"Well, I think. It's hard to tell," I say, thinking. "Hazel and Slate kept Sienna off balance, so that was good."

She grins at me viciously. "I hope they knocked her on her ass."

Chuckling, I raise her arm and kiss her knuckles. "You're a violent little thing."

"I think you like it," she purrs.

"I like everything about you," I reply, my voice low. Her back muscles tense as she shivers lightly. Our steps have slowed, putting us at the back of the pack. Gently, I tug her to a halt.

"What?" She cocks her head, looking between me and our packmates disappearing between the trees.

"Nothing," I say. Marigold wrinkles her nose. "When we get back, it'll be dinner and then Hazel invited us over for a game night. If I have to wait hours to taste you, I'm going to lose my mind."

"Oh," she says, a faint blush staining her freckled cheeks.

She's eager for my mouth, slipping her hands around my neck and up into my hair. Our kisses are playful and heady. My blood tingles and sparks, like she's an electrical charge.

With little pushes, she walks me backwards until my back hits a tree. Her hands tug at my shoulders until I scoop her up under her thighs. With my arms busy lifting her, I'm at her mercy as she slips her cold fingers under the neckline of my shirt and trails her hot mouth down my throat.

She pauses on my circle of scars, the mark of her claim. I can feel her deep satisfaction through our bond.

"I want to take you home," I breathe. Holding her tight, I push my back off the tree and spin until she's pressed against it. Her eyes glow blue-green, her lush mouth open in surprise. I lean down, trailing my lips over her ear. "Or maybe I'll fuck you up against this tree."

"As appealing as that sounds, we should go, or we will miss dinner," she says breathlessly.

"We can eat at home," I reply, licking her throat. She shudders.

"But I want to go to game night," she manages to say, the words uneven.

"Alright," I say, ceasing my torture. Her feet lower to the leaves and I take a half-step back. Mild disappointment swirls between us, and I'm unclear if it's mine or hers. Hand in hand, we resume our walk. "You know what would make game night better?"

"What?"

"If we got some pickles."

She snorts, shoving me back. "You're ridiculous."

"What? They're a good snack," I jest. Her giggle is my favorite sound in the world.

WANT MORE?

Want a bonus short story featuring Hazel, Slate, Jasper, and Marigold?

Join Aly Hollis's newsletter for updates, or follow on social media! See all her links here...

FAMILY TREES

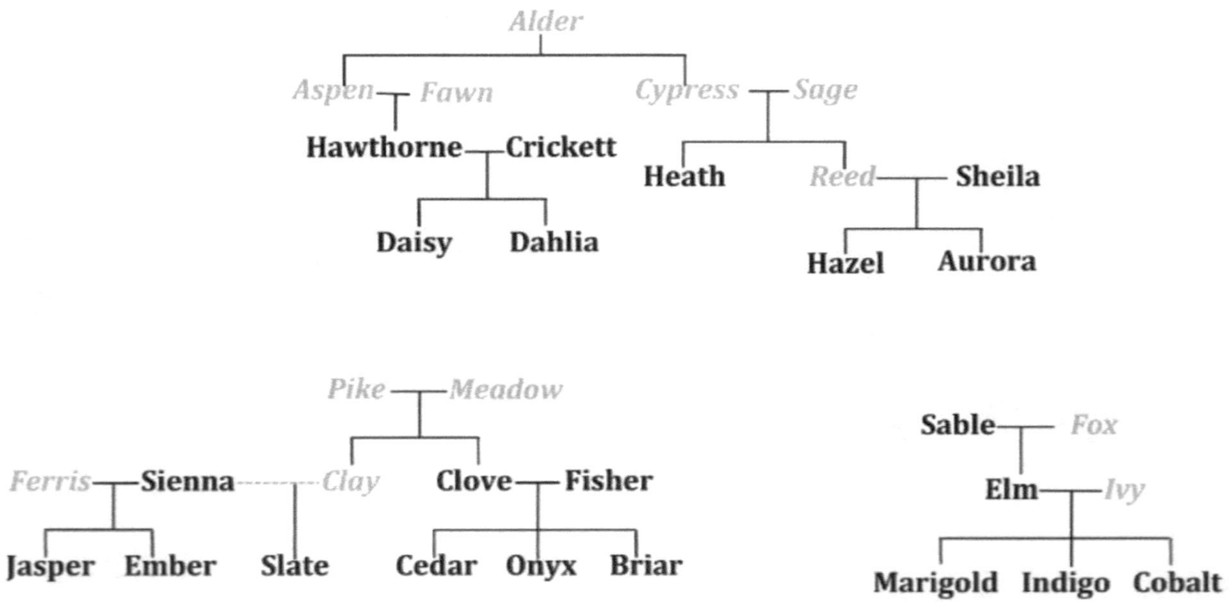

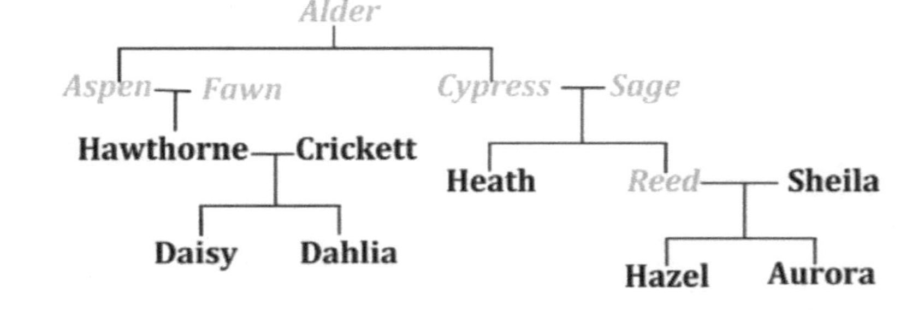

PACK LEADERS

The Bracken Creek Pack
Alpha - Heath
Betas and Heirs - Hazel and Slate
Gamma - Hawthorne
Delta - Fisher

The Ironcrest Pack
Alpha - Zephyr
Beta - Beryl
Gamma - Dell

The Granite Ridge Pack
Alphas - Ferris and Sienna
Beta - Aries, and later Orion
Heir - Ember

The Valley Pack
Alphas - Cashel
Beta and Heir - Malachite
Gamma - Zinnia

The Raven Pack
Alpha - Nyx

SECRETS AND S'MORES

Ember

"Look who's here lurking in the shadows," a low voice cuts through my reflective bitterness. Onyx moves through the darkness like he belongs here. Bathed in dim reflections, his hair is ashen and his skin bronze as he steps closer.

"Maybe I'm trying to be less of a bitch."

"What a noble cause," Onyx says, his eyes scanning me. "Look, I'm sorry. Marigold says I have to apologize.

"I don't want your apology."

"Alright, but I'm trying to do the right thing." His forearms rest against the wall as he leans into my personal space.

"I doubt that. Back off."

I try to ignore him, but his inhale is audible. "You smell good."

"Too bad you don't," I snap, even though it's a lie. I can smell his citrus soap mingling with sweat and something that reminds me of a bakery, like fresh baked bread.

The asshole smiles down at me. I hate that he's a head taller than me. I hate that he's pretty.

"Why are you still here?" My arms cross over my chest.

"Maybe I'm drunk and horny and I like it when women are mean to me," he purrs.

"You're pathetic. Find someone else to annoy." His eyes light up at my insult. I guess he was telling the truth about liking mean women. Then he's going to *love* me.

"Are you lonely since Hawk left you?"

He's cruel, cold and mocking, and I should not be attracted to him, but all the hairs stand up on my arms at his nearness.

"Like you always feel, since no one wants you?" My whisper is ragged, holding none of the malice I should feel. He should fear being this close to me. The last time we clashed, I made him bleed.

He's near enough I can feel the heat rolling off his skin. My hand presses to his chest, and I mean to push him away, but my intoxicated body reacts without my permission, brushing down the faded fabric and across his torso. Damn, he's a wall of stacked muscle.

"Ah, seems someone does want me." The bastard is delighted at my moment of weakness.

"Fuck off," I grumble.

His hand grabs my wrist, his thumb over my pulse. The contact of his skin scorches me. "Your heart is beating like a hummingbird."

"I'm considering all the ways I'd like to kill you," I bluff. "It's a very appealing idea."

He cocks his head, his eyes glittering with intelligence and mocking humor. "I don't think you are." His gaze drops down, to where my body has leaned into him. *Shit.*

He lowers his head toward mine and my lungs tighten. "I think you're thinking of *other* things you'd like to do to me."

"I'd settle for strangling, disemboweling, or a simple guillotine." I'm aiming to wipe the smile off his face, but instead it widens, pleased at my threats.

"We both know that isn't what you want."

His warmth is too tempting and it makes me dumb. He dips his head, lips near my ear. "I'm going to kiss you and you aren't going to stab me. Understood?" The touch of his breath triggers a shiver I try to hide.

I should shove him away. I should punch his handsome face. Unfortunately, my willpower is in tatters. A low moan of agreement escapes my throat. I mean it as a growl, but I'm too lost in the feel of him.

"Answer me," his command pulls a gasp out of me and my mouth opens. He reaches up and runs his thumb over my bottom lip.

"I won't stab you right now," I say, though it comes out as more of a whimper. My hands tighten against the fabric of his shirt and pull him against me, and at the same moment, he grabs my ribs possessively, pushing me against the wall hard enough my body jolts.

My vision glazes over. It's perhaps one of the stupidest things I've ever done, but damn if his mouth doesn't feel good against my neck. His tongue licks against my skin and his teeth graze, sending electricity zinging through me.

Something in the back of my mind yells to stop. He's the enemy, and he's made his opinion of me clear. Just because he's sexy as hell doesn't mean I should let him use me like this. But the way his hands run up my side and skims the underside of my breasts has me melting. My anger slips through my fingers, evaporating in the heat of him.

Sighing, I arch my neck as he presses forward. The shadow of a beard along his jaw scuffs my throat and my hands come up to reach for him, wanting more. Like lightning, one hand grabs both my wrists and pins them above my head.

"I still don't trust you," he says, his lips still against my skin.

Good. He shouldn't.

ONYX

Years ago, my brother, cousin, and I went cliff jumping at a river a few hours away. Over and over, we plunged off the rocks, aiming for deeper water, knowing that one slip could mean death. The rush was addictive.

That's what kissing Ember is like.

It's the last thing I should be doing, but I can't resist.

I can't keep my gaze away from the way her dark green hair highlights the emerald in her hazel eyes. Her heart-shaped face glows in the low lights.

My first mistake is getting too close, maybe because I feel guilty or maybe to feel the thrill of irritating someone who clearly would like to murder me.

But when her scent reaches me, all of those thoughts evaporate, and all I can think of is touching her. She's soft wildflowers and the sharp, metallic scent of lightning, so alluring I'm leaning in too close.

She wants me too. The glow of her eyes is a thin halo around her blown-out pupils.

My hand tightens around her wrists, stretching her out for me to taste. She's so pliant, melting against me - the opposite of her prickly personality. It's heady, the way she obeys my silent commands, opening her mouth for me. She kisses back fiercely. Her teeth nip at my tongue, sending a jolt straight to my hard cock pressing against her supple body.

I sweep my mouth to her jaw, wanting to taste more of her. A hushed noise from her throat sends my head spinning. It's walking the edge of a blade and getting away with it, and she feels so good.

"You kiss better than you fight," I whisper against her skin.

Her chest heaves as she struggles to get enough air to say, "Unfortunately, you don't."

Huffing a laugh at her insult, I use my free hand to tip her chin up so she's forced to look me in the eyes. "Don't lie to me. You've been enjoying this too much for that to be true."

"You're pathetic," she growls.

It's ice hitting my overheated skin. What the fuck am I doing?

My fingers are stiff as I release her and take a forcible step back. The cool air washes over me.

"Better pathetic than a psycho," I mutter defensively. Those startling eyes narrow and then she's moving, stalking off into the dwindling crowd.

Snarling, I adjust myself, gulping down the night air to try and calm the inferno raging through me.

That shouldn't have happened. I try to picture her months ago as she viciously slashed a knife against my side and cut into my skin. That's the woman I just kissed - someone who would gladly gut me.

But now all I can recall from that moment is the way her curves felt in my arms, still naked from shifting. Even then, it had been wildly distracting. That's how she managed to hurt me, or at least that's what I tell myself.

What's wrong with me? That was a fight, not a flirtation. Though I shouldn't be surprised. She's exactly my type - feisty, strong-willed, unpredictable.

Acidic disappointment eats away at me. If I had kept my mouth shut, it could still be on her body. I can feel the ghost of her up against me.

THANK YOUS

Thank you to my husband for supporting my writing habit, and my kids who love telling their teachers that their mom writes fantasy books.

Thank you to Ilea and Anandi for your editing insights. This story wouldn't exist without your encouragement.

Thank you to my author community, to Tereza Kane (Storm and Sea Saga) and Harlowe Savage (Monarchs of Eros) for being my writing buddies.

And thank you to my mother for proofreading my story even when I told you not to read it. I will never get over the embarrassment of you sharing my spicy werewolf books with all your grandma friends, but I appreciate the support.

ALSO BY ALY HOLLIS

Bracken Creek Wolves:
Campfires and Canines
Moonlight and Mischief
Secrets and S'mores
Wolves and Watercolors
Snow Drifts and Soulmates *novella*
Blood and Brambles *novella*

Sablewood Trilogy
Raven Rebel
Ember Queen
Fated Traitor

Standalones
Wish Me Freely
Selkies and Saltwater
Blood Sugar

Seasons of the Alphas
Shifters' Fated Summer
Breeding Meadow
Knotting Autumn
Winter's Heat

ABOUT THE AUTHOR

Aly Hollis lives in the Southwest with her family, two enthusiastic heeler dogs, two judgmental cats, and an adorable turtle. She's written fiction since she was a child, but Campfires and Canines was her first book to be completed, edited, and published. It received such a great response, Aly wrote and published three additional novels and a novella in the Bracken Creek world.

When Aly isn't writing, she loves crafting, drawing, and debating book tropes with her friends.

www.ingramcontent.com/pod-product-compliance
Lightning Source LLC
Chambersburg PA
CBHW020310160726
47992CB00004B/1467